# Whatever Starts On The Streets... Stays On The Streets

A NU Direction Publishing
A division of MeJah Books, Incorporated

Note: This book is a work of fiction. Names, characters, places and incidents are products of the Author's imagination or are used fictitiously. Any resemblance to actual events or locales or persons, living or dead, is entirely coincidental.

Published by A NU Direction Publishing
A division of MeJah Books, Inc.
Tri-State Mall, Suite #12-13
333 Naamans Road, Claymont, DE 19703

Library of Congress Control Number: 2006935274
ISBN 10: 0-9765733-3-4/ISBN 13: 978-0-09765733-3-3
Copyright © 2007
Whatever Starts On The Street...Stays On The Street
Story by Derrick Phillips
Editing: A NU Direction Publishing and Ms. Germaine
Cover Concept and Text Formation-Jewel Sanchez, jwlsnchz@yahoo.com and Diane Barnes
Cover Graphics- Kevin Carr of OCJ Graphix
Printed and bound in the United States of America. First Edition

Whatever Starts On The Street...Stays On The Street

# Whatever Starts On The Streets... Stays On The Streets

## By
## Blue Gambino

# NOTE FROM THE PUBLISHER

A NU Direction Publishing/MeJah Books Family: Diane Barnes, Jewel Sanchez, Jordan, Vince Seaton, Kevin Carr, Marilyn DeGannes and I, thank everyone for their continued support of the services we provide to the community. A special thanks to my HipHop4Life customers who continue to support MeJah Books Inc. and the books published by A NU Direction Publishing.

In supporting A NU Direction Publishing you are giving a man/woman an opportunity to start over and for this, we are grateful.

A book comes about because of the faith, caring and hard work of the author and many other people. A huge investment of time and resources was required to bring this project from a draft to a work of fiction. We are deeply grateful to the many friends whose generous support…enabled us to complete this project and make it available to the readers.

Blue, I am proud of you and this is the realest book the streets will ever read and will forever talk about.

Emlyn DeGannes
MeJah Books, Inc.
A NU Direction Publishing

# NOTE FROM THE AUTHOR

Finally, to everybody that buys this book I sincerely, "Thank You." Some people thought a book about a little city wouldn't do good. "But Real Recognize Real". I'm declaring myself the authority on Street Lit from this day forth. If you think this is hot, I got a slew of fire coming at y'all in the near future: "She Came Between Us", "Little City-Big Gangsta", "When Dreams Become Nightmares Parts I & II", "Can't Miss Parts I & II", "You Deserve Better" and I'm still writing. Plus, I've been down 8 years, wait till I get back to the street and catch-up, it's going down! So stay tuned for plenty to come from your boy, BLUE GAMBINO. I'm every bit of the MONSTER they say I am and I'm just getting started.

In closing, addresss all comments and/or questions you may have to: Derrick Phillips, #E.Z. 3576, 500 E. 4th Street, Chester, PA 19013.

# DEDICATION

This book is dedicated to all the real gangstas that stuck to code of the streets; Dudes that played by the rules and respected the game because they love the game and every thing that come with it. Dudes that was dealt a bad hand and played it with their poker faces; refusing to fold under pressure while maintaining their honor and dignity when faced with adversities. Unfortunately, for a lot of real dudes the repercussions were life in jail or death. However, a real soldier will embrace death before living with dishonor... firmly believing that:

Whatever Starts On The Street – Should Stay On The Street.


Dedicated to:
Vincent "Taterhead" Williams
Nolan "N.Y." O'Neal
Damon "Flame Calione" Hastings (RIP)
"ACE CAPONE"

# Acknowledgements

All praise is due to God. Without him, none of this would have been possible. Although I got 8 ½ years for watching a crime occur and refusing to snitch I am contented with what God has decreed for me. Truly believing that HE is the best of planners and "for every hardship there is relief."

I'd like to start by thanking A NU Direction Publishing, Ms. Emlyn DeGannes and the extended family I have now gained. I appreciate this opportunity more than words can express. Thank you for everything you have done with my book and all the time ya'll put into getting it ready to be presented to the world. Hopefully, all of the hard work will take us to the best sellers list.

Next, I'd like to thank my mother Debra Jackson. Your love and loyalty has been unconditional throughout all of the trials and tribulations I've faced in my life. Even as you endured your own hardships, you still do your best to help me, however you can. Hopefully one day I will be able to buy you a house and make sure you are set financially. Though it will never express how much I love you and appreciate all you have done for me, it will definitely be a good start. To my Grandmom, Patricia Bivens: Thank you for being here for me when all your children abandoned me. I love you to death and hopefully I'll be able to take care of you as well. To my Aunt Patricia and Aunt Neet- Thank You. To my sisters Myra and Danika, y'all know y'all got a brother-right? I'm still alive. Aunt Vanessa, well at least you took the book to the publisher for me. Aunt Pam, you did send me one check, guess you got me, right?

And for everyone else, if you're wondering why ya name ain't listed, "ASK YA'SELF" what have you done to deserve an acknowledgement. When I touch **SOON**, give me the same amount of space you giving me now. If you are wondering, that means you and when I touch, I'ma ride by in something husky banging T.I. "You Don't Know Me."

To my business partner Tarik Morris: You the closest thing to a brother I got, the most loyal nigga in the world. I appreciate everything you are doing for me. You showed me how real niggaz ride b/cuz I definitely forgot. Now you gotta drop ya book "The Choices We Make" on our company "The Homicide Division" so we can murder da book game; the streets need us, they tired of buying soul food from the Chinese store. They want comp from dudes that spit it how they live it, ya dig?

To the dudes that got genuine love for me and looked out for me; I got some major love for y'all dudes: Geez, Leem, T-Bone, Rock, Lil Omar, Wes, Markish, Tyress, B-wright, and my man Eddie Gilbert.

To the other cats I met throughout this 8 years: Fookie, Hak, C-Doe, Vaughn, Lil-J, Skip, BooMatic,"Lil"Cook, Justice, Nitty, Bub, Saleem, Looney Tunes, Haz Chiley, Ma-D, S.A., S.T., E.Dub and Marvin Williams. (a real good dude.)

To everybody else, if we really cool you ain't worried about no shout outs b/cuz you know when I get on, you straight.

To Chester, the city I wear on my sleeve, the city I was born in and will probably die in; shout-outs to everybody-haters included.

To my peoples from Coatesville, Oxford, West Chester, Darby, Sharon Hill, Philly, N.Y., D-Ware, Pittsburg, Jersey; all the states systems and anybody I forgot-much love. I ain't got enough paper for everybody; I got you next time.

Finally, to the few people that went home and kept their word, the few people that played their part out in the real world when it counted the most: Scotty, Biggs, Loc, Jamir (Miz), Mike Miles, Sincere (Ty-Ty), E. Marvels and D.J. - Good Looking, "Much Love."

# THE REALEST BOOK THE STREETS WILL EVER READ

In the concrete jungle that we  hustlers call the streets... There are certain rules that we must adhere to...
We cannot adhere to the rules of the court or the laws of the land...
We lost that privilege when we chose to indulge in the criminal activities of the underworld...
now, as hustlers, gangstas, murderers  and convicts, we  must follow a different set of rules...A simple code that states...

## WHATEVER STARTS ON THE STREETS... STAYS ON THE STREETS...

# CHAPTER 1

Doc came speeding down Twenty-fourth Street from St. James. He bent a left on Madison in front of Larry's Pizza Shop. The system in his BMW 745 was crazy, so people heard him coming a mile away. Doc quickly shut the car off and walked across the street to holler at his team.

Flame and Blaze were both sitting on Juanita's steps surrounded by Nikki, Shakeya, Charnetta and Simone. They were on the usual dick-eating shit that most chickenheads be on when they're around guys with money. Each of the girls had their favorites, so sometimes they even got into dick-eating competitions.

That was the funniest shit in the world to Doc. Nikki was Blaze's personal pom-pom girl, and Charnetta was Flame's. On a good day, if Doc was lucky he might even catch them arguing over the two. Nikki would act like Blaze was God's gift to the world, and Charnetta would dispute it by claiming Flame was sexier than the sunset on a deserted beach. Then they'd argue about who had what and who had the best sex. They'd come an eye blink away from fighting and maybe, if it got really bad, they would stop speaking to each other for a week or two. The craziest part was that none of them were an actual girlfriend.

They were the *two o'clock in the morning girls*. About two o'clock, after all the bars closed, *maybe* if they got extremely lucky, Blaze or Flame might take the chicks to a cheap hotel. But Doc hated all of the two o'clock in the morning girls, and the feeling was mutual. He was a narcissist and possibly the most conceited nigga on the block. None of them could understand why, because he was far from the most attractive person on the block. But who needed *their* approval? Not Doc. He could care less what they thought. He believed they only despised him because he disrespected them at will. Doc treated them like shit, and that was an understatement.

He shook Blaze and Flame's hands before sitting down on the steps.

"What's the deal?" he greeted, happy to see his peoples for the first time in three days.

"Same shit," Blaze replied.

"Yeah," Flame chimed in, "tryna get this mothafucking money."

"Yo, y'all seen Wally?" Doc asked.

Both Flame and Blaze shook their heads no. Then, out of the corner of his eye, Doc caught Shakeya whispering something to Nikki, which made Nikki's face ball up.

Now to some niggas, Nikki and Shakeya might have looked all right. Especially when they threw their little outfits on and got their hair done, you couldn't tell them shit. But to Doc, those bitches were gutted. Shakeya looked like Mya on crack. And even with the little feathered hair-do she was wearing that made broke niggas wanna holler, she still looked like a peacock in the face to him. And Nikki? She had her moments. Mainly when her long hair covered her face, so you had to get up close and personal to see her flaws, like lips blackened from smoking weed all day, everyday. Or teeth so fucked up from a candy addiction that they'd make you wanna throw up when the bitch smiled. But to a quarter ounce, ball-game flipping-ass nigga the two of them belonged on the cover of a magazine ... *Easy.*

Still, Doc wasn't going to put up with them bitches biting his back out right in his face.

**2**

"Damn," he protested, "Why the fuck y'all always talking about me? Y'all should get paid for being on my dick, then maybe y'all could get rich. Dick-eating bitches," he groused.

"Boy, ain't nobody talking about you!" Shakeya responded.

Then Nikki added her two cents.

"And we definitely ain't on ya dick. Don't get that fucked up," Nikki said, her face and tone full of absurdity at the very thought.

Flame and Blaze's laughter didn't help Doc take it on the chin too good either. But he kept his mouth shut because he knew if he argued with her he would more than likely punch her in the mouth. He looked over at Flame to change the subject, saying, "Yo, what y'all doing tonight?"

"I don't know. We wanna go down the Metro if everybody up to it."

"Yeah, it's dollar night," Blaze added.

Dollar night at any bar in Chester was a good night, because it was guaranteed to attract piles of women. But dollar night on Third Street, that shit was like being at a Mardi Gras or a Greek picnic. Corner to corner crowds.

It was the beginning of summer, and the three bosses on Twenty-fourth Street all recently bought new cars. Flame was in a Denali, Blaze was wheeling an Escalade EXT, and Doc was pushing a BMW 745. It was a week ago Friday that the trio hit the city showing off their new toys.

Shit like that made people talk in a small city like Chester. The only other block that did the same thing was the Dog Pound. On New Year's, the bull J-Rug grabbed a Chrysler 300, Scotty was in a Dodge Magnum, Ronald a S-500, Bey was pushing a Tahoe, while five or six other niggas were all up in some new shit following them, when they came through Third on New Year's, ten deep. All *new* shit with papers in the windows. They shut shit down.

That's where Doc got his idea. He went to his squad and suggested that on the first day of summer they were going to hurt the city. The only problem was, his squad wasn't eating like the Dog Pound's squad. The three main suppliers, Doc, Blaze, and Flame were the backbone of Twenty-fourth Street. Everybody else was fucked up.

On the low though, Doc's young bull, Wally, was supposed to cop something that day. Only Doc knew about it. He wanted to be around to see the faces on niggas when his young bull came through. Only he couldn't stand sitting around the *porch-monkey*, hood rats that surrounded his team.

"Yo," Doc said, "I'm about to hit the liquor store right quick. Y'all niggas want something?"

"Grab a case of Dom Perignon" Blaze said, pulling a knot from his pocket and peeling off a thousand dollar stack.

Flame peeled off three hundreds with his cheap self and asked for some Hypnotic and Dom Perignon.

"All right. I'll be right back," Doc said, heading for his car after he collected their money.

Doc was just pulling out when his young bull came screeching around the corner. Not a second after Wally double-parked in the street; Blaze's young bull Biggy bent the corner and skidded up to Wally's bumper.

The rims on Wally's X5 were so sick that it took Doc a moment to notice the paint job; they were still spinning with a lime-greenish light inside of them; pearl white on white with Ben Franklins painted all over it.

"This mothafucka's crazy!" Doc exclaimed, as he turned off his car and climbed out to admire Wally's truck, astonished at how flawless the paint job looked as he walked around the truck.

Wally and Doc didn't always have to talk to understand each other, so when their eyes met, Wally cranked the system up.

♪ *I'm out for presidents to represent me/ Get money/ I'm out for presidents to represent me* ♪. The Jay-Z song was so appropriate that it made Doc laugh.

"You stunting," Doc drawled out so Wally could read his lips.

Wally just pulled his hat down over his eyes, already slouched low in the seat with a look that said, *I know you love me for this one, old head. I'm shitting hard.*

Doc came around to the front of the truck and peeped the nameplate. What he saw made him throw a *you-outta-control* face at Wally.

"The President?" Doc said.

Wally nodded.

Blaze and Flame made their way to stand beside Doc to see what he was talking about.

"Now ya young bull the president, huh?" Blaze said, half hating half astonished.

"Yeah, this nigga is stunter," Flame added.

Nobody noticed Biggy's car. It wasn't like it wasn't nice, it just didn't have that Team Baurtwell customized paint. Biggy was in a Lexus GS 400, jet black with peanut butter guts. And after Wally got done stealing the show, Blaze and Flame walked over to Biggy's car to say what's up. Doc walked around to Wally's passenger window and stuck his head in.

"So, what you think?" Wally asked, already knowing the answer.

"I think you stunting right now," Doc replied, feeding his ego.

"Hey, Laneer. I like ya truck. It's real cute," Shakeya said, all in the driver's side window, addressing Wally by his real name.

"Cute?" Wally said to Doc, not even looking at Shakeya. Wally just flicked the remote to his CD changer to his Ludacris CD. "So, what you about to do, old head?" Wally said nonchalantly to Doc.

Then, suddenly, a message came blaring from the speakers: ♪♪ *Move bitch, get out the way/ Get out the way bitch, get out the way* ♪♪

"You ain't got to be acting all like that, Laneer. That's corny," Shakeya voiced angrily.

But Wally was on a roll, so he rolled the window up on the bitch. And knowing Doc wouldn't miss an opportunity to cuss Shakeya out, Wally called out, "Hey, old head, tell that dick-eating bitch, my name Wally."

"You dick-eating bitch, stop calling my young bull Laneer. His name Wally!" Doc hollered at her. But after the fact he told Wally, "you stunting too hard."

Wally slid over to the passenger's seat and unlocked the doors so his old head could hop behind the wheel. Doc wasted no time coming around to the driver's side.

"You know they gonna start hating ya guts now," Doc stated as he climbed in and adjusted the seat.

"Who is *they*?" Wally responded.

Blaze followed suit and hopped in Biggy's car and high-beamed Doc so he could pull off. Flame saluted his team as they rolled out. He still needed to sell the rest of his coke before they went out, so he passed up on the ride to the liquor store.

Twenty minutes later, they pulled back up on the block with enough liquor to throw a block party. A cooler was in the back of Wally's truck filled with ice, a case of Dom Perignion, a case of Hypnotic, six bottles of Hennessy and Patron and a few bottles of Belvedere. All the liquor was for when the bars closed. Then they would more than likely head uptown to an after-hours spot, and after that they'd probably go straight to the hotel. Even though they all had their own apartments, the unwritten rule was that nine out of ten girls they met on the first night weren't trustworthy enough to go to their houses. Plus they all had girlfriends, all except Doc. Not to mention they were all a bunch of fronting-ass niggas.

When they pulled back up on Twenty-fourth Street the block was packed. Tyran was in Blaze's money-green Benz S-500, with his cousin Tommy while B and Duck were in Flame's S80 Volvo wagon. Plus there were twice as many dick-eating bitches around.

As Doc got out of Wally's truck to pass out the liquor, he noticed bad-ass Juanita. She was the queen of the two o'clock in the morning chicks. Juanita was probably the only chick on the block that nobody fucked, but everybody wanted. She was tall, about five-ten, five-eleven, light-skinned, with green eyes and a body that screamed, *If you ain't fucked me, you ain't had good pussy!* She could easily pass for Lisa Raye's little sister on her *worst* day.

The only person that she had sex with in the last year was Doc's nut-ass little brother Ali. Doc couldn't stand Ali, but he tried to conceal it as best he could. Doc could never get past how his brother shitted on him while he was locked up. Ali was rumored to be rich, but he fronted on Doc like Doc wasn't the one who gave him all the connects that he had. Not to mention Ali let niggas come to court and testify against Doc when he could have easily paid them off. If they didn't have the same blood running through their veins, Doc would've *been* bodied the nigga.

After Doc passed out liquor to all his young bulls, he couldn't help but offer Juanita something.

"You want something to drink, Queen Bee?" he asked, bringing a smile to her face.

"Yeah, give me a bottle of Dom, Mr. President's *old*

**7**

*head*," Juanita replied, her sweet voice making Doc want to stiff her even more.

Doc walked to the rear of the truck and grabbed a bottle of Dom Perignon. Handing it to her, he made sure to size her up with his eyes as she took it.

"Thank you, Doc."

Doc sat on Juanita's steps with his team, bidding with his squad another half hour before they were ready to go. Around midnight they loaded into their rides and pulled off.

Third Street traffic was backed up all the way to Townsend Street. Cars moved at a snail's pace toward the local bars. The eight-car convoy from Twenty-fourth slowly rolled up Third hitting the horns at various people they knew. When they got to the Metro, since there was nowhere to park nearby, they bent a left on Hayes, drove down to Second, and doubled back up the alley on the side of the Metro.

The scenery was wall-to-wall people. It looked like it was a concert or something. Doc hopped from his *Quarter to 8*, which was leading the pack, and sat on the hood. Directly across the street he saw his homey, Turk, and a pile of Dog Pound niggas, about twenty deep, in the middle of a crap game. He knew it was Turk because he saw the midnight blue Escalade with the Lamborghini doors.

Right in front of the bar were the niggas from Third Street. McCaffe and Bennett project niggas were posted up in front of the Chinese store. But more importantly was the fact that bitches were everywhere, and they all had on next to nothing.

Doc, Blaze, and Flame all sat on Doc's car with the young bulls surrounding them, making their appearance like bosses do. Shortly after, all three of them made their way to the bar, stopping briefly to holla at the Third Street crew out front. As they squeezed inside the bar, Doc felt like the president as he continued shaking hand after hand.

"Grimy, what's up? ... Jerv, ...What's good my nigg?"

By the time Doc finally reached the bar he felt like he hollered at everybody *in* the mothafucka. It was cool though, because it wasn't like that for everybody. Everybody didn't have the type of love Doc had.

Blaze made his way to the back of the bar and posted up with some chicks he knew, while Flame ordered shots for everybody. All of them got girls, but Blaze thought he was a real live pimp.

Blaze was a half-black, half-Puerto Rican pretty boy, tall and slim, with the good grade of hair most of them pretty niggas had. He was the type that made it hard to get women, because he was on everything walking with a skirt. He got the name Blaze because he was always the first to shoot some shit up. He carried guns like Footlocker carried sneaks. Blaze always claimed his fight game was pro, but in the ten years Doc had known him he never saw Blaze punch anyone. Blaze will talk that fighting shit, but before a nigga could get a chance to get out on his skinny ass, he'd shoot the party up and hit twenty people that ain't have shit to do with shit, and possibly kill three or four mothafuckas that did.

Flame, on the other hand, was the complete opposite. He'd punch a nigga's lights out. Niggas always slept on the curly-headed, brown-skinned bull with the sleepy eyes that always made him look high. Mainly because Flame was just a cool dude. But if provoked, he'd fuck a nigga up *or* shoot it out, choosing to shoot it out as a last resort. Doc had personally watched Flame fuck up ten to twelve mothafuckas.

Now Doc, at sixteen, was a gangster's gangster. He ain't give a fuck if you wanted to fight, shoot it out, or use bottles in a bar fight. It was whatever, because he grew up getting beat up, and spent most of his life in and out of jail working on the solid reputation he was known for. And now, two-dozen shootings, a few D.L. bodies, and forty or fifty prizefights later, he was a certified hood legend. He looked it too, with a husky build on a six-foot frame, chocolate brown skin, and deep brown eyes that said *"Thug"* more than *TuPac's* did in his prime. Not to mention all the prerequisite battle scars: the bullet holes from being shot everywhere from leg to head; the stab wound from the time he was kidnapped when he was eighteen; and a grocery list of other marks that each had its own story.

The three of them were in the bar for about ten minutes when gunshots erupted out front. They didn't really pay it any mind, until moments later, when Tyran ran into the bar hollering their names.

"Yo, Doc, Blaze, Flame hurry up, we out!"

The trio ran outside into a thinning crowd. Then the shocking news came.

"Yo, Wally just slumped a mothafucka!  He hopped in ya car and bailed, Doc!"

"Damn, what happened?" Doc asked.

Tyran began to explain the situation while they ran to their cars, but the details were sketchy. Most of the young bulls had already bailed, leaving behind the three old heads and Blaze's young bull.

The dead body was laid out a few feet from where Doc's car had been parked. Doc hopped in Wally's truck and pulled off. He whipped out his cell phone and dialed Wally to see what happened. The phone rang once before Wally answered.

"Yeah."

"Yo, what the fuck happened!" Doc barked.

"Man, these bitch-ass niggas rolled up on me on some hating shit. And while I was arguing with Bang, his nut-ass homey tried to snatch my chain. So I slumped that pussy."

"What you and Bang was arguing for?"

"Cuz, that nigga rolled up threatening to rob me if I ain't

**10**

break down. So I'm tryna tell him to pump his brakes, and his man stole me and grabbed my chain. So I let the nine rip through my jacket pocket, hitting the nigga in his face. You feel me?"

Doc just shook his head. He was mad he wasn't there to prevent the entire incident.

"So where you going?" Doc inquired.

"I'm on my way out ya crib, that's why I grabbed ya car."

"All right, look, I'mma try to find out what's going on. I'mma hit you up tomorrow. Just lay low until I find out the deal, All right?"

"All right, old head, I'll holla at you tomorrow."

Doc hung up and called to the car behind him, saying, "Where y'all tryna go, Flame?"

"We going to our bar. B's on the other line. He's breaking the shit down now. They all over Jack's."

Jack's was the local bar that the Twenty-fourth Street dudes usually hung in. The crowd was usually Eastside dudes and chicks that they saw every day, all day.

Doc pulled up right in front of the bar and parked. Moments later Flame and Blaze pulled up. Blaze of course had three chicks in the car with him. Doc noticed that all of his young bulls were already there, and directly in front of the bar was Ali's Escalade.

*Bitch-ass nigga*, Doc thought as he climbed out of Wally's truck.

Doc, Blaze and Flame all walked into Jack's and found a table to talk in the back. Then two young bulls from Twenty-fourth Street pulled up chairs. They started explaining the story, and for the second time Doc was mad he wasn't there to squash it.

"You know the bull Bang and Wally started arguing, right?" B recited. "Well, the bull they call Donny walked up and hyped that shit up. It wasn't no heated argument before he added his two cents. I think Bang was just talking shit on some playing shit."

Blaze's young bull, who was sitting in the bar, strolled up on the conversation just as B finished with the story.

"So what happened to Bang?" Flame asked.

"I think he got hit in the arm. He ran off holding his arm, feel me?" Tyran added.

"All right, first and foremost, nobody has seen nothing," insisted Flame taking control. "We ain't going to give them more information than they already got, okay?"

"Yeah," Doc added. "If there are witnesses, it's going to be us and them, and we ain't see nothing. And if they did, they going to wish they didn't."

"Yo, was any bitches out there?" Blaze asked.

"Yeah," B said. "Those bitches Michelle and Lisa were out there, dick-eating Wally's truck. But it was some other bitches out there too. They were standing right next to us."

"All right, I'm on that," Blaze assured his team. "Look, from here on out, it never happened; we don't know shit."

After their conversation ended, Blaze and Flame made their way over to the bar to holla at the chicks Blaze picked up. Doc sent Duck to the bar to get him a drink, staying at the table to holla at the rest of the young bulls. Doc spotted his little brother, Ali by the door and knew that they had walked directly past him without him saying a word. It made Doc wanna punch him in the mouth, but he refused to let his anger get the best of him.

"What's up?" Duck hollered across the bar to Doc, noticing his anger.

"Ain't shit, pimp!"

Doc was more mad at Wally than anybody. Technically, *Wally* was Doc's little brother. He'd be sick if they locked his favorite young bull up for life behind some dumb-ass shit, because Doc knew prison better than he knew the streets.

Doc was just coming home from a bid that came courtesy of some snitch-ass niggas and bitches on his block. But in jail he met some of the most thorough and smartest niggas in the world. And to him, prison was a place where the man stored you to make money off you while you lost everybody and everything you loved. He just couldn't imagine seeing his young bull letting life pass him by and becoming a memory over a chain. They had stacked too much money and climbed too far up the ladder of success to let some shit like that ruin their lives. Maybe Doc was getting soft, or maybe he was maturing. He wasn't sure. But what he was sure of was that one day soon he was going to get his priorities straight. This could very well be his wake up call telling him it was time to retire.

# CHAPTER 2

Two o'clock came quickly, and before Doc knew it the bar was about to close. The bartender yelled for last call, and people ran to the bar to buy their last drinks for the night. A few minutes later, people started heading out to the streets.

Doc was debating if he was sober enough to take the forty-five minute drive out to Oxford, or if he was going to stay in the city at his ducky apartment. Blaze invited him to the hotel as he left out the bar, but Doc declined. Flame, on the other hand, was more than happy to take Blaze up on his offer. He hollered at the chick from down Third Street. Blaze nodded too, shot some game, and passed her the keys to his Denali.

"Yo, I'mma pull around front so she can follow me," Blaze notified Flame as he headed toward his truck.

Doc and Flame made their way out front and took the opportunity to talk for a minute.

"So, what you going to do tonight?" Flame asked.

"I don't know, I might shoot to the crib and holla at my young bull," Doc said.

"Well, I'mma holla at you tomorrow," Flame said. "Call me in the morning."

Flame hugged Doc and gave him a firm handshake before stepping off. As Doc was about to walk to his car someone called out to him. He looked back and saw Charnetta approaching.

"Yo, what's up?" Doc asked her.

"Can you drive me and Juanita home?"

Doc looked a few feet away and saw Juanita talking to Ali. It didn't look like she needed a ride to him. Still, Doc told Charnetta it wouldn't be a problem. But just as Doc was crossing the street a car came speeding in his direction and, then, from nowhere, shots rang out.

Doc ran for the safety of the sidewalk, taking cover behind the closest available vehicle. He inadvertently tackled Juanita in the process of diving behind Ali's truck, as machine gun fire ripped through all the parked cars on the block and took a lot of bystanders by surprise.

Ali had been standing in the street unlocking the door to his truck when the shooting started. The fact that it shocked him made him react too slowly as he attempted to run for cover. He only got as far as the front of his truck before bullets tore through his flesh and riddled his body. Ali's momentum carried him face-first into the pavement. Juanita screamed and Doc shouted, as his body fell inches from where they were laying.

When the shooting stopped, Doc checked to see if his brother was cool. He knelt down next to Ali to see if he was still breathing. With the last breath of life left in his body, Ali attempted to talk.

"Yo," Ali murmured, then coughed up a clot of blood. He looked deeply into Doc's eyes and saw the pain and concern.

"Hold on, nigga," Doc coaxed, "you going to make it. The hospital is right across the street." "Somebody get an ambulance!" He yelled.

"Yo, I ... I ain't gonna make it to no hos ... hospital. Just mak... make sure you take care of my kids for me," Ali whispered.

"I got you. Don't worry about it. You going to be here to do it yaself."

Ali, realizing he didn't have much time left, grabbed Doc's hand as tight as he could.

"I'm not gonna make it, bro. I love you, man.... Make sure you get them niggas," Ali insisted with tears filling his eyes.

Realizing Ali was probably right, Doc kneeled all the way down to hug his brother, vowing, "I got you, dog! I swear on my mom, I got you!"

The tears were falling uncontrollably for Doc now, as he held his brother for the first and last time. Then someone tapped him on his shoulder, bringing him out of his zone. Doc looked up at Blaze and saw tears falling from his eyes too.

"Yo, they killed Flame, and shot B and Duck up," Blaze informed him.

Doc gazed down the street and saw his right hand man laid out in the middle of the street.

"I'mma fucking kill them pussies!" Doc snapped, running down to holla at Flame. But it was too late.

Flame had been standing in front of his Volvo talking to Duck and B. And since Duck and B were in the car, they were both still alive. B was bleeding badly from a bullet wound to the neck, and Duck was hit in the arm. But Flame was dead. The truth of the situation was just settling in as the ambulance and the police were pulling up.

Blaze suggested that they should leave to avoid questioning, but Doc wasn't registering what he said.

Officer Minor was the first on the scene, and he immediately started badgering witnesses for information. But by then Blaze was gone, with the Third Street chicks following him in Flame's Denali. Tyran was the last to leave, practically running people over as he sped off. Biggy walked up on Doc and volunteered to stay to make sure their squad was all right. That's when Doc snapped back to reality.

"Yo! Make sure nobody's talking to these fucking Jakes!" Doc told them before heading for Wally's truck.

"Excuse me, sir. Is that your truck?" Officer Minor asked.

"No," Doc replied as he hopped in the truck, "It ain't mine. Why?"

"Well, whose truck is it, and why are you driving it?"

"Yo, what is you asking me a hundred questions for? Did I do something wrong?" Doc replied, angry and agitated.

"I don't know, maybe you did. I'm just trying to find out who it belongs to."

"Look, this my brother's truck – the guy they just loaded into the ambulance. Right now I just wanna go to the hospital and find out what's going on. You dig me?"

Officer Minor was saying something else, but Doc paid him no mind. He merely went in his pocket and pulled out his cell phone to call his brother's baby's mom, Shana. She became hysterical as Doc broke the bad news to her.

Standing there listening, Officer Minor started feeling a little sympathetic towards Doc, but was still mad at the way Doc was handling the situation.

"Yeah, Shana," Doc continued into the phone, "me and my mom will meet y'all at the hospital… aiight?"

"Look, excuse me, buddy," Officer Minor cut in. "Was your brother down on Third Street tonight in this truck?"

"Shana, I'mma call you back, the police in my ear... All right... Yeah, I'll see you later. Bye." Doc hung up the cell phone then turned around to face the cop with his rock on. "Yo, what's up, man? I just told you that my brother just got killed. Can you at least have enough respect to let me call my family?"

"I'm sorry to hear that, but I need to know who was driving this truck earlier," Officer Minor replied.

"You asking the wrong person, because I don't know!"

"Well, where's *your* car?"

"Right there," Doc pointed. "The burgundy Escalade. You

want the keys or something?" he questioned, while shoving the keys at the officer.

"Listen," Officer Minor said, voicing his own impatience. "I could easily lock you up and impound the truck and have you answer all the questions I want."

"Do what you going to do," Doc retorted. "It'll be fucked up, but it won't be as fucked up as watching my brother die tonight!"

Juanita walked up, crying all crazy and hopped in the passenger's side. Charnetta climbed into the back, sobbing just as freely.

"Doc, can you take us home, please?" Juanita said.

Doc turned to face Officer Minor, and the cop stepped away from the car. For right now he would let Doc leave, but it was far from over. Somebody would go to jail for being in that truck, the officer was sure of that.

Doc drove straight to Charnetta's house and dropped her off first. Then he pulled around the corner in front of Juanita's house. She was hesitant about getting out, and Doc took that as a sign.

"You wanna shoot out to the Embassy with me?" he asked Juanita.

"If you want me to."

Doc took that as a yes and put the car in drive. As he pulled off, his thoughts were consumed with avenging his brother's death, so he was mostly silent on the ride out Essington. He just listened to the music and smoked one cigarette after another. He picked up the cell phone a few minutes before he pulled into the hotel parking lot and asked Blaze for his room number. After hanging up, he went in his pocket and slid out a knot of money.

"You got your ID on you?" Doc asked Juanita.

"Yeah."

He peeled off two hundreds and handed them to her, asking, "Get us a room?"

"Okay," she replied as she took the money.

Doc found Blaze's truck in the lot and parked in the slot next to it. After he turned the car off, he grabbed some liquor from the cooler and threw it in a brown bag.

Juanita paid for the room and headed toward the elevator with Doc directly behind her.

"You gonna be at Blaze's room for a long time?" she asked.

"I don't know. Why?"

"Because I want you to hurry back so I can tell you something."

Doc gave her a head nod and got off the elevator on Blaze's floor. He was hoping Juanita really didn't want to talk, because he didn't care to hear stories about *Flame* all night. He'd rather get some of that hot gushy pussy to take his mind off the pain he felt.

Doc walked down the hallway to Blaze's room and knocked on the door. The chick that opened the door was completely naked, and her body was nice. Doc became instantly aroused. He walked in the room, closing the door behind himself, as she stood directly before him like a centerfold.

"I hope you came for me," she said coyly. "Or should I say I hope you *cumming* for me?"

She approached Doc and slid a hand down deep into his pants. Astonishment crept into her face as if she found something a bit more than she expected.

"Hey, shorty, hold up," Doc said, almost reluctantly. "Give me a minute to holla at my mans right quick."

Doc brushed past her and walked further into the room. The sight of Blaze lying up under the covers with her friend let Doc know that it wasn't a good time to talk.

"I ain't think you was gonna show up," Blaze declared,

with a hint of relief in his voice. He had the look of a person just rescued from a deserted island. Although Tyran took one of the girls off his hands, Blaze was still stuck with two, and he was glad Doc showed up to lighten his load.

───────────────────────

Wally rolled into the Nottingham Towers' parking lot and killed the motor. He hopped out and searched through a ring of numerous keys until he found the one that would unlock the vestibule door of Doc's apartment building. Once the door was unlocked, he went into the building and walked the carpeted hallway until he came to Doc's first floor apartment and let himself in.

The two-bedroom apartment was tastefully decorated, filled with the nicest things money could buy. Wally sat down on the leather couch and picked up the remote to the plasma TV mounted on the wall. The 64-inch flat screen looked more like a movie screen than an actual television. It was equipped with surround sound, DVD, and Direct TV. Wally skimmed through the channels to find a movie, which took a few minutes. Afterwards he kicked his shoes off and laid his cell phone and I-phone on the glass coffee table. The table was trimmed in gold and embellished with diamonds. Doc hated for people to set stuff on the table, but Wally didn't care.

He got up before getting too comfortable to raid Doc's mini-bar. He walked inside the kitchen and opened up the cabinets over the sink; the crib was as familiar as his own.

"Let's see, what do I want?" Wally mused aloud, glancing at all the bottles of liquor in the cabinet.

He settled on a fifth of Hypnotic, then opened another cabinet to get a glass and filled it with ice before heading back into the living room. Wally sank into the couch again and flicked through the channels for another few minutes before he settled on Comic View. Just as he lay back to relax, his cell phone rang.

---

Juanita unlocked the door to the hotel room, walked in, and relocked the door. She walked to the back of the room and sat the bag with the liquor in it on the table. Juanita wished she had brought a change of clothes, but was satisfied with the designer bra and panty set she was wearing.

She kicked off her Chloe sandals first, and then wiggled out of her tight D&G capri jeans. She then pulled her matching D&G shirt off over her head. She stood in front of the mirror briefly to glance at herself. Content with what she saw, Juanita continued to undress and walked to the bathroom.

She ran a warm shower, and as soon as she stepped in, her tears began to mix with the water. She cried softly over Ali, wondering how she would feel in the morning if she decided to sleep with Doc. Secretly she was planning to leave with Doc from the moment he set foot in the bar. She was only feeling bad because she couldn't help but feel responsible for Ali's death. She had intentionally stalled Ali to ask him a bunch of stupid questions just so he would notice when she left with Doc. Now she felt like maybe he'd still be alive if she hadn't stopped him. Her conscience was eating her up.

*It's not ya fault. You didn't know they were going to start shooting. It is ya fault. Don't fool yaself; you wanted to flaunt it in his face. And now he's dead.*

Juanita was starting to think she was crazy, but she knew she couldn't be if she could think rationally. A couple of minutes later she got out the shower, dried off, and walked into the room and pulled the bottle of Dom Perignon from the liquor bag. She gulped down a mouthful, then another, and then another until the bottle was halfway empty. But the Dom Perignon wasn't strong enough, so she opened a bottle of Hennessy and swallowed a mouthful of that, wondering w*here Doc was.*

Juanita sat on the bed naked for a minute to roll her weed up before she slid back into her tight bra and panty set. Then she popped the Hennessy again and walked to the door to stuff a towel under it. Moments later, she sat back down and lit the weed up.

---

Although the time seemed inappropriate to talk to Blaze about business, Doc sat around long enough to let Blaze know he was really upset. Then Doc took the chick into the bathroom and got some head before rolling out.

When he got to his room, Doc could smell the aroma of weed in the hallway. He tapped on the door lightly and waited a few seconds before Juanita opened it. The tight Chanel underwear she had on momentarily made him lose his train of thought, he was breathless. He stepped into the room and eyed her closely as she shut the door. Juanita sashayed back to the bed, grabbed a towel, and tried to fan the smoke. Doc offered a solution to the problem by walking past her and opening the balcony door.

A bit embarrassed, Juanita said, "I guess I should've been done that?"

Doc just shrugged his shoulders then grabbed the bottle of Hennessy off the table as he sat down. He kicked his shoes off and slid up against the backboard of the bed to watch TV.

*Make ya move,* he said to himself. But just as quickly as

the notion popped into his head he shook it off.

"What took you so long?" Juanita asked.

*I was getting my dick sucked,* he thought to himself. But what he actually said was, "I was hollering at my man about some *real* shit. I ain't know I took that long."

"You didn't. I was just teasing you."

Juanita got up from the bed and walked to the table. There she picked up a paper cup and filled it from the bottle of Dom Perignon beside it. Then she returned to the bed and sat next to Doc. She looked straight ahead at the TV, not really paying attention to what was on, quietly fantasizing about what he would say or do to try to get her. By the time a commercial came on she was starting to think that maybe he wouldn't make a move at all.

"You watching this?" she asked, knowing he wasn't either.

Doc just shook his head no, drank the rest of the Hennessy, and got up to get the other bottle out of the bag.

Juanita walked over to the TV and intentionally bent over so Doc could get an eyeful of her ass. She flicked through the channels and stopped on the same channel before looking back to see if Doc was paying attention.

"How about this?" she asked him. "This looks good?"

"Yeah, it's cool."

*It's the same fucking channel,* she said to herself. *What the fuck, I guess I got to stand here all night for him to get the picture.* But another voice within her said, *Why is you trying so hard? Fuck him. Sit ya high ass down.*

She changed the stations again, hoping to find something for real this time, before looking back one more time. That same voice came to her once more, *if you don't sit ya dumb ass down, girl!*

Doc wasn't paying attention to anything except the bottle he just opened. He was drinking like it was going out of style, and Juanita was starting to think he was going to pass out in the very near future.

The last time she had sex was so long ago that her pussy was literally as tight as a keyhole. She sat back down, wondering if she would seem like a whore if she came right out and asked for it. She felt like she really needed a hard fuck to relieve the stress, though she was thinking she'd probably have a better chance of meeting her favorite star than getting some good sex tonight. Then Doc finally said something.

"Yo, you got some more weed?"

"Mm-hmm. I got a half a blunt and another bag. Want me to roll it up?"

"Naw, just give me that half a blunt, if you don't mind."

She reached for the blunt and her lighter on the table and passed them to him.

Doc accepted them and went out on the balcony to smoke.

———————————

By four in the morning everyone in Blaze's room was sound asleep, except Blaze. He lay up silently by himself mourning the loss of his best friend and contemplating his next move. He thought about the littlest details, over and over again, knowing that if he wanted to get away with murder, it was going to have to be planned right.

Blaze knew from the look on Doc's face when Doc came to the door that he meant business, but Blaze considered himself the sharpest out of his squad. He knew going to the hotel and having an orgy with two chicks would make people think he wasn't stressing about the situation like that. Demeanor was everything to him, and he never wanted somebody to be able to look at the way he was carrying himself and be able to call his next move. While everybody thought he wasn't sweating shit, he would be the brains behind the whole operation that would get all of his enemies killed and be the last person people suspected.

*One thing was certain; somebody would pay for killing Flame. If not the person who did it, then his mother, father, kids, grandmother. Somebody,* Blaze thought to himself.

Blaze wouldn't rest until they were dead. From that day on he planned on letting niggas know why they called him Blaze. 'Cause he was gonna ride until the wheels fell off.

# CHAPTER 3

A half an hour passed before Juanita decided to go check on Doc. "You all right out there?" she called, sounding seductively sweet.

"Yeah, I'm cool. I was just thinking, you know?"

"Yeah, I feel you," she said with compassion. "You wanna talk?"

Doc just looked at her stupidly. "About what?"

"I don't know ... about you?" she replied, reaching. But it was worth a shot.

*About me?* he thought. *Naw, bad idea.*

It was a mistake Doc only made once in his life. He still couldn't believe that he let somebody get past his wall, because he always kept his guard up. Doc was betrayed by everyone he ever trusted, so it made him an extremely cold person at times.

He was the child of Sharon, a single mother who had him at an extremely young age, and Duron, Sr., a so-called pimp-drug addict-con artist, and the slimiest nigga Doc ever met in his life. His dad walked back into his life when he was twelve, the same time Sharon was in and out of the hospital fighting cancer. That's when Big Ron decided he wanted to be a father. They got along at first, but after Sharon lost her fight with cancer and died, Doc was devastated. Doc turned to the streets, totally disregarding the warnings his father gave him.

He started hustling on the harsh streets of the projects first. It took a minute for niggas to accept him, but he was out

**26**

to make a name for himself. He was one of the young gunners that was quick to get in some dumb shit. It was Doc's way of venting all the anger and pain he kept bottled up. He lived his life being the headliner of the dumb shit like *fighting over the High, down at the parade shooting and hopping on dudes down Reflections...."*

That was excitement for him, he was an adrenaline rush junkie. The only problem was, hustling around Buckman and the McCaffe was a lost cause. The McCaffe was breeding gangsters like farmers breed cattle. That made Doc feel like he wasn't reaching his potential. He wanted to be a hood legend, but staying in that neighborhood was like being on the same team as Kobe Bryant, A.I., and Shaq. They were all in their prime; there was too much talent, no way a nigga could shine.

Buckman had an all-star team and it wasn't as many play-ers as it was in other hoods so Doc shined up there easily. The only problem was the police were running down on the block everyday trying to lock dudes up and going to jail wasn't an option. However, in the projects it was niggas with names on every corner, which made him less of a target to the police. Plus, they had a host of young bulls coming up that was put-ting in work daily like the young bull Wally, N.Y., Mean Sheen, Ike and so on. Them niggas were getting in shootings every day, robbing niggas, pistol whipping chumps, the works.

Doc being who he was could've stayed up in the projects or around in Buckman and been cool, especially on the money tip. But he wanted to be the leader, the franchise player, who carried his whole team. Therefore, he had to migrate. His goal was to go somewhere and be the center of attention. Considering Chester's size, it didn't take long to find the per-fect block. He got in his set trip bag and tried hanging every-where. Until finally he found the block he was looking for, Twenty-fourth Street.

He stumbled across the block one day while dropping his young bull Wally off and saw that it was flooded with money. The only person holding the block down was skinny-ass Blaze. The rest of the niggas on the block ain't want no trouble from a young project nigga that could go to any block, in any hood, and drop seventeen a night. And that was bullets *or* ounces. He was a nigga that knew a lot of people and was well respected. Now all he needed was a block to run, which is exactly what he did. He turned it up ten notches. He started fucking with the bull Blaze, shot a couple niggas on the block, beat a couple niggas up, and in six months Doc and Blaze had the block locked and niggas were terrified.

Two years later, after a couple of shootings and a murder, Doc was locked up. The shit that hurt Doc the most was the D.A.'s main witnesses. The people who actually got Doc convicted were in fact his own young bulls and one of his young girls. He hired the most powerful lawyers money could buy to come from up under the rock with his life. He spanked the murder because it was all hearsay and ended up copping out to seven and a half to fifteen years for two shootings. You would think a thing like that would change him, but now, nine years later, he was ready to put it all on the line again. He was going to ride, and slump anybody he believed had something to do with Flame and Ali's murders.

This time, however, Doc had more at stake. He wasn't the same young bull searching for attention. He was one third of a dynasty. Doc, Blaze, and Flame all put up one  hundred and twenty-five  thousand dollars to score twenty-five bricks a week. Then they took eight a piece and split the last odd brick down in breakdowns; nicks they sold or used to pay crack-houses.

They actually had a trash bag full of nicks from all their flips. When they started scoring a year ago, they frontlined the extra nicks. Now, eighteen months later, they wouldn't dare front any coke.

Doc was putting coke out Oxford, West Chester, Coatesville, and in St. James. Blaze had coke out Lancaster, Scranton, and Chi-Chester. And Flame was supplying Sharon Hill, Darby, and Upper Darby. Plus they all split the Twenty-fourth Street money. It was a win-win situation that couldn't get any better. But now they were faced with a crisis. Flame was dead and Doc's most loyal young bull was on the run. How could shit get any worse?

"So I guess you don't wanna talk, huh?"

Doc snapped out of his daze and looked at Juanita. He didn't know how to say what he wanted to say, but he could tell by her facial expressions that she was reaching.

"You know why I don't like talking?"

She shook her head no.

"You know that bitch, Keisha, from 21$^{st}$ Street?"

"Yeah, I know her," Juanita said.

"Well, that bitch and a couple of slimy-ass young bulls I was fucking with got me knocked for that last bid I did?"

"Are you serious?" Juanita asked, shocked.

"Yeah, they tried to get me booked for life. But look at me now...crazy, right?"

"Yo, I heard about that too."

Juanita looked at Doc more closely. There was something about him that seemed so vulnerable it set her body on fire. She couldn't hold back any longer. She leaned in and gently took hold of his chin and kissed him. That kiss lead to another, and then another, and before she knew it, Doc was laying her down on the balcony's thin carpet.

He slowly climbed on top of her, sucking on her neck, leaving purple passion marks everywhere. Then he worked his way down to her breasts, discarding her bra on the balcony floor. Her nipples stood up, perky and stiff, as if they were just released from cruel confinement. Doc twirled his tongue around them and nibbled on them softly. The erotic faces Juanita made helped Doc become completely aroused. He slid further down her stomach, sucking and kissing every part of her flesh. He continued down to her legs and feet while maneuvering her tight panties off at the same time. He climbed in between her legs face first. The teasing was done, now she was about to have it her way like Burger King.

His soft wet tongue caressed Juanita's clitoris with a steady stroke as if he was painting a fence. He kept the pace rhythmic until she reached an orgasm, but for her the fun had just begun.

After she ejaculated, he eagerly stuck his tongue inside of her cookie jar. As soon as she was thoroughly excited again he stopped. Then he mounted her like a cowboy on a horse, and thrust his erection deep inside her. He was hard as a jackhammer prepared to fix the road inside of her love tunnel.

*Oh, good God Almighty*, Juanita groaned within herself. *Where has he been all of my life?*

Doc withdrew out of her slowly, leaving a small portion of himself within Juanita before lunging back down deep into her ocean of love. He was long stroking the shit out of her, and she loved every stroke of it.

To Doc, sex was like a sport, and he knew exactly how to sink the balls in the pocket with his pool stick. Twenty minutes later he went from long stroking to doggy style. Then he went for the golden gloves. He jabbed strong and hard with his super hard fist. He beat the pussy up like *Mr. T* beat *Rocky* up in the movies. The noises she made only made him go harder and harder, until his body finally locked up and went limp as he filled her with his fluids.

"Oooh! Uhh! Yeaaaa!" he moaned with delight.

He rolled off of her moments later and cuddled with her to watch the sunrise. After the sun came up, even though they

**30**

both were tired, they headed to the shower then returned to the bed for rounds two and three.

──────────────────────────

Tamia was worried sick about Wally. Duck had called from the hospital to tell her that detectives were looking for him. Tamia hung up and immediately called Wally to find out what was going on.

Wally was too smart to explain the whole situation over the phone, but he did let Tamia know shit was serious. He made her pack up all his money and coke and leave the apartment that night. He told her to stay at her mom's house down Delaware because he was sure the police would run up in there soon. He wasn't worried about the police as much as he was worried about niggas finding out where he lived, and running up in his house trying to hurt his girl. That was his worst fear of all.

Wally assured Tamia that he would meet her early tomorrow morning, and together they would go find a new apartment. After he hung up, Wally sat on the couch wondering who was reliable enough to run his five crack houses.

"Damn, I really fucked up this time," he mused aloud.

Wally was your typical placement kid; he'd spent more time in placements than he did on the streets. He usually caught most of his bits for drugs, although he did have two attempted homicides on his jacket; one for shooting a nigga in the chest three times.

That one happened during a fight down the carnival. The McCaffe niggas ran into their archrivals, The Gardens. In the middle of the huge fight, guns were drawn. At that time Wally and N.Y. were both fifteen. One of their enemies, Harp, pulled out his gun first and shot at Ike and it was then an eye for an eye. Out of nowhere Wally and N.Y. popped up and saved the day, shooting up three or four of their adversaries.

Fortunately nobody died, but Wally and N.Y. both managed to get locked up and placed in juvenile detentions until they were eighteen. Since then Wally pretty much stayed out of the way, until now.

He was a product of the streets, with the same sad story most kids his age told, parents on and off drugs, older brother died while he was young etc., but when he started getting major money, all of that didn't seem to matter anymore. He didn't have time for the dumb shit. But like they say, *"more money, more problems."*

Wally turned the TV off and tried to get some sleep. He knew he'd have a busy day to look forward to, so he decided to get as much rest as possible.

"Where the fuck this nigga at?" Blaze mumbled impatiently to himself as his phone rang for the fifth time. Two rings later...

"Hello?" Doc's half-asleep voice croaked over the line.

"Yo, it's check-out time. Where you at? What, you staying another day?"

"Naw."

"All right, well, I'll meet you in the parking lot," Blaze said, then hung up.

Doc took a minute to get himself together, then went to wake Juanita up.

"Yo, it's check-out time, boo," he said to her.

"Damn... we ain't leaving yet, is we?" She muttered, groggily with sleep. Even with cold in her eyes and her hair everywhere, she still looked good.

"Yeah, beautiful," Doc said regretfully. "I gotta go handle something, but I'mma call you later."

Doc climbed out the bed and put his clothes on. He

walked into the bathroom and washed his face and swished some courtesy mouthwash inside his mouth a few times. Juanita's actions echoed his when he was done. Ten minutes later the two of them strolled down to the parking lot. Blaze was sitting in his truck listening to the radio when he saw who kept Doc company last night.

"Yo, I'mma follow you to drop the queen off," Blaze said jokingly. "After that, you can ride down Third with me."

Doc and Juanita climbed into Wally's truck and sped off, headed for I-95. He got off at the Widener exit five minutes later and headed for Twenty-fourth Street. Tyran got to the block first and parked Flame's Denali, then he hopped into Blaze's Benz S-500 with the chicks from down Third Street. Doc pulled up second and kissed Juanita passionately. As soon as Blaze pulled up, Doc told Juanita he'd see her later before he hopped from Wally's X-5 to Blaze's truck.

"Keep an eye out on Wally and Flame's trucks," Doc instructed Juanita. "And call me if you see any suspicious looking cars pull up."

Blaze was on his job, already making sure that when he dropped the chicks off down Third, they'd gather up as much information as possible. The incentive he promised them was a thousand to five thousand dollars. They claimed they'd do it for free, but he threw the numbers their way to make them work harder. Blaze wanted names, and if he had to kick out some Prada boots or a few Chanel and Gucci outfits, it wasn't a problem.

With the chicks dropped off, Doc, Blaze, and Tyran cruised out to Highland Gardens two cars deep. It was a hell of a risk, driving around up there without a gun, but it was a risk Doc was willing to take. Doc and Blaze had connections with major niggas in every hood, so getting shot or killed wasn't that big of a concern.

They pulled up on the infamous Culhane and Boyle and parked. As they got out the truck they noticed niggas was reaching for their guns. Doc was too smart to over sport his jab, so he called out to one of the only niggas he had love for and trusted.

"Skate, let me holler at you gangsta."

Skate said something to his squad that Doc couldn't hear, and they put their guns away just as fast as they pulled them out. Big Skate walked across the street to holler at Doc.

"Doc, what's up with you?"

"Ain't shit. I'm chilling, big homey. What's with you?"

"You know me, I'm just holding down my spot," Skate represented. "Ain't shit changed."

Doc's voice went from cordial to serious as he said, "Yo, I know you heard about the shooting last night cuz that was one of ya homies. One of these niggas killed my mans and my little brother."

"Yo, you know how this game go," Skate said, without the slightest bit of compassion. "You don't need me to explain it. Shit happens. The young bull that slumped the bull from our block responsible for that?"

"I'm saying, I dig that and all, but they hit two niggas that ain't have shit to do with it."

Skate stared at Doc with the dumb face. He was trying to keep his composure because he had love for Doc, but Doc wasn't understanding that.

"You might not had shit to do with it either. But if I wasn't out here," Skate gave a subtle tilt of his head in the direction of his crew across the street, "them niggas wouldn't be tryna hear it. They was ready to cut at y'all. Bottom line, everybody got somebody that love them. And just like you love ya peoples, we love ours. Now me, personally, I ain't have shit to do with it neither. So the best I can do is squash it with my team if you squash it with yours."

**34**

Doc looked at Skate, and to avoid having them suspect anything, Skate pulled his coat to something.

"Yo, I can only squash that shit around here. Now Bang and them from the cutoff, I ain't sure if they gonna let that shit ride all like that. I understand that's ya brother. But put ya vest on before you go around there on this same vibe."

Doc bobbed his head, letting Skate know he understood before climbing back into the truck.

After Doc gave Blaze the run down they drove up to the corner and made a left, headed for the highway. But before they cleared the block, Doc and Blaze could tell by how niggas were acting that they were leaving hostile territory. The two of them would take Skate's advice, because the situation was destined to get worse. And if there was going to be a war, Doc and Blaze would damn sure prepare the troops. So, effective immediately, the whole block would be put on dress code, meaning, everybody on the block would have to get a gun if they didn't have one, and wear all black.

Now it was all about who was going to strike first.

———

B and Duck didn't get out the hospital until six o'clock in the morning. They were badgered by the cops for a whole hour. The police asked a hundred questions, trying to use bits and pieces of information they already had to trick B and Duck into giving them some more.

To B and Duck the assumptions they came up with were as ludicrous as a talking dog. They couldn't wait to tell their squad the shit they heard. Both of them stayed over Duck's house and woke up early in the morning to holla at Blaze and Doc.

When they got to the block, they automatically knew something was wrong. Wally and Flame's trucks were parked at the corner, but the cop parked behind them was not a good sign.

B knocked on Juanita's door, wondering why none of her dick-eating friends were on the block yet. Juanita's squad was like the daily paper; they knew about everything. Then everything they find out they run back and tell Juanita.

One good thing about Juanita was that she was totally against the cops. She'd let a nigga stash their coke, guns, or whatever illegal shit they had whenever the cops hit the block. She was like a big sister, and nobody dared disrespect her like they did her friends. Besides, all the dudes wanted to fuck her, but none had ever been lucky enough.

She had told niggas time after time that she would never fuck any of them, because a month or so later she knew they'd be disrespecting her if she did. And since niggas knew she was probably right, they respected her gangster.

"Yo, you seen Doc or Blaze?" B asked Juanita when she finally answered her door, cranky from having her sleep interrupted. The first thing she noticed was the police car and asked, "How long them police been sitting there?"

"I don't know," B said. "We just came out and knocked on ya door."

"Hoping Doc or Blaze was here, right?" she said, finishing the sentence for him.

"Yeah, pretty much," B and Duck both replied.

"That's probably the same thing they thinking. Go around back. Take the long way," Juanita instructed.

She closed the door and headed straight for the phone.

# CHAPTER 4

Doc and Blaze took a week to come up with a plan to retaliate on their adversaries. On the day after Flame's funeral, Doc got the call he was waiting for. Their connect, Ace, called to inform them that he got what they needed, and suggested they meet on South Street at six o'clock. Doc looked at his watch to check the time, it was two o'clock. So that meant he had a few hours to burn. He called Blaze and relayed the information, and Blaze told Doc that he was on his way.

It had been a rough week for the two loyal friends. The police impounded Wally's truck, but since they were two steps ahead of the police, before Tamia went to get it back, they briefed her on what to say. Of course, the cops hassled her and threw all types of crazy accusations in the air, but she stuck to the script. The police only had hearsay.

According to their information, the truck either belonged to Laneer Jones a.k.a Wally or Duron Thomas a.k.a Doc. It wasn't a shocker that Tamia Adams had the appropriate paperwork for the vehicle; they had figured that out when they ran the tags. What they didn't expect was that Tamia Adams would be a successful corporate lawyer with bank statements that said she didn't need no drug dealer's money to buy a nice truck.

They still had three witnesses who put the truck at the crime scene. But she quickly claimed the truck was in use by her deceased boyfriend, Ali Thomas. Ali couldn't be questioned to deny the story, but it came out that he wasn't just a local drug dealer; he was also a prominent businessman.

After her interview, Tamia called Wally and ran back the entire conversation. He in turn called his old heads and briefed them on what was going on. That helped them to keep alert on the block. Then the dress code went into effect. That puzzled the police and had people coming through fucked up.

Doc locked Juanita's spot down, so it was always heavy artillery on the block at all times. Plus, he and Blaze went to Shana's house, and she gave them all the coke that was stashed around the crib. In return they told her if she ever needed something to call, and they showed her where Flame's ducky apartment was. He kept a nice bit of money stashed there, and crept his little chickens there once in a while.

Other than that, the only thing Doc and Blaze were doing was sewing up all the spots Flame had locked down. They went and hollered at his workers, loyal customers, and people who ran his crack houses. They promised to treat them the same way Flame did and gave the appropriate people their cell phone numbers. After making sure everything Flame had was stable, they split it down the middle.

Next, they got with Ace and told him they wanted to hire some professional hit men. It was Friday night, and that was the best time to hit niggas where it hurt. Everybody and their mother were out on Fridays, so it wasn't a job that needed that much planning. Plus, with hit men, it'd give them perfect alibis.

Wally and Tamia got an apartment in the same complex as Doc. It was far from the city, but to avoid going to jail, it was ideal. Tamia didn't care if they had to move to Cuba, just so long as she didn't have to lose her soul mate. She loved Wally more than life. Maybe it was the confidence in his swagger, or maybe it was that he was the most sensitive nigga Tamia knew; she didn't know what it was, but they had almost six years in. She was with Wally when she was just a skinny little girl with a dream. Tamia was far from ugly, but she actually didn't blossom until three years ago. She was about five-foot-nine and a well proportioned one hundred and forty pounds. Her hair was long and brown, the same color as her eyes.

Wally, on the other hand, was a six-footer with a medium build and reddish-brown hair. His high-yellow complexion was sprinkled with freckles the color of his hair. But to Tamia he was her Denzel Washington. She wished desperately that they could have a baby because that was the only thing they were missing.

---

B and Duck were posted on the block, chilling. The day had quickly turned into night, and neither one of them had seen Doc all day. Duck was a compulsive gambler, so he was still thinking about a crap game more than anything else. He was the type that would gamble on anything, sometimes he would even make shit up.

"Yo, B, I bet you twenty dollars Doc pulls up before Blaze."

B cocked an eyebrow at him. "How you know they ain't together?"

"I don't."

"I'll take that bet," offered Juanita.

"Why? What you seen them already?" Duck asked.

"Naw, I ain't seen them yet. I just figured Blaze might show up before Doc," she explained.

She almost had him, but the sight of Shakeya and Nikki whispering to each other made Duck skeptical.

"I got a better bet for you," said Duck. "I'll bet you fifty dollars the cops come around here in the next ten minutes."

"Hell naw! That's a stupid bet," Juanita declared. "The cops ain't been through in at least twenty minutes, so I know they'll come through in the next ten."

"You good, you real observant," Duck said with a sly grin. "All right then, I got another bet for you..."

By the time Duck got done coming up with bets that Juanita successfully picked apart and showed the flaws in, Doc pulled up with Hollywood in the passenger seat of a rental.

Doc hopped out the car and stopped momentarily to shake hands with B and Duck before he ran inside Juanita's house. Inside, he ran up to her room, grabbed a gun, and dropped a brick inside the dresser drawer. Once downstairs, he kissed her softly before heading out again.

"Where you going?" she called after him.

"I'll be back. I gotta make something happen right quick."

Doc jumped back into the rental and pulled off. He drove down Third, and from Third on to the highway.

"You think you can find ya way?" Doc asked his passenger.

"Yeah," Hollywood replied. "What's the name of the street again?"

"Highland Avenue."

"All right, I got it."

They cut back through the Gardens just so he could familiarize himself with the faces. Doc didn't do any pointing, but he did spot a few of the dudes he was looking for.

"Yeah, they was out there," Doc said

"So, what make you think they gonna be at this bar tonight?" Hollywood asked.

"Everybody be at this bar. But if they ain't, they'll definitely be out here."

---

Blaze and Tuna got with Haz, a smoker Blaze knew, who set them up with a new squatter. They met two blocks from a used car lot where Haz worked and gave him a ballgame. Then Blaze dropped him off back down Erie Ave. From there they drove straight to Chester. Since the car was tinted, Blaze took Tuna on a tour of the city to get him familiar with the terrain. Later, the two of them pulled into the car lot to meet Doc and Hollywood.

*Midnight for the Twenty-fourth Street bosses.* They were already in their rentals and prepared to move out. All the young bulls on the block pulled up, ready to ride out at quarter to twelve. The small fleet of cars hit the road shortly thereafter, about twelve o'clock in the morning. They drove down Third first, pulling up at the bar and parking as close as they could get. If they weren't successful there, they planned on hitting Boots & Bonnets.

Before hopping out the wheel, Doc chirped in on Tuna's cellular. Hollywood picked up to the sound of the squatter's system banging that Styles P shit. Their conversation was brief, but long enough for Doc to know Hollywood and Tuna were on point.

The whole team dipped up in the bar, hollering at various niggas and chicks. The McCaffe bulls were up in the joint deep with their trademark red scarves. Doc walked over and shook a few hands before walking up to the bar and buying it out.

He was posted up with C and Thaddie Ock from the

Bennett, busting it up about coke prices. Blaze was sitting across from Doc, hollering at a handful of chicks. The night was pretty much going smoothly until them niggas he was looking for walked in. Doc immediately excused himself to go make a phone call.

Out front of the bar, Hollywood got a description of the clothes from Doc before they disconnected. He made his way closer to the entrance door and waited for his victims to come out.

N.Y. caught a glimpse of his worst enemies the same time Doc did. N.Y. drew his nine out and cocked it.

"Be easy," Shyne urged N.Y. "not inside the bar unless you have to."

The Garden young bulls had to be about ten deep squeezing their way through the packed tavern. They posted up at the bar, grabbed some drinks, and hollered out to a couple niggas they fucked with before edging up on the wall.

Doc had already put shit together. So he was lounging, just checking out the crowd, when he peeped the Killer Hill old heads: Maine, Skate, and Dre walked through the door with their guns ready.

*Damn, they going to kill each other!* Doc realized. He caught Blaze's eye across the room, rubbed his nose, then shot his gaze towards the McCaffe niggas. Blaze looked around and smiled when he saw what Doc wanted him to see. Blaze rubbed his nose back, thinking, *Yeah, I smell you, nigga.*

Around one, after some major dirty looks, Killer Hill rolled out. As they filed from the pub on their way to their cars, Blaze called Hollywood's cell phone. "Here they come. They deep too," he said.

Hollywood and Tuna waited patiently. Once their unsuspecting victims walked past them and was clear of the crowd, Hollywood swung two Mac-11s out. The shots cut into the night air like fireworks on the Fourth of July. The old heads that came out behind the young bulls tried to pull their weapons, but Tuna whipped out an Uzi and started firing as quick as Hollywood did. Skate, Maine, Huck and the rest of the old heads ran back in the bar. While a few young bulls were unfortunately cut down by the Uzi.

The shots caused pandemonium inside the bar. And as Skate and his squad tried to run back in, the McCaffe niggas tried to run out. The shots firing from inside the tavern stopped them dead in their tracks. Skate pulled out his four-pound first and hit Dirk in the chest. Five shots from Huck, hit three other people. Ike and N.Y. took cover and started firing back.

Bitches were screaming and falling like they just got the Holy Ghost in a Southern Baptist revival meeting. Then a stampede rushed for the exit. Blaze dove behind the bar when the bullets started flying and pulled out his .40. Doc ducked down on the side of the bar and drew his laser-sighted Glock 9. Most of the niggas in the pub had guns, so everybody was looking for somebody to shoot.

Then suddenly, just as quick as the shooting started, it ended. Hollywood and Tuna drove from the crime scene, heading toward the highway. Skate's team made it outside moments later, stopping momentarily to observe the casualties on the ground. They scattered with guns in hand to various cars and pulled off. The McCaffe came out next, dispersing in various directions to the sound of police sirens racing to the scene.

Blaze passed his and Doc's burners to a cooperative female companion to stash and continued to sit at the bar and drink. The owner was trying to force people out and close the joint, but the majority of the crowd had already left.

There were four dead bodies inside the bar, and the police were asking a lot of questions. Doc and Blaze fell back to see who'd talk to the cops and who didn't. The owner tried to downplay the whole incident, claiming that the shooting started out front, and when everybody ran inside they got hit from gunfire from shooters outside. Naturally he couldn't identify anybody, so the police tried to find someone else to snitch.

Out front, the detectives didn't waste time yellow taping the crime scene. The ambulances rushed two people to the hospital, while the coroner was called for the other four.

―――――――――――

"It was them fucking McCaffe niggas! I'm telling you, Maine!" Skate hollered as they pulled up at their mom's house on Boyle Street.

Skate parked, then swiftly walked into the house. Tia was sitting on the couch when Skate stormed through the door. She instantly knew something was wrong when her brother didn't bother to say anything to her before running up to his bedroom. Skate grabbed fifty thousand dollars he had stashed and put it in a duffel bag, along with his AK, AR-15, and some extra clips. Then he ran down the stairs.

"What you about to do?" Tia inquired as Skate headed for the door.

"Nothing, what you all in my business for?" Skate barked as he continued out the door.

When he got back outside, his team was double parked next to his car, talking to his brother Maine. Skate hopped back in the driver's seat and threw the duffel bag on the back seat.

"Y'all grab y'all heat?" Skate called over to the other car.

"Yeah, we ready. How you wanna do this?" questioned Huck who was rolling down his ski mask with nothing but retaliation on his mind.

"Look, they know our cars, so we might as well park on Clover Lane and cut through the backyards," said Skate.

"Sounds good to me," agreed Huck.

They drove down toward the A-Plus and made the left on the little street that led to Renshaw Road. From there they turned onto Keystone, then made another left then a right on Pine Lane. They drove down to the middle of the block between Twelfth and Tenth and pulled over and parked. They hopped from their cars—motors left running—and cut through a walkway into an alley. When they got to the alley they cut between a couple of houses and came out in the projects.

All four men were strapped with heavy artillery. And they found the niggas they were looking for sitting on a transformer relay box. Skate and his bulls came out shooting. Round after round of sub-machine gunfire cut their unsuspecting victims down like a lawn mower.

N.Y. was sitting on the green box arguing with niggas around his way about revenge on their enemies. He was furious, and honestly contemplating riding by himself. No sooner than he sat down, shots came whizzing by his head. The loud sound of the automatic weapons immediately sent him into action. He jumped up, sprinting for cover as he pulled his gun out. As soon as he got behind a car, he returned fire.

The shooting lasted for almost five minutes before Skate and his team retreated for their cars. They all made it back unscathed and made off for the highway.

Skate and Maine as usual stayed at a ducky apartment down Delaware in those types of situations. They would merely lay low till the smoke cleared, hoping that their names didn't come up in the middle of anything. Tonight they were more paranoid than usual. But then leaving at least five bodies in the projects and Lord knows how many others at a bar will do that to you. Shit was definitely crucial right then, but they were the realest of the real, so they would unquestionably go out with a bang if it came down to that.

In the McCaffe, police were everywhere. Nosey onlookers were rapidly gathering. And friends and family of the deceased victims were distraught or hysterical.

N.Y. and Shyne were as far away as possible. After the shooting ceased, they hopped in their car and pulled off to their destination, Fairhill Street, up Philadelphia. They needed some weed and wet to calm down and relax. N.Y. had his theme music on, of course. And as the words blared through the speakers, he visualized himself catching his adversaries and blowing their brains out.

♪♪ *I'm gone ride/ I'mma ride till the wheels fall off/ I'mma ride like I'm nailed to a cross/I'm gone ride...I'mma ride like a suicide bomber/bringing drama like a Una Bomber...* ♪♪

He chanted the words in his head right along with the song. For him, life was like a movie starring N.Y. "The Notorious Young Bull," a skinny twenty-one-year-old who was light brown, wavy-haired, brown-eyed, and weighed a hundred and twenty pounds at the most. He stood five-eight, maybe five-nine, though he couldn't be exact, because it had been a very long time since he'd last seen a doctor. Most chicks thought he was all right looking, but his wild and crazy nature never allowed them to look at him as the boyfriend type. He still managed to get plenty of pussy though. Probably because he didn't run his mouth as much as the typical nigga on his block. He'd been a seasoned veteran for years now, with at least twenty-five shootings that included being suspected of three murders under his belt. He was a #1 shooter, so for him life was far from a game; it was more like a war where battles were waged every day.

———————————

Juanita pulled up on Twenty-second and Dickerson so

Doc could holler at Hollywood. Doc found him sitting on some porch steps and cheerfully handed him a bag, saying, "Aye, good looking, playboy. I'mma get back at you if I need you again. All right?"

"Yeah, that's what's up. Next one, we can cut this in half, you feel me?" Hollywood insisted as he grabbed the bag, that contained a half a brick and ten thousand dollars.

They shook hands and Doc returned to his car. He was eager to get Juanita home so he could tear her back out. The Armani Exchange jeans she was wearing were so tight they looked like they had been sewn together after her ass was already in them. She had a tight Armani Exchange blouse to match, and some Prada boots. On a scale from one to ten, she was pushing a nine and nine tenths. She looked at Doc occasionally as they conversed, flashing a smile that melted him like butter on hot popcorn.

An hour and some change later, she pulled over in front of his apartment out Oxford.

Doc called ten minutes prior to make sure Wally was at his own crib and not at his. Wally let him know everything was a go, once Doc got him on the phone. It had been a long time since Doc really cared about a woman, so he wasn't used to going through what he just went through to make things perfect, but Juanita was worth it.

Deep down inside, Doc was just hoping that the evening meant as much to her as it meant to him. It was a big trust issue for Doc, and now that he trusted Juanita enough to let his guard down he hoped and prayed that she didn't let him down. His first step was taking her to his house. Once she saw how beautiful he had things arranged, he was expecting her to realize how big a step he was taking.

# CHAPTER 5

Wally got back in the apartment at about a quarter of four in the morning. He wasn't in the apartment five minutes before Doc called from a gas station a couple of miles away, asking, "Yo, you take care of that for me?"

"You know I did," Wally replied. "It took me a minute to find some flowers, but it's all in place."

"All right, good looking. I'mma holla at you in the morning."

Doc was just hanging up as Juanita came back to the car from the store carrying cigarettes and sodas. She noticed that Doc had slid to the driver's seat, so she walked around to the passenger's side and hopped in the car.

"Put this on," Doc requested, handing a scarf to use as a blindfold. Juanita accepted the scarf held out to her, but was clearly uneasy, as she said, "I'm not going to remember where we at Doc, please don't make me go through this" she pleaded.'

"Don't you trust me?" Doc asked.

She gave a modest yet affirmative nod of her head.

"Well, put it on for me then. We ain't got far to go."

Though she frowned her face up, she did as he asked. Doc hoped the blindfold would add a little extra element of surprise for what he'd set up for her once she took it off. Otherwise all the running around Wally just did to make everything perfect would've been for nothing.

Earlier Doc had asked Wally to pick up five dozen red

**48**

roses and spread the petals of three dozen of them in a trail
leading from the door, into the bathroom, where petals from
another half dozen would be scattered over a hot sudsy bath,
and end in the bedroom. There the remaining dozen and a half
would be scattered over the bed. But that was only part of
Wally's work. He also put two bottles of Dom Perignon on
chill, and left two candles burning in the dining room and put
one each in the living room, bathroom, and bedroom. That
gave the house an incredible glow with the lights off.

Then Wally took the food he picked up from Denny's and
put it on plates and left them warming in the oven. When he
was finally done making sure everything was perfect, he
turned the CD player on, pushed repeat, and left.

It had taken Wally about an hour to run around and get
everything, which wasn't bad, considering it was on such short
notice. Still, he was done and out the house five minutes
before Doc called. Wally hoped Tamia didn't wake up in the
short time he was gone, but just in case, he took pictures so he
could prove where he had been and what he'd been doing.

Arriving at his apartment building, Doc parked then made
his way around to Juanita's door to help her out the car. She
was feeling some type of way but figured it was almost over,
so she decided not to complain as Doc led her from the lot to
his front door. "Please don't be upset at how my house looks,"
he said humbly. Then he keyed his door.

Juanita made no comment, she didn't want to say the
wrong thing. She simply untied her blindfold. When it dropped
from her eyes, her heart fluttered. She stared around the house
in astonishment, wondering, *how did he do it?* Juanita stepped
over the threshold and into the living room.

The music playing softly in the background caught her ear
right away. It was Jagged Edge's *"?I Promise?,"* a classic, and
it gave her a tingle inside her soul. Doc reached for her hand

and lightly held it as he led her toward the kitchen. He pulled the warm plates of food from the oven and sat them on the table.

"You something else, you know that?" Juanita informed him.

"I would be flattered if it wasn't somebody as beautiful as you saying that."

"Where's ya bathroom?" she asked.

"Follow the trail," Doc smiled. "You can't miss it."

Juanita walked back toward the bathroom, and the scent of vanilla candles brought her to near arousal. The bathroom was elegantly decorated. The red, white, and gold Versace shower curtain was pulled back so that the tub full of suds and red rose petals could be exposed. The toilet seat, floor rugs, and hand towels were all color coordinated by the same top-notch designer as the shower curtain. Juanita was thrilled. She couldn't believe that Doc lived in such a meticulously lavish apartment.

She strolled back into the kitchen, only to find Doc devouring a plate of steak and eggs. He paused momentarily to gulp down a mouthful of Dom from the bottle, then said, "Yo, if you want some orange juice or apple juice or something, it's some in the fridge. I'mma alcoholic, I pretty much drink this shit all day. Plus I got a bad habit of drinking out the bottle, so I made sure I chilled two bottles."

He looked at her for a second, waiting for a response. When she didn't say anything he just dove back into his plate.

*He even sexy when he ghetto, girl*, Juanita's thoughts whispered. *This might be the one, for real. I'm telling you!* She slid into her chair, quickly said grace, and began her meal.

After Doc was done eating, he got up and walked to the bedroom. He pulled some lingerie from his closet that he had picked up for one of his chicken heads from Oxford. He didn't know if it would fit Juanita, but since it was a nightgown, he assumed it would. Plus it still had tags on it, so she could take it back if she wanted. He walked back to the kitchen and showed it to Juanita.

"I took the liberty of picking a little something up for you. I didn't know what size you were, so I grabbed a five-six."

"I just happen to wear a six, so I guess it'll be fine," she replied, all the more taken with him.

She ate a little more before excusing herself from the table. She picked up the nightgown. And after he walked her to the linen closet and handed her a towel and washcloth, she walked into the bathroom and closed the door.

The bathwater was still fairly warm, so she didn't have to run too much hot water. She just stripped naked and soaked inside the tub, thinking how sweet Doc would feel inside her. Fifteen minutes later she was squeezing into the Victoria's Secret gown. She didn't bother to put panties on, since she had no intentions of keeping them on.

When she finally walked from the bathroom she made her way to the bedroom, expecting Doc to be in there. She glanced at the bed and noticed the roses... and the whipped cream and bowl of strawberries on the dresser. *This is too much*! She thought.

Juanita went back into the living room and found Doc fast asleep on the couch. Instead of just nudging him awake, she gently unzipped his pants and pulled his penis out. She started by orally pleasuring him, which woke him up immediately.

Their sex-fest started in the living room, detoured in the shower, made its way to a kitchen counter top where they quickly grabbed some alcohol from the liquor cabinet before ending up in the bedroom. Once there, their souls met as their bodies intertwined in feverish ecstasy.

The police wasted no time trying to put a halt to the sudden increase of violence in their small city. Within the last week, eighteen people had been murdered, eight or nine more shot, and twelve robbed. Not to mention the burglaries and other various crimes.

The lead detective, Barren Finkle, was working diligently to find and arrest the perpetrators responsible. It was a hard job, but somebody had to do it.

Finkle already had three arrest warrants issued, and APBs out for a couple of suspects. For the latest shooting inside the projects, it was much harder to persuade a witness to come forward. But after a meeting with the Chief of Police, all officers patrolling that area were instructed to pick up known criminals and bring them in. With a little bit of harassment and a few petty cases they expected to have all the information they needed. If that didn't work they would just hit the streets hard making sure anybody and everybody involved in any type of criminal activity went to jail for something.

The block was packed Saturday afternoon. The women were out in full force enjoying the sun. The hustlers were out in full force lusting over the women as money came from every nook and cranny. Then, out of nowhere, around three thirty, right before the shift was supposed to change, cop cars rushed the block. Niggas tried scattering, but the police were coming from every angle. At the end of the sweep fifteen people were arrested, but the main person the cops were looking for had left the block a mere five minutes earlier in a truck covered with Ben Franklins.

Blaze was furious when Tyran, Biggy, B and – all his main workers – called from the police station asking for bail. Tyran got caught with a gun, Biggy had some weed, and B had fifteen dimes in his possession. Altogether Blaze kicked out fifteen thousand dollars just to get those three out. Then there was the *other* twelve niggas that hit his and Doc's cell phones. To avoid niggas from snitching on their block, Doc and Blaze always assured all their workers that if they ever got arrested to never worry, because they'd be bailed out within the week. So now they had to stay true to their word.

It cost another twenty thousand dollars, but within two days everybody was back on the block. They all told Doc and Blaze the same story: "The police want Wally." They claimed that until Wally was arrested the police would come through and lock people up every day.

At first it sounded like a joke, but two days later six people left the block in handcuffs. This time Doc and Blaze were wearing a vest. They were both charged with concealing body armor and given bail of five thousand dollars each. And a charge that usually only required someone to sign for their bail to get released was now becoming their biggest problem. Not only did they have to pay their bails, but the police were also confiscating their bulletproof vests. Duck had been caught with one on the first sweep, and now they were locking the bosses up for the same bullshit. For them it was definitely time to get some high-powered lawyers.

The first stop in the Gardens was Boyle Street. CID stormed two houses on Saturday, two on Sunday, and by Monday the blocks were a ghost town.

Dennis Wilson a.k.a. Skate managed to elude arrest, but not his brother Maine and a group of their young bulls.

Unfortunately for the cops not much information came out of the Gardens; however, they did manage to keep a lot of the people they picked up on bench warrants. The cops were mad Skate's brother Maine and his bull Rat made bail, but as soon as they surfaced again, Detective Finkle intended on making sure they were arrested again and again.

---

N.Y. got up from the bed fully clothed. He checked his pockets for his cigarettes while pondering what he would do for the day. After lighting a smoke, he fished around in another pocket for his phone, surveying the room. It was filthy as shit. The floor was covered with all kinds of trash; open food containers that had sat for three or four days, dirty clothes that were just thrown about after being worn continuously and all kinds of other shit, not to mention the flies and roaches. It was times like these that made N.Y. mad he ever got in the game.

For that brief moment he actually considered going to his girl's house, but that was out of the question. So he dialed his house, hoping that maybe he could swing by to take a quick shower and change his clothes.

N.Y. had been on the run for three months now, and just when he let his guard down the police ran up in his girl's crib and almost locked him up. Had he not been on the couch sleep they might have gotten him, but he heard them pull up. He quickly hid in a cabinet under the sink and stayed there for the forty minutes the cops spent searching her house looking for him. Luckily for him they searched upstairs instead of down-stairs, otherwise he'd be in the county locked up.

Since that close call three days earlier N.Y. had been post-ed in this crack house. He detested staying in a place like that at night, but it was the last place people expected him to be. Besides, he didn't have much choice since the cops swarmed his girl's crib until he could get his money right.

"Hello?" came N.Y.'s sister's voice on the third ring.

"What's up, Karen?"

"Nothing. Where you at, boy?"

"Up the way," N.Y. replied. "Why, what's up?"

"Because Linda called me and said they up they're look-ing for you."

"Who's looking for me?" he asked uneasily.

"Who you think looking for you, the fucking police," Karen said hotly. "You were in a shooting or some shit last night?"

"Who told you that?"

"That's irrelevant. Just get from up there, 'cause the police been up there all day."

"All right. But listen, I'm on my way over right quick to take a shower and get dressed."

"Well, hurry up," Karen said impatiently. "You know it ain't safe here. So come on while it ain't that many people outside. And use the back door so nobody sees you."

N.Y. hurriedly made another call to Mean Sheen to get a ride, and Mean Sheen informed him that cops were parked around the block. *Ain't this some shit!* N.Y. thought with some consternation. These pussies want me bad as shit! *What, they gonna shut the whole project down?* N.Y. grabbed his jacket from a hook on the back of the door on his way out the room. He hustled down the stairs, stopping to give Ms. Ann, the house lady, two dimes to cover his overnight stay before leaving out the back door.

He cut across the basketball court and walked through the playground, headed for Clover Lane. When he got there Mean Sheen was sitting inside his Cutlass, waiting for him. N.Y. climbed into the car, slouching down in the seat so that he could barely be seen.

"Where we going?" Mean Sheen asked.

"Take me to my sister's crib."

---

By the end of the week the young bulls on Twenty-fourth Street were tired of the cops. They secretly formulated a plan to bring an end to the problem. They knew there was no way they could tell Doc, however they thought maybe Blaze might listen. So they asked him to meet them at the crack house.

When Blaze got there, Tommy, Tyran, B, Biggy, and Duck were all sitting at the table.

"So, what's the forecast?" Blaze inquired.

Tyran, being Blaze's favorite young bull, took the initiative of talking.

"Old head, we know you losing a lot of money out here. Not only with the bails every other day, but then you paying for lawyers and shit. Plus we ain't making as much money as we was. So it's taking us longer to score. Niggas out on the block naked, scared to carry guns *or* wear vests...Man, shit is fucked up."

"So what do you suggest we do about it?" Blaze asked, not really getting Tyran's point.

"It may sound fucked up," Tyran continued, "but the only way to get the cops off our backs is to give them Wally."

Tommy pointed out, "he ain't originally from our block."

"Technically, he from the McCaffe, for real-for real,"

Biggy added.

"And whose idea was this?" Blaze asked.

"All of ours," B said.

Blaze wasn't convinced. Everybody there was on his direct payroll except one person. And since that person was the only one he hadn't heard from yet, Blaze said, "What do you think, Duck?"

Duck locked eyes with his boss and saw the seriousness in his face. "Blaze, I'm fucked up," Duck said frankly. "I ain't got no stash, and I spend money too much when I ain't gambling it all away. If I go to jail I'mma be assed out, so I ain't tryna go to jail."

Duck's face was stone cold. He had a look like he was being robbed and he feared for his life. It made Blaze bust out laughing, which caused everyone else to laugh, or at least smile. But the break in the room's tension was only temporary, as Blaze became serious again.

"Well," he said, "if this happens, Doc is gonna feel some type of way. Especially with Wally being his main young bull." He paused for a moment to look everybody in the face. "So when Wally gets knocked, we never had this conversation. Something like this could get niggas killed, and I honestly don't approve of this shit. But I can't stand losing money every week neither. So look, I'mma holla at y'all later, and I'm glad y'all called me and talked to me. And like I said, this conversation dies right here."

Blaze walked around the table and shook everybody's hand. On his way outside, Blaze said, "Yo, Tyran, let me holla at you out front right quick."

Tyran followed him outside. They stood by Blaze's car while Blaze made sure that Tyran would take care of expressing how serious the meeting was. He also informed him that if somehow it got out somebody would be dealt with. Blaze wanted Tyran to plan it out precisely so that it didn't look obvious. Then Blaze hugged his young bull, and they parted company.

―――――――――――

The girl talk on Twenty-fourth Street was in full swing. Juanita had been away for over a week, and her girlfriends wanted to know where she'd been hiding. Juanita couldn't wait to let it out, so she immediately started boasting about her romantic week with Doc. She was giving up all the intimate details, explaining every second of every minute of every hour, while her girlfriends clung to every juicy word. Juanita went on about the action in the bedroom for two days straight, and how, on the third day, he whisked her away to Atlantic City for another two days on the beach and the Taj Mahal. But their last day, Juanita assured them, was the most intimate. And, yeah, she gave up tapes about that day too.

The girls never really got much of a chance to share their stories very much, because there were always guys around. But for some strange reason there wasn't a guy in sight that day.

"Girl, this is like a good movie!" gushed Simone.

"Who you telling?" said Charnetta. "This shit better than the soaps! "

All the women laughed.

"Don't tell her that, girl," Nikki interjected, her voice dripping jealously, "cause we all know Doc ain't shit with his fake Casanova ass!"

Juanita stared at her before saying, "Don't be jealous, bitch."

"Jealous for what?" Nikki replied.

"Cause my man know how to treat a lady, and you wish

you could find somebody half as good," Juanita proclaimed, rising to Doc's defense.

"Please. Next week he'll be cussing you out too."

"So what! The dick will still be mine, and it taste good, feel good, and last long."

"Like Big Red," Charnetta and Simone chimed in, bringing the three of them to laughter.

Nikki still didn't think it was funny, even though that was the group's favorite inside joke. She just never imagined that they would be making the joke about Doc. She sat quietly then, and listened as Juanita continued to explain how she and Doc had sex way into the early hours of the day past sunrise.

"You think he baby daddy material, Juanita?" quizzed Charnetta.

"I don't know yet! But if he keep this shit up he'll be *husband* material," she said with a smile as wide as the Mississippi.

Talk continued about Doc for a few more minutes, until Blaze pulled up and cut their conversation short. When he jumped from his truck, Nikki's whole demeanor changed. Her savior was now on the block, and she tried desperately to make him seem like the most important person in the world.

For some odd reason Juanita detested it more than usual. She started to see what Doc was talking about, and on top of that she could see how arrogant Blaze was. It didn't stop Nikki from practically panting like a thirsty dog. It took about ten minutes before Juanita was sick to her stomach. And once she got like that, she started thinking of how to make Blaze and Nikki feel stupid.

Being on the run was nothing new to Wally. The shit was so normal that when he wasn't on the run or in trouble with the law he started to feel strange. Since the cops were constantly sweeping every day there was no way for him to get money out there. He sat down and had a talk with Doc about his financial situation, and of course his old head put something together for him.

Doc told Wally not to worry, then popped up the next day with a trash bag half full of coke. He told Wally to off the coke and break the profits down the middle. Wally had the option of putting some young bulls on the payroll, but that would mean less of a profit for him. But since Doc was the major distributor in Oxford it wasn't really a problem getting rid of the coke. Doc just told all his customers it was a drought and let Wally take over the operation. He let Wally push the remainder of his coke in weight for hiked up prices, and after that Wally was out on the block's frontline.

It had to be an easy quarter a million worth of twenties and dimes. Wally didn't have the time to sit down and count them out, because it would've taken all day, so he just hit the block.

The money out Oxford made Wally wish he would've found a small town to hustle in a long time ago. It poured from all directions like a thunderstorm. By the end of the week, Wally had pulled fifty thousand dollars easy.

He had people coming for double-ups, junkies spending their checks and trying to sell TVs and stereos. Shit was crazy. He didn't know what Doc put in the Starburst-colored bags, but whatever it was, it was working.

# CHAPTER 6

It took Wally nearly two months of serious grinding to get rid of all the coke. He didn't spend a lot of time with Tamia, and he knew she was upset. He didn't think about it much until he finished paying Doc a hundred thousand dollars for the trash bag of coke. After that was taken care of Wally went straight to get his girl a present.

He had put in an order for a jet-black Benz S-500 with hot pink interior. The hot pink was piped in black, so it made the car unique. Originally Tamia wanted something completely pink, so Wally intended on getting his and hers matching cars. But when the dealer announced the price tag he decided to improvise.

He got the Benz wrapped with a bow and pulled in at his apartment complex, camouflaged by all the cars and called Tamia.

"Yo, I need ya to come out front and help me with something."

He hadn't bothered calling her all day up until that point, so Tamia was naturally irritated. She breathed hard into the phone before telling him she was on her way. A minute later, Tamia was outside looking in the direction of her parking spot, thinking, *Where the hell is he?*

Tamia gathered that Wally wasn't in the lot and was turning to head back inside when she heard a horn beep. She spun back around and watched a beautiful car driving slowly across the parking lot with a bow on it.

*Oh my God!* She silently screamed. She ran top speed

toward the car. Wally threw it in park as she neared and hopped from the driver's seat with a smug grin on his face.

"Thank you! Thank you!" Tamia screamed excitedly.

"This ain't for you," Wally said, but his grin said otherwise.

She hugged him passionately and smothered him with kisses.

"Yeah, right," she replied when she finally took a breath. Then she nearly dove into the car to get behind the wheel. Wally walked around to the passenger's side. For an hour she chauffeured him around in her new car before returning to the apartment and doing what grown folks do.

Wally spent most of the rest of the day laying up with his girl before giving Doc a call to see what the crew was up to. Doc said they'd probably ride down to Thunderguards around midnight or so. Wally said he'd be there. But first he had to go put a serious spin on Tamia to make her think it was all business. That went pretty well after he promised to stay out of Chester. He got dressed and bailed out around eleven thirty to go meet Doc and the rest of his bulls in Delaware.

Wally found a good parking spot right in front of the club. Doc, Blaze, and three cars full of young bulls showed up ten minutes behind him. They didn't notice Wally as they drove by, but when they walked up to head into the club, Wally hit the convertible top and called out to Doc.

"Old head, what's the deal?"

The whole squad turned and caught a glimpse of Wally's new car.

"Goddamn!" Duck exclaimed.

Doc was all smiles, but Blaze didn't see what the big deal was. Tyran and B were instantly jealous and mad at the fact that they were getting locked up every day while Wally was buying new cars. Tommy and Biggy were kind of happy to see Wally, or at least they pretended to be. Rick didn't bother

speaking at all, but that was him. He didn't care about anybody but himself. It was surprising to even see him with the
squad, because nobody really fucked with him like that.

They talked about everything that was going on as they
walked into the club, and the new news around the way was
the fact that Dee was home. He was an old head from the
block that got knocked for a dime on a robbery.

Once inside the club everybody branched off, mingling
with the women who were scattered about. Wally sat around
talking to Doc for about twenty minutes. By then he had to go
to the bathroom, so he told his old head he'd be back and
headed toward the back. When he got done using the bathroom, on his way out, Wally bumped into a familiar face. N.Y.
was laid back in the cut with about six dudes from the
McCaffe.

"Weezy, what's the deal, gangsta?" Wally called out.

N.Y. quickly spotted the person who called to him and
loosened the grip on his six-shot .25. He snuck the gun deep
inside his boot, just in case he ran into problems.

"Yo, what's going on, Wally?  Where ya been, cuzz?"

"Laying low. The police looking for me all crazy,
nawmean?"

"Yeah, they on my heels too, but I'm riding – I'm shooting at them too. You ain't heard?" N.Y. boasted.

"Naw, what happened?"

"I got into a high-speed chase with them pussies coming
from my mom's crib. And they almost had me, but I bailed out
busting at them bitches."

"Yo, you outta control!" Wally hyped with a smile.

"Yeah, I'm on the armed and dangerous, most wanted list,
feel me?"

N.Y. talked about his misfortune like it was the best thing
that could've happened to him. It kind of made Wally feel like

he wasn't riding right. After talking to N.Y. for a while Wally passed him a number and told him to holler when he needed to lay low. Then Wally went back to hang with his team, running into Duck posted on a wall by himself first. Duck was drunk as shit. As soon as Wally came up beside him, the first thing Duck said was, "Yo, stay outta Chester."

"Why you say that, Duck?"

"Yo, you ain't hear it from me, dog. Just stay away for awhile," he cautioned.

That was all Duck managed to say before spitting up all over himself. The exchange baffled Wally, and immediately made him start scrutinizing his team. Before the end of the night he thought he understood what Duck was talking about, because everybody except Doc seemed distant. Before he left for the evening, Doc told Wally he would try to buy the rest of the bagged up coke Blaze had. Then he shook a few hands before parting ways. All during his drive home, all Wally could think about was Duck's warning.

---

Doc knocked on Blaze's door and waited for an answer. He had called Blaze earlier and told him he was on his way, so he didn't expect Blaze to take so long opening the door. Doc planned on hollering at his mans about the rest of the bagged up coke he had. Doc figured on the strength of who they were he'd be able to get the coke for a hundred grand, maybe two at the most.

Little did Doc know Blaze had short-changed him considerably on the split. Blaze counted out all the coke the night Flame was killed. He took fifty thousand dollars in twenties out the bag that night and put them out Scranton and Lancaster. By the time Doc asked about the bag a couple of

days later, Blaze had already clipped half of it. And he would-
n't say anything about it. That's how he was.

Blaze opened the door after a few minutes to let Doc in.
He'd been in the process of running money through his
money-counting machine when Doc knocked. And since he
didn't trust anybody, he quickly threw the quarter of a million
he had in rubber bands in a duffel bag in a closet. The rest of
the money laying around wasn't that big a deal since he was
pretty sure it was Doc at the door.

Blaze walked back to the kitchen table and sat down.

"What's the deal?" Blaze asked.

"Ain't shit," Doc returned. "I wanna know what you going
to do with the rest of that coke in the trash bag."

"How much was it?"

"I don't know," Doc replied with a hunch of his shoulders.
"I ain't count it. But Wally said it was two hundred grand."

"You trust that nigga like that?" Blaze asked, voicing surprise at Doc's unconcerned response.

"Yeah, that's my young bull. I ain't worried about him trying to get over on me. Blaze, he's had too many opportunities
already. If he wanted to burn me for something he would've
been did it when I was worrying about that type shit. We got
years in, that's like my little brother."

Blaze was baffled. Mainly because he didn't trust a soul,
but also because it made him wonder who else Doc trusted to
that extent.

"So if you would've gave the bag to Duck you wouldn't
have counted it?" Blaze asked, watching Doc closely to see
how he'd respond, wondering if his best friend actually had
that much trust for his team.

"Hell yes! Duck's a compulsive gambler. That nigga will
gamble on how fast the wind blows. His nature will *make* him
skim a couple dollars."

*The nigga not as crazy as I thought he was,* Blaze decided. So he said, "What you going to give me for the rest of it, and do you want to count it first to see how much it is?"

"I figure it should at least be two hundred," Doc said. "Since you was supposed to give me half of the bag last time, and on the strength of who we is, I figured you'd want about fifty."

Blaze was happy with the response. He didn't want to tell him that there was about three hundred thousand dollars left. He just told Doc to give him the fifty thousand, and another twenty-five if it was over two hundred. Doc thought Blaze didn't count the coke, that Blaze was guessing it was over two hundred thousand dollars. And since Doc didn't count the last bag of coke, Blaze was indirectly trying to insinuate that Wally skimmed a couple dollars off the top. Secretly Blaze knew that he gave Doc two hundred thousand dollars the last time, plus or minus a few bags. And now, since Blaze knew it was three, this was his way of testing his homey to see if he was as veracious as he claimed he was.

"You know that means you gotta take time out ya busy schedule to count this bag," Blaze advised with a grin.

"No big deal," Doc responded, "I'll do it now."

Blaze went to get the coke and gave it to Doc. While Doc counted out the coke, Blaze went back to counting his cash, which came out to a $1.5 million dollars.

By the time Doc got done counting, Blaze had cooked and bagged up a brick to run out Lancaster.

"So what you get?" Blaze asked.

"It was three hundred thousand," said Doc.

"So that mean you owe me twenty-five grand."

"That still don't mean my young bull skimmed off the top," Doc defended.

"I ain't saying he did, gangsta. Why you barking at me?"

Doc just looked at Blaze. Naturally Blaze was smirking

back at him. Even though Blaze said nothing else, Doc felt obligated to explain.

"I bet you when I drop this shit off, he give me a hundred fifty back if I tell him I don't know how much in there."

"Bet fifty," challenged Blaze...

For the brief moment Doc took to think about it, Blaze brought him back to reality.

"When you first came in here," Blaze said, "You didn't need that brief second to decide. That's all I was saying the whole time, gangsta. Don't leave a door open for a nigga to get over on you, because everybody, no matter how cool they is, will try you if they think ya slipping."

"Tyran's my fucking heart, but I would never, and I mean never, give this nigga shit without knowing what it was I gave him."

By the time Blaze and Doc were ready to leave, Doc's whole thought process had been manipulated. Blaze took off for Lancaster to drop off some coke and pick up some money, while Doc was heading toward Oxford. The two planned to meet again in two days.

It took Doc an hour to get to his apartment. Once he got situated he called Wally and told him to run over right quick. He opened the door five minutes later and let Wally in.

"Yo," Doc said, "I just grabbed the bag from Blaze. I need a fifty from you to pay for it."

"How much in there?" Wally asked, not liking the idea of having to come up off fifty thousand dollars.

"I don't know, I ain't count it. But it's probably two hundred, maybe more."

"You wanna count it right quick?" suggested Wally.

"Naw, I trust you. I gotta take Blaze the hundred grand and pick some money up from round the way." He lied so Wally wouldn't get suspicious.

"All right. What, you want me to go grab that now?"

"Yeah," said Doc. "If you got it, that's what's up."

"All right, I'll be right back."

Wally grabbed the trash bag, threw it over his shoulder, and hurried home. There he grabbed a bag from his stash and put it into a plain paper grocery sack. Then he took the money to Doc and told him he'd holler later.

Doc put another fifty in the sack and threw it in his closet. Then he called Juanita to see if she'd found her new apartment.

Since their relationship had become serious, Juanita believed it was time to move away from the block; which sounded good to Doc because he didn't like spending the night at her house. It was too close for comfort. Plus he detested her hating-ass girlfriends. The only one he was starting to like a little bit was Charnetta. For some reason she had become extremely thorough in the last week or two.

After talking to her and finding out where she picked an apartment, Doc grabbed fifty grand from his stash and headed for the city.

───────

It had been two and half months since Juanita started messing with Doc. To her it was possibly the best time of her life. Not only was Doc spending crazy time with her, but he also gave her the money for a new apartment, promised to furnish it, and told her she could live anywhere she wanted; just as long as it was outside of Chester.

She found a beautiful place in East Oak Lane. Once her application was approved, she put down a deposit and the first and last month's rent.

All of this was like a ghetto girl's dream come true for

Juanita who, by profession, was a private duty nurse and understood what it meant to struggle. That's how it was when your mother got turned out on drugs when you were twelve and chose the streets over her maternal responsibility. Or if your father was Baruti, the neighborhood dope man, who got indicted for interstate trafficking when you were fifteen. From there Juanita lived with an aunt until she turned eighteen. Yet, it was during that time with her aunt that she resolved to beat the odds, to work hard and stack money. She moved out and got her own apartment. The first two years she lived on her own was hard but she was content then something happened to change all of that.

One day, when Juanita came home from work, she ran into a burglar. She was so tired from the constant work that she couldn't even fight her assailant off. He ended up brutally raping her. It did something to her mentally. Not only because she didn't really have the friends and family to support her through it, but she was also a virgin. Juanita reported the incident, and a week later the police apprehended her attacker—a guy who lived on her block. That devastated her because she had spoken to him on several occasions.

No longer feeling safe on Third Street, Juanita moved to the east side. She still felt leery talking to guys in her new neighborhood, but she did, however, reach out to a few *girls* who lived on the block.

By having girlfriends she basically stayed up on top of everything and everybody. Especially with the nosey girl-friends she had. It took two more years before a man got close enough for Juanita to let her guard down again. When she finally did, it was with Ali. Ali, the sensitive, sweet-talking pretty boy. The guy all the girls wanted but none of them got.

By then she was crowned the leader of her girlfriends and had the same rep as him; the girl everybody wanted but who was untouchable. So fate landed them together for a couple of months, but Juanita was far too mature to play the silly games Ali was into. They broke up, having sex off and on for about a year.

Then Doc came home, the older, more mature version of the perfect guy. There was always something about him that Juanita liked, but she wasn't in a rush to make a move. Neither did she expect for them to ever be together, since she'd previously been with his brother. No, she wasn't that type of girl. But it happened, and now she didn't regret one moment of it. She was attracted to that cocky, confident attitude of his that made her feel safe. He was also very frank, even when it offended people. Most of her girlfriends only disliked him because he told it like it was and never bit his tongue. That always amused her, because most of the time he just said the shit everybody else wanted to say but wouldn't. And now she was finding out that underneath all his sarcasm was the sweetest person in the world. That's what counted the most to Juanita, and it made her feel lucky to be with him.

She began packing her clothes and personal belongings after their conversation. Doc assured her that she wouldn't need anything else, but there were still a lot of things she wanted to take that had sentimental value.

Charnetta was with Juanita as she packed, persistently trying to talk Juanita into leaving her the apartment. But Juanita knew none of her friends were financially stable enough to take over the lease. Besides, she wanted to keep it for herself if things didn't work out. There was always the possibility of renting it out, because she could use the extra money. But she planned to talk it over with Doc to see what kind of ideas he had.

Juanita continued to pack her clothes reminiscing of all the good times she had at her apartment and fantasizing about her future.

The gambling finally paid off for Duck. It was late in the game, but somehow he pulled a rabbit out of a hat. He went down to the casino the night before with five hundred dollars to his name, hit the crap game for seventeen thousand dollars, and for the first time in his life he knew when to quit. He couldn't see something like that in his future with a telescope. Even though he had handled large amounts of money before, for some reason, that day, he finally knew what to do with it.

The next morning Duck left a message on Doc's phone before heading to the auction with his uncle to get a car. He dropped six thousand dollars on a platinum Denali and pulled up on the block a couple of hours later leaving niggas astonished.

"Damn, what the fuck, you robbed somebody?" B asked amazed at how fast Duck came from nothing.

"Naw," Duck replied with a chuckle, "I just made some major moves."

Duck knocked on Juanita's door after shaking B and Tyran's hands, hoping Juanita had hollered at Doc. Duck had ten grand to spend, and since Doc was going to front him whatever he spent, he couldn't wait to get his hands on that brick.

Charnetta opened the door a hot minute later.

"What's up, Duck," Charnetta greeted, looking over Duck's shoulder and admiring the truck parked at the curb. "Who's truck is that?"

"Oh, that's mine," Duck replied. "Where Juanita at?" he asked, brushing past.

Charnetta did a double take, looking at Duck then back at

the truck. At the sight of Duck's Denali, she bit down on her luscious lips while sizing him up. The sound of a money machine could be heard as her mind rambled to figure out how much the truck cost. She batted her hazel eyes concluding that the truck cost at least ten grand. Looking at the wall mirror, she gave herself a once over. Her Cavali jeans were fitting so tight that if she passed gas they might bust at the seam. Her half shirt exposed a washboard stomach and a pierced belly button. It also accentuated her thirty-six, C-cup that she refused to restrain with a bra with such cute outfits.

Duck was paying her no mind now that he was in the living room calling for Juanita.

"Aye, Juanita! Let me holla at you!" he yelled up the steps.

Juanita promptly appeared and came down.

"What's up, Duck?" she asked.

"'Aye, where my old head at?"

"He ain't get here yet, but he supposed to be on his way. Why, what's up?"

By now Charnetta was standing on the side of him, looking him dead in his face. Duck was six feet tall and weighed two hundred and ninety-four pounds. Although he was overweight, it looked natural on him. His full beard was shaped up very sharp for once but he kept his head shaved bald to hide his receding hairline. Usually his baggy sweatsuits were wrinkled and bore food stains. Today however, things were different his red Monkey jeans were crispier than new money. The Gino Green Global t-shirt he wore matched his jeans and butter Timbs perfectly. The Jacob watch he wore said a mouthful.

"Hold this for him," Duck said, pulling out a brown bag and handing it to Juanita. She accepted the bag and knew at once that it was money.

"What, you owe him this?" Juanita asked, curious more to know where he got it from.

"Naw, I'm tryna make a move with him. Plus I'm about to make a run right quick," Duck stated before spinning back out the crib.

The truth was that he didn't want to fuck his money up gambling, so he thought it would be best to give it to her. After he left, Charnetta, went straight into dick-eating mode, "Girl, this mothafucka got a hot-ass truck out front. How much money you think in the bag? You got to see this truck though. Hurry up before he pull off," she insisted, leading Juanita to the door before Duck was gone.

"You see that jawn?" Charnetta went on. "I wonder where his broke ass got all this money from. He was even looking sharp and everything."

Juanita watched Duck drive off with B and Tyran joining him. But her mind wasn't on the truck. She was estimating how long it would be before Charnetta sucked Duck's dick. That thought made her wonder how she had hung around those crazy-ass bitches for so long. Juanita was so happy she was leaving.

# CHAPTER 7

At his apartment in Nova Vista, Doc thought about leaving the money until Juanita was ready to furnish their new apartment. But he quickly changed his mind, figuring the less she knew the better. It wasn't that he didn't trust his girl, because he did. But it was a known fact that pressure busts pipes; if she were ever in a situation where it was a matter of giving up secrets about him, stacked against her life, he just couldn't call it.

Doc owned two apartments and a house. The apartment he was currently utilizing was Flame's. The lease was paid up for a year, and since Shana had no desire to stay in it, she gave the keys back to Doc only after finding Flame's money and removing things she viewed as valuable or sentimental. It was very convenient for him, because both of his apartments were outside of Chester; one out Oxford and one out West Chester. His house was the house his mom wanted to buy before she died. It was a two-bedroom house in Buckman Village on a quiet tree-lined street. He didn't keep coke there because his dad still lived there. Doc didn't drop by much and although he had a room there with a lock, he never spent the night. He more or less took care of his father, paid all the bills, bought food, and once in a while gave his dad clothes.

Doc ran upstairs to grab a brick out of Flame's bed. The box spring was specially made to stash money, but Doc used it to hide coke. After grabbing the brick he left to go to Juanita's house.

Duck had been leaving messages on Doc's phone all day,

so Doc wanted to hurry up and get his money before Blaze got to it. On the block, the first thing Doc noticed was the platinum Denali. He wasn't that impressed by it because he could buy ten of them. What was impressive was learning that it belonged to Duck.

Doc crossed the street to Juanita's house. Duck, B, and Biggy were sitting on her steps, kicking it.

"What's the deal, y'all?" Doc greeted, shaking hands.

"Ain't shit. We chilling," they replied.

Then Doc walked up in Juanita's house with Duck following him.

"Hey, baby," Doc said to Juanita, who was sitting in the living room with Charnetta watching television. He and Duck kept walking back to the kitchen.

"Yo, I don't know what you did, but I'm proud of you," Doc told him once they were in the kitchen and out of ear – and eyesight of the girls. "I personally think you shoulda got ya stash up before you bought that truck, but it's definitely nice. So, look," Doc pulled a brick from his pants pocket and handed it to Duck, "get this back to me soon as you can, and I might be able to help you make a major move."

"Like what, old head?" Duck asked.

"One thing at a time, youngin'. Get this money right, and when you've shown me that you're really tryna eat, I'mma help you shut this whole block down."

Duck shook Doc's hand and promised to get back to him in two or three days. After Duck left, Doc went into the living room and sat next to his girl. He kissed her softly before asking how she was doing.

"I'm cool," Juanita told him. "I packed up a lot of stuff."

"Didn't I tell you you ain't need nothing," Doc reminded her.

"I know, baby. I just packed clothes and sentimental

things. But I don't wanna just leave all this stuff. What should I do, sell it?"

Doc glanced at Charnetta, who was practically staring down their throats. Then he looked back at Juanita.

"We'll sit down and talk tonight, okay?"

"Okay," she replied. "What, you getting ready to go somewhere?"

"Yeah, I gotta make a quick run. But I got something in the car for you. C'mon and take a walk with me."

He took her by the hand and led her out to the car. He climbed in behind the wheel and unlocked the door so she could grab the duffel bag on the floor.

"Make sure ya nosey ass girlfriend don't look in there," Doc admonished.

"What's this?" Juanita said as she hefted the bag.

"It's the money for your new house."

"Oh," she sounded as a thought popped into her head, "I got that money Duck gave me."

"Yeah, I know. Hold on to it. I'll be right back."

Juanita carried the bag swiftly into the house, she was as excited as a little kid on a class trip. She couldn't fathom how much money was in the bag, but from the weight of it she knew it had to be quite a bit. Once she was inside her crib she locked the door and ran straight upstairs, eager to look and see if it was really all money. She unzipped the bag after she was in her room, and it was just like Doc said—all cash. For the first time in her life Juanita could've actually screamed.

"What's that?" her nosey friend inquired from the doorway.

Juanita quickly zipped the bag up and looked at Charnetta.

"It's just some clothes he's going to change into tomorrow," Juanita lied, her mind racing. All she could think about was how much fun it would be decorating her new apartment. She got up and threw the bag in her closet before heading back down the steps. She wanted to tell Charnetta the truth so bad, but she knew why he told her not too. Because Doc knew as well as she did that Charnetta would be jealous...very jealous.

***

Against Maine's better judgment, Skate took their two hundred and fifty thousand dollars up to New York. He planned on buying fifteen bricks. Ten they could push weight with and five they'd break down and bag up nicks for their Delaware spots. Maine was worried that something might go wrong, so he and three of his young bulls followed Skate up in two cars. Despite his bad feelings, everything went according to plan, and they made it back safely.

Maine was still upset that they spent damn near all their money. They had about a thousand dollars left between the both of them. Considering that they dropped fifty thousand on bails in just the past two months, scoring with that much money was a considerable risk. Though they had a tight knit squad, not being able to pay bails could kill their loyalty.

Skate wasn't worried about it like Maine was. He bagged up a brick of nicks and flooded Claymont, Delaware. In two days he pulled forty thousand dollars out of two crack houses and had boosted his clientele dramatically. Maine bagged up five bricks in quarters, halves, and ounces and hit the Gardens. The prices for ounces in the city ran between seven and eight hundred, so he sold his for six hundred and fifty dollars. Plus, since Maine didn't put any cut on his coke he undercut a lot of competition. In two weeks he pulled out two hundred and thirty-four thousand dollars off the ten bricks he sold, while Skate grossed two hundred and fifteen thousand dollars from the five bricks he sold frontline.

Just when they thought everything was going great, something had to go wrong.

They were at the *Roc the Mic* tour up Philadelphia, having a great time and enjoying their success, when they ran into some real nut-ass niggas. They scuffled inside of the concert. But when they ran outside to their cars, shit got ugly.

———————————————

Daneya and Tamera arrived at First Union Complex hoping to catch somebody scalping concert tickets. They waited until the last minute to buy tickets, so of course it was sold out. They were the ultimate jetsetters, so it felt crazy for them to not be inside of a concert of such magnitude. They walked around out front, mingling with numerous wealthy looking men, hoping that they might luck up and get inside. They were both very attractive, so it wasn't nothing for them to work men

Daneya a sexy, one hundred and twenty-five pounds, stood five-ten with long jet-black hair. Her skin was like a cup of Starbuck's creamy mocha, and her eyes changed colors weekly because she'd rather wear contacts instead of glasses. Daneya was twenty-two and older than her protégé, Tamera, who just turned twenty-one but had the mind of a thirty-year-old. Tamera was the more mature of the two because she thought things through more than her home girl. Although Daneya was more outspoken, Tamera was more decisive.

They had stood around out front of First Union Complex for two hours by the time they decided to leave. They headed through the parking lot toward their car, when six guys came running past at top speed. They didn't think anything of it at first.

"Yo, we should ask them if they got some tickets. I bet

you they leaving," Daneya said, voicing one of her bright ideas.

"They was probably fighting," Tamera said.

"Probably. So you know they ain't gonna need no tickets. I'm gonna ask them. You with me?"

Tamera eyed her friend up and down while she thought it over. What did they have to lose? So she decided to go along with it.

---

N.Y. was damn near going crazy when 50 Cents hit the stage. His squad was about twenty deep and they were drinking and getting high up inside the concert. The night was going great until N.Y. saw Skate, Maine, Huck, and a couple other niggas he hated. He tapped his old head, Shyne, on the shoulder, hollered out to Mean Sheen and Ike, and in minutes the whole crowd of niggas that came with them was splitting up to surround Skate and his team. They snuck up on Skate from all sides, and from the crowd N.Y. suddenly jumped out swinging. A brief scuffle broke out, and McCaffe niggas were coming from all directions. The H.G.s had to retreat.

They punched their way out the crowd and ran out to their cars. N.Y., Ike, Mean Sheen and E. Marvels were right on their ass. Mean Sheen got to his car first and unlocked the door in seconds. He and Ike both grabbed their guns and continued to run after their enemies.

Shyne and a couple other niggas were all breaking to their cars to get their guns when Skate and his squad came running back.

Mean Sheen started firing first, missing Skate but hitting the girls that were running with them. Skate ducked down behind a car just as Daneya caught two in the back.

"Get down!" Skate screamed at Tamera wondering what had made the women run in their direction in the first place.

Maine came running to defend his brother, letting off about ten shots from his Mac-11. He and Skate tried to back Mean Sheen and company up, but there were too many of them shooting. N.Y. and E. Marvels were trying to sneak up close to them, but the other niggas from their projects had their attention diverted when a parking attendant pulled up on them. N.Y. immediately spun around and put six rounds in the truck, making it accelerate away. Then Skate and Maine hopped in a car that pulled up on the side of them and sped off.

"Fucking pussies!" N.Y. screamed as he ran back to his old head's car.

"Yo, they left they girls," Mean Sheen reported.

"Man, they ain't with them niggas," E. Marvels said as he ran past Mean Sheen and hopped in the car with Ike.

They all sped off, leaving only one victim in the wake of their reckless shooting rampage. Daneya lay on the ground bleeding to death as Tamera screamed and yelled for help. "If only we woulda left," Tamera kept saying. "If only we woulda left."

---

It took about two and half weeks, but when it was done, Juanita's home was truly perfect. A black and white rug that stood up like a farmer's crop set the living room off. Anyone coming to her home had to remove their shoes because aside from it being comfortable and beautiful, the rug was expensive as hell. Her black leather sofa set was trimmed with ostrich feathers, and her end tables were encrusted with diamonds just like Doc's. She had a 64-inch TV mounted on the wall, accompanied by a Bose surround system. In each corner of the living room stood a 4-foot black vase with designs of white roses on the sides, trimmed with what looked like diamonds, containing four-dozen white roses each. The walls were beautifully adorned with paintings. Her favorite was one that depicted a shabby old house on a barren street with two malnourished kids standing out front. They had tears in their eyes and snotty noses. Juanita felt the picture expressed her childhood. She called it, "Where's my Mother?" It kept her grounded to her roots.

The rest of the crib was just as meticulously decorated. She did an exquisite job and got as close to perfection as possible. An easy one hundred thousand dollars went into decorating it, ten thousand dollars of which was her money.

Everything was so surreal for Juanita. Just waking up in a house so lavish was an adrenaline rush all by itself. She wasn't too thrilled with Doc's decision to rent her old apartment to Duck, but the arrangement that Doc made was a win-win situation. Duck agreed to pay all the bills and give Juanita five hundred dollars every thirty days. Plus he agreed not to trash her furniture and belongings, so she couldn't complain. Besides, she was more concerned about making Doc the happiest man in the world, because he was without a doubt making her the happiest woman.

Too bad Juanita's girlfriends weren't happy for her. Besides Charnetta, the few girlfriends she did have were jealous, extremely jealous.

She found out from Charnette that Shakeya and Nikki felt some type of way, especially after Duck moved in. They even went so far as to call her a sell-out and a nut-ass bitch. It didn't bother her at first, but as the day-to-day talk grew, so did her anger. Juanita knew that it was only a matter of time before she fucked one of them bitches up. Starting with Shakeya, then working her way down the list.

---

After a month of hard work, Wally was sitting on about a quarter million. He was figuring in about a week he would be done knocking off the coke. The day after he got the coke, he called his old head and told him how much it was. It kind of surprised Doc and Wally didn't know why.

"Yo, you know it was three hundred thousand," Wally informed him.

"Damn, so it wasn't two hundred, huh?" Doc replied.

"Naw, but I ain't expect it to be that much on the nose if you ain't never count it."

"Yeah," Doc said, "how about that."

*Blaze had counted the first batch,* he thought.

"So why you ain't pocket the other hundred thousand? Ain't like I woulda knew."

"What?" Wally said, as if Doc just cussed at him.

"Why I'mma do some shit like that? You give me everything I want. I would never steal nothing from you. That's crazy," Wally said, refusing to believe Doc would even think something as absurd as that.

"Naw, I trust you, nigga," said Doc. "If I ain't trust you, I would've counted that shit. I just wanted to see what you was going to say."

"Come on, old head, I'm getting a hundred and fifty gees off this flip. I promised Tamia a house and everything. I ain't into that slimy shit; I'm tryna get money."

They kicked it for a few more minutes about some other shit. Doc told Wally about everything that was going on and made mention of the shoot-out up Philadelphia at the concert, then they hung up.

No soon as Wally got off the phone with Doc he called N.Y. Wally wanted to make sure N.Y. wasn't caught in any bullshit. During their conversation Wally came to the conclusion that the police weren't hip that it was them shooting yet, the Chester Police was still on their asses for a bunch of other shit.

When they hung up, Wally had made arrangements to snatch N.Y. and Var up for a week and let them stay out the hustle spot. Wally had a coke house that wasn't really fucked up like that. One of his customers sold him a trailer, and in no time Wally hooked it up real nice. He planned on letting N.Y. and Ike lay low for a week or two. It wasn't like the little town he was in wasn't jumping, because every time he ran to the bar to make a sale, chicks practically threw themselves at him.

It was a little too close to home for Wally, but in a couple of months, after he moved wifey out Maryland, he planned on scooping up all the broads.

He promised Tamia a house as soon as he got the money right to stop her from nagging him about his work hours. So far she was laid back about shit.

Plus Wally knew he couldn't blow the spot up the way he wanted to until he moved from the vicinity he was hustling in. The cops were already on his head, but he didn't show his face enough for them to match a face with a name. Still it didn't change the fact that his name was as hot as fish grease.

# CHAPTER 8

Blaze got up early Saturday morning and called Doc. "Yo!" came Doc's sleepy voice from the other end of the line.

Blaze said, "Yo, what's the deal? You know we suppose to see Ace today."

"You riding up there this early?"

"Yeah, I'mma shoot to the shop and get it done early."

"All right," Doc replied, "cover that and I'll bring my half when I pick the package up."

"All right, meet me at my crib around one this afternoon."

After setting up their appointment, Blaze hung up and called their connect. He told Ace he needed twenty-five bricks and where he would meet him. Blaze then loaded three hundred and seventy-five thousand dollars into a duffel bag and headed to meet Ace.

Blaze estimated that in another year he would be worth $10 million. He was already sitting on $2 million. Once he reached his goal he'd go straight legit. It wasn't really a hard goal to reach, as long as he didn't have to keep paying lawyers and bails. His bills for his house and apartments weren't that high, the notes on his cars were paid off, and he had A-1 credit from financing his house.

His job on record was a personal trainer. Since he networked with so many people, he paid a legit business to list him as an employee to legitimize his income. It was a job that paid a salary commensurate to that of his clients and Blaze kept very rich clientele. That's what networking was all about.

In another year or so Blaze planned on retiring a very rich

man to maybe start a modeling agency, a record company, or a restaurant. He'd have the option of doing whatever he wanted.

━━━━━━━━━━━━━━━

Things couldn't have been going better for Duck. Thanks to Doc he had the block on smash and moved in Juanita's a week after she left. The crib gave him a crazy advantage over a lot of the niggas on the block, not to mention since everybody hung in his house. He made all the junkies knock on the back door to score. Sometimes they would come for Biggy or Tyran and Duck would lie, saying they weren't there so he could serve them himself. Then he'd tell smokers not to knock on his door looking for anybody else if they already beeped B, Tyran, or Biggy. He might've let his niggas get a couple dollars, but his rule was, after midnight nobody hustled out of his crib. Since everybody got drunk and crashed in the living room or down the basement, his competition was literally sleeping on the job.

Even though Duck had everything going great, he was hardheaded. Doc distinctly told Duck not to make Juanita's house a hangout. Of course Duck couldn't understand where he was coming from because her house was already a hangout. So the last time Duck scored, Doc tried explaining what he meant. He told Duck that not only is having niggas hanging out all day going to draw money, but it would draw cops and stick-up boys, but by then it was over Duck's head. The house was seeing more traffic than a toll bridge. One smart thing he did was start messing with Charnetta.

Charnetta suddenly became interested after his overnight success. So Duck, being the guy he was, decided to utilize her.

He kept all his drugs in her crib, and gave her keys to the truck and house so she could drive to get coke whenever he needed some. It was only right because she had a license and he didn't. She was less of a risk factor.

Another smart thing he did was stashing all his money at his mom's house. He was buying two bricks from Doc now, and owing him for two as well. In return, he refused to leave his money with Charnetta and have her leisurely spending whatever she wanted to. He'd spend all his money gambling for all that. So Duck was finally on track. He didn't intend on letting anything stop him.

He woke up early to breakfast in bed one Thursday morning. Charnetta fixed him cheese eggs, grits, and beef bacon with toast on the side. Since B and Kiana were still asleep in the guest room, she fixed them breakfast too. Duck was happy she woke him up early because it was the first of the month. He only had about twelve hundred dollars worth of dimes in the house, so he asked her to go get him something from her house when she got the time. He figured he needed a quarter brick – that's how he bagged all his coke up, in quarter brick packs. A big freezer bag would usually hold four and a half ounces worth of dimes and four and a half worth of ballgames and quarters. He had two freezer bags already bagged up, and two whole bricks left.

Customers were knocking on the door soon as he got up, so after Charnetta ate, she hopped in Duck's truck and drove home to take care of business.

Tyran showed up at about noon. He had an ounce of weed and two boxes of blunts. He came right in, greeted Duck and B, then walked straight from the living room to the kitchen, looking for food.

"Damn, where the food at, Duck?" Tyran inquired.

"That shit gone already, playboy," said Duck.

Tyran took a couple of minutes to fix a bowl of cereal and

rejoined his squad a few minutes later with the weed.

"Man, where Charnetta at? How she playing, not fixing the kid no breakfast?" Tyran rambled. Then he pulled the weed out and tossed it to Duck so he could begin to pearl the blunts.

B suggested, "She probably thought you was going to eat at home for the first time in ya life."

"Look who's talking, Mr. Never-Miss-A-Meal," Tyran teased.

Moments later the weed was in the air and the small group of men were taking turns beating each other on the PlayStation for cash bets.

Biggy joined the party about an hour later with a bottle of Belvedere and a case of beer. Ten minutes after Duck sold all his coke, Charnetta showed up with enough coke to hold him over until the next day or maybe later that evening, depending on who else had coke on them.

---

After laying low for nearly a month, N.Y. and Var needed to get back to the city. Wally was also eager to get out, not having been in the city in a long time. He dropped his money off in the projects and headed straight over to Twenty-fourth Street. He was missing his squad and wanted to see how everybody was doing. Doc had told him that Duck was shutting the block down, so Wally wanted to see how Duck was living. He drove the Benz because he knew his truck would draw attention on him, and he didn't want any trouble with the law.

Wally pulled up onto Twenty-fourth Street in front of Juanita's house. He could tell by the cars up and down the block that everybody was in there. He knocked on the door. A hot minute later Charnetta opened up with a look of astonishment.

"Hey, Wally!" She greeted as if she was happy to see him.

"What's going on, Charnetta? Where Duck at?"

"Come on in," she invited.

Charnetta stepped aside to let him in and closed the door. She strolled into the living room with Wally following her.

"Aye, y'all, guess who here?" she announced, stealing everyone's attention in the crowded room. The emotions were mixed, and it was easy for Wally to read faces.

Shakeya and Nikki frowned their faces in disgust, as if they were looking at a bum standing in the doorway. Kiana and Kelly were more curious as to who the newcomer was. Tyran and Biggy were shocked that Wally had showed up out the clear blue. Duck and B smiled warmly and immediately got up to shake Wally's hand and hug him.

"What's good, playboy?" B said happily.

"Ain't shit. I was missing y'all niggas!"

"Long time no see, cannon," Duck said, shaking Wally's hand after hugging him tightly. "Have a seat somewhere, fam." Duck sat down himself and picked up the control for the PlayStation, enthusiastically asking, "What's going on with you?"

"Man," Wally said, "I'm chilling. I'm just stacking my change, nawmean?"

"What's ya name again?" Kelly interjected.

"My name Wally. Why, who you?"

"I'm Kelly. Me and my sister, Kiana, just moved around here." She asked seemingly interested, "where you from?"

Wally gave Kelly the once over. She was very attractive with long black hair, baby brown eyes and a very petite body. Though she had nice sized breasts and a fat ass, she wasn't as well proportioned as her twin sister Kiana. That was the defining characteristic that separated them. That and the small beauty mark on Kelly's cheek.

Everybody in the room laughed almost simultaneously at Kelly's question while she tried to figure out what was so funny.

"He used to be from around here, but he on the run now," Shakeya explained.

"I can see some people still stay in other people's business. I guess some things never change," Wally said sarcastically.

Wally walked over and shook Tyran and Biggy's hands before sitting on a crate in front of the TV next to B and Duck.

Biggy got up and grabbed a beer for Wally and himself from the freezer, and B passed Wally some weed. They conversed about the neighborhood news, and B and Duck informed Wally of how shit had changed.

Five minutes after Wally showed up, Tyran's cell phone rang. And after a quick conversation he told his niggas he was going to make a sale and would be right back. Tyran shook everybody's hands before spinning off to take care of business. After busting it up for fifteen minutes, Duck suggested that he and Wally take a ride in his new truck.

"Yeah, it's so much shit out there I didn't know who was driving what," Wally said with an expressive smile.

"What you pushing, the X-5?" Biggy inquired.

"Naw, I got the Benz with the coochie-colored seats."

Since none of the women on the block had ever seen Wally's car, they all got up, one after another and followed B, Wally, Biggy, and Duck out front.

"That's me over there," Duck said, pointing to his truck.

He threw Wally the keys so Wally could test-drive it, and Wally tossed Duck the keys to the Benz.

"What, we going on tour?" Wally asked as he hopped in Duck's truck.

"That's what's up," said Duck.

B walked over to Duck's truck and hopped in with Wally, and Biggy rode in Wally's car with Duck.

After an hour of riding around the city, Duck and Wally pulled up and parked back on Twenty-fourth Street. As they pulled up they noticed Blaze, Tommy and Tyran climbing into their cars and leaving. Wally didn't think much of it at the time as he got out of Duck's truck and traded keys back on their way into the house.

"Yo, I'mma go grab a pack of cigarettes right quick," Wally informed his three homies.

He walked across the street to the Chinese store, grabbed a pack and a peach Snapple, and came right out. He stopped momentarily to crack the Snapple open to drink a little bit to wet his throat. For that brief second that he diverted his attention, a black Expedition swiftly pulled into the parking lot. Wally started towards Duck's house, not really paying attention to the truck when the doors flew open.

"Freeze! Put your hands up!"

The command from the undercover cops startled Wally. In the time it took for him to look up, he could see the cops were out of the truck and ready to close in on him. His instincts kicked in and he took off running.

The first warning shot fired into the air by Detective Jones shocked Wally but didn't stop him from hauling ass. He didn't get too far. Once Wally got on the main street, cop cars swarmed from all directions. He tried cutting toward an alleyway but got tackled in the process.

After a few minutes of police brutality, they loaded Wally in a car and took him to the stationhouse. During the ride Wally expected at least one other person from the block to get locked up too. After the detectives questioned him he knew he'd been double-crossed.

N.Y. jogged straight to Shyne's house when Wally dropped him off. He knocked on the back door before opening it and walking in. To most people in his project Shyne was the heart of the project, he was a very skilled fighter and a gangster's gangster. To N.Y. he was like the big brother he never had.

"Shyne!" N.Y. called out from the kitchen, as he walked through the downstairs.

Shyne was upstairs when he heard his young bull call out to him. He quickly got out the bed with his female friend and went to the steps to greet his young bull. "You know that's how people get killed; walking in my house like they live in this mothafucka," Shyne announced, not entirely joking. "Where you been, man? I was starting to miss your punk ass."

N.Y. gave a chuckle as he sat down, turned on the TV, and said, "I was laying low out Oxford with Wally. That nigga got shit on smash, cuz. Straight up."

By now Shyne had walked down the steps to take a seat on the couch next to N.Y. They shook hands and Shyne asked, "What, you thinking about getting that nigga?"

"Naw, he from our block. That nigga looked out while I was down that thing. I was only supposed to stay a week, but he let me and Var ride for a month. The only reason he brought us back is because we wanted to come back."

"Well, don't tell me about how good the nigga doing 'cause I don't wanna hear that shit, straight up," Shyne said tersely. "You know Mean Sheen caught them Garden niggas over Debbie's bar the other day and cut at them."

"Yeah?" N.Y. said curiously. "Who got hit?"

"Nobody. You know y'all dumb-ass young bulls don't kill

shit but car tires and stop signs."

They both laughed.

"Yeah, right, nigga," N.Y. said. "Them niggas got nine lives, but they down to about two or three now and I'm ready to flatline 'em. So what's the plan for today, now that the kid's back? I'm ready to get into some dumb shit."

"Well, I got the smut jawn, Shelly, upstairs. You can go try to hit that while I take a shower. And after that we can go uptown, get some weed and wet, and before the night's over we'll find some dumb shit to get into."

N.Y. smiled as Shyne got up to head upstairs. For the first time N.Y. finally realized what he was missing...excitement.

---

The news came as a shocker to Doc. Duck didn't get into the particulars, but he didn't have to because Doc knew what needed to be done first and foremost.

As soon as Doc hung up with Duck he called his lawyer, Omar Dickens. Omar Dickens was possibly one of the sharpest lawyers in Philadelphia. Doc knew the rinky-dink lawyers in Media wouldn't be good enough to help Wally spank the case. After a ten-minute conversation, Omar Dickens had the particulars of the case and scheduled a time for Doc to come and drop a fee for his services. He assured Doc that as soon as they hung up he would get on Wally's case and work on getting him a bail.

Doc had already grabbed his hundred thousand dollars from Wally. He wasn't sure how much money Wally had of his own, so he would take twenty thousand dollars to Mr. Dickens in the morning and also pay Wally's bail. That's what friends did; they showed up when you needed them the most.

The bar was packed as usual when Tommy and Tyran walked in. Most of the niggas from their block were already there except for Doc and Blaze. Tyran wasted no time hollering at the owner and buying the bar out. He gave Mr. Jack fifteen hundred dollars and the bartender announced that all drinks were on Tyran.

The atmosphere suddenly changed, as females rushed the bar to get free drinks. Tyran grabbed a tall glass of Belvedere and cranberry juice, then found a table in the back with his team. He couldn't wait to tell them the good news. So when he sat down at the table with Biggy, B, and Duck, he blurted out, "Yo, y'all know Detective Nutsack said that our block ain't gotta worry about detectives for a year," he boasted. "Yeah, when I told him where Wally was at, I practically had that nigga eating out my hands." No one at the table commented, still, they all toasted to their success, not knowing how short-lived it would be.

Duck finished his drink and excused himself from the table to see why Charnetta was calling him. He walked to the bar, where she informed him that one of his customers, Greg, wanted to meet him to buy an ounce of coke. At first Duck started to pass it up, but since she volunteered to go get it, he told her to tell Greg to meet him at the bar.

Charnetta got right on top of it. It was a rush for her to pick up Duck's coke and bring it back. Charnetta was starting to believe that she could get money on her own now that he taught her how to bag coke up and sell it. She was even debating on buying a couple of ounces of her own to sell when he was asleep at night. She already sold a good portion of his product late at night when everybody was sleep, *so how would he know if she pushed her own coke?* Charnetta hadn't completely thought it out yet, but it was an idea she was having.

Ten minutes after picking up the ounce, Charnetta was back at the tavern. She pulled in front of Greg's car and threw a finger up, signaling Greg to wait, as she hurried inside to pass the coke to Duck.

"He out front, baby. I told him to hold up."

Duck took the coke and made his way out to Greg's car. He climbed in the passenger's seat and closed the door, expecting it to be a quick transaction.

"What's up, Greg? You got the money?" Duck asked as he handed Greg the ounce.

"Is this good stuff?" Greg asked in a drunken slur.

"Come on, dog, I always give you good stuff."

Greg wanted to taste the coke, talking about how good the coke was until you bought something big and a whole bunch of extra shit, while he opened the sandwich bag and stuck his finger in it.

"Yeah, this is good," Greg said as he tried to sit the coke down in the armrest, but he fumbled it. "Ah shit!" he exclaimed as he tried to reclaim the bag from where it had fallen between the seats.

"I got it," Duck volunteered as Greg went in his pocket to get the money.

In the time it took Duck to reach between the seats the police swarmed in. As he sat back up to hand the bag back to Greg, he was caught red handed.

"Police! Don't move!" a detective commanded.

Duck couldn't accept it being a coincidence that the police rushed up on him and caught him in the act, so he punched Greg as hard as he could and tried to continue hitting him as the police yanked him from the car. They brutally slammed him on the ground, putting their knees in his back to cuff him. A second later he heard screams from the bar as they went through his pockets and grind his face into the pavement. Charnetta was hysterical as Duck was muscled into a police car. As he was carted off to jail, all Duck could think of was, *I guess they won't have to worry about detectives for two years now.*

# CHAPTER 9

Charnetta was furious when Duck got locked up. She would have almost gotten herself locked up if her friend Simone hadn't pulled her to the side, calmed her down, and reminded her that she had to be on point in case they hit the house. Charnetta instantly woke up then. *Shit! The house!* She thought.

She screamed out to Duck, telling him to call, and hurried off in the truck. As she was pulling off she noticed something that left her puzzled for the entire ride home. She caught Tyran talking to Detective Nutsack. She hastily assumed that he had something to do with Duck getting locked-up and started pre-meditating ways to get even.

It took Charnetta only a few minutes to get home. She rounded up all Duck's coke and loose bags and hid them out-side. Now she desperately needed somebody to talk to who might be able to help Duck, so she called Juanita so she could get in touch with Doc.

———

Blaze pulled up not long after the confusion had ceased and walked into the bar. He knew his squad would be inside celebrating, so he decided to slide through and show his face.

He walked through the crowded bar to the back table where his young bulls were usually stationed. When he got within eye contact, he could tell by their faces that something was wrong. He pulled out a chair and sat down, wondering what had happened.

"What's going on?" Blaze asked. "I thought y'all niggas was celebrating."

The faces were filled with mixed emotions. B looked the maddest, but Biggy had an upset look about him too.

"Yo, you know they just locked Duck up," Tyran disclosed.

"For what?"

"They said he's been serving an undercover for two months," Tyran painfully explained.

"Fuck!" Blaze exclaimed.

He immediately thought the worst that Duck would break under pressure. But then it dawned on him that he wasn't Duck's supplier. Now that Duck was gone that meant more money for him.

"Yo, it ain't a big deal," Blaze said casually.

"Doc will bail him out tomorrow."

"I don't think so, old head," Nutsack said. "Duck ain't getting a bail because he got detainers for not going to court. I asked him can we come pay his bail, and he said it would be a waste of time."

Blaze didn't show anything on the outside, but to him it was good news.

"All right, it still ain't a big deal," Blaze insisted. "Ain't like he got a murder case. We'll get him a lawyer tomorrow."

Blaze got up, walked to the bar, and got a double shot of Hennessy and a Heineken before returning to the table. By then Tyran had shook off being upset to discuss what chick they would be going home with. Biggy, on the other hand, was telling Blaze how he thought he himself might've slipped up and served the informant on a previous occasion. Blaze assured Biggy that he would get in touch with a lawyer in the morning to straighten it out.

After that, Biggy seemed less concerned and ended up following Tyran through the bar to find some late-night sex. B of course was taking shit more seriously than everybody, because in the last month he and Duck had become extremely close. This time he sat by himself while his team went ho hunting. He honestly thought that somebody at the table had set Duck up. He just didn't know who.

———————

It took Wally forever to see the judge. At eight o'clock he finally got in and was refused bail. Afterwards they let him get his phone call and he called Tamia to tell her to go get her car. By nine that evening Wally was on his way to the county lock-up. There he was strip-searched, had his clothes taken, and was given some red pants and a shirt. He was classified to maximum security and given a pillowcase containing two sheets, a towel and washcloth, and some other toiletries. Then he received a bag lunch and was taken to 8-D.

When Wally hit the block he heard a few people call out to him, but the guards took him straight to his cell. He was celled up with a guy named Troy. Wally found out by eleven o'clock that night that Troy was knocked for killing his girl-friend for fucking another man.

At about twelve thirty runners came out on the block and somebody knocked on Wally's door to holler at him. He looked up from his bunk, half asleep, to see who was calling him.

"Yo, what's happening, playboy?" hailed M.B.

"Yo, what's going on with you, M.B.?" Wally returned.

"Hop down and holla at me, my nigg. I know you need a cigarette."

Wally jumped down from his bunk and ambled over to the door to holler at his mans from the McCaffe. M.B. bent down and slid three cigarettes and a lighter under the door. In a non-smoking facility, Wally didn't realize how much the smokes meant until his cellie begged for a short.

M.B. told Wally how shit usually ran on the block and promised to get him some shower shoes and new underwear. They talked about the streets for a while before M.B. told Wally that he'd be out for his two hours between nine and ten in the morning and he'd see him then. Then M.B. said he had to get back to sweeping floors and cleaning showers, so he'd let Wally get some sleep.

---

Tamia couldn't help crying after she hung up the phone with Wally. She was extremely distraught. She called Doc's cell phone and asked him if he could help Wally get out of jail. He told Tamia that he had already called a lawyer and that she shouldn't worry. But when she hung up she still couldn't help but feel like all her dreams were flying out the window.

Tamia had just convinced Wally to give the game up, and Wally had promised that after getting rid of the rest of the coke he had, he would buy a house and move out of state to start over. Now, even though she had three hundred thousand dollars in cash in the house and seventy thousand dollars in her bank account, all the money in the world wasn't worth her baby's freedom. Tamia had too much time in, and even though it sounded crazy, she would give everything up to start over again. She just wanted the old Wally back that she fell in love with a long time ago.

"Chow up!" the block officer yelled. Wally's cellie, Troy, woke him up before running out the cell to get his tray. Wally thought about laying in the bed but he was too hungry. He got up and wiped his face with a washcloth before walking to get his tray. When he got in line he was shocked as shit to see Duck a couple of people in front of him.

"Yo, Duck, what the fuck's up?"

Duck turned around with the shit face and looked at Wally.

"Yo, what's up, dog?" he said.

"What you get locked up for?" Wally asked.

"Man, they banged me for selling to an informant."

"Why you ain't come in with me?"

"Man, they caught me down Jack's later on that night," Duck explained.

"Yo, take your trays back to your cells and lock in," bellowed the Correctional Officer.

Wally and Duck looked around at the few people eating on the block and wondered why the guard didn't say anything thing to them. But they didn't question him. They just picked their food up, told each other they'd holler later, and locked in.

The doors popped again at nine o'clock and Wally hurried to the phone to call his girl. For an hour of their recreation time, he and Duck talked to their girlfriends. They set up visits for Saturday afternoon and told their girls that they loved them and missed them dearly.

About a hundred people were housed on the block, and Duck and Wally knew nearly half of them. From the top tier people called to them that wanted to talk, but neither were really in the mood to be bothered.

Wally had a lot of questions for Duck. He knew someone

had set him up from the way the cops were talking when they arrested him. They told Wally that he might as well turn his homies in because they had turned him in. Wally knew something was fishy about how they got him, but he still wouldn't talk. Not Wally. He was a gangster's gangster. But still, why had Duck told him to stay away from the block?

By the time they locked in, Duck had spilled his guts and explained everything he knew. He also told Wally that he believed niggas got him knocked too. Niggas seemed happy he was locked up from the way his calls went with B and Charnetta.

Charnetta refused to let Tyran and the rest of Duck's so-called friends in the house. She let B in because B didn't come to her house asking how much money was coming and where Duck's coke was. He was the only person who was genuinely concerned. She told Duck how Tyran was talking to Detective Nutsack and put it in Duck's head that his friends were jealous of him. Of course now Duck was really empathizing with Wally and felt bad he hadn't said something sooner.

When they went in their cells, Wally laid in his bunk thinking of how he could get back at his block for the slimy shit that they did. After an hour or two he had it. He knew exactly what to do.

---

Early Friday morning N.Y. got a phone call from Tamia. She was crying and upset and trying to explain the news she got from Wally. After hearing what happened N.Y. understood why she was upset.

"Look, calm down, Mia. I'll handle it for him. Tell Wally

I'mma get on top of it immediately."

When N.Y. hung up he didn't waste any time putting together a plan. He took a quick shower and threw a black sweatsuit on. Before leaving Shyne's house, he woke Shyne up and told him he had something to take care of. N.Y. then called Var and Mean Sheen and told them to meet him on the block.

Since he was on the run, when he got to the block N.Y. stood in the shadows on the porch of an abandoned house. Before long Var pulled up and hopped out looking for N.Y. He was also dressed in a black sweatsuit, gloves, and a mask in his back pocket. N.Y. slid out from the porch and called to Var to let him know where he was. Var spotted him and made his way over.

"What's going on, N.Y.?" Var greeted with a handshake and hug.

"I just got a call from Wally's girl, she said them niggas on Twenty-fourth Street got him locked up."

"Who?" Var demanded to know.

"Everybody except Doc. They supposedly had a meeting or something, so he sent me the young bulls Tyran and Biggy's addresses and told me to handle it."

"We on it," Var declared.

"Cool. I'm waiting on Mean Sheen, he suppose to bring me an AR-15 around."

Var wrinkled his brow, "you think you need heat like that?"

"Yeah, I'm tryna take care of some other shit too," N.Y. explained.

A few minutes later Mean Sheen pulled up and N.Y. and Var hopped in his car. Mean Sheen drove down to his stash spot and passed off two vests, a Calico, and the AR-15. He told Var and N.Y. to give him a call if they needed him and dropped them back off at Var's car.

They drove around to the young bull Larry's crib and got him to tell them where one of his stolen cars was. Larry led them to a brand new Camry he had just dent pulled, charged them two hundred dollars for it, and rolled out.

Twenty minutes later N.Y. and Var were parked in front of Tyran's apartment. Since they knew Tyran lived by himself, N.Y. got out the car with his nine and knocked on the door. He kept his back to the door, so whoever answered it couldn't see his face.

"Who is it?" Bianca queried.

"It's Biggy," N.Y. replied.

As soon as the door opened, N.Y. spun around and rushed in. Since he had a nose and mouth mask on he only shot Bianca in the leg twice. Tyran, of course, came running out from his room to see what was happening. N.Y. charged at him, letting bullets fly.

"Shit!" Tyran exclaimed as he ran back to get his gun.

But it was too late. As he reached under his bed to get his .45, N.Y. put four bullets in his back. Tyran slid to the floor with his hand barely clutching the gun. N.Y. stepped up on him and put two in his head. There was no point in leaving him with the money since he was dead, so he decided to interrogate Bianca.

"Bitch, where the fuck's the money at?" N.Y. demanded pointing his gun at her, his eyes full of threatening menace.

"I don't know! It's a little bit in the closet, but that's mostly drugs!"

Bianca was balled up on the ground crying, nursing her leg, and praying silently that the intruder didn't kill her.

N.Y. hurried to the closet and tore through it quickly trying to locate the money and drugs. After a minute of throwing shit around he found a duffel bag with ten thousand dollars in cash and two bricks in it.

*Jackpot!* He thought as he grabbed the bag. Thank God for small apartments.

Just in case the cops investigated, he left Tyran with his gun and opened up one of the bricks and shook a little bit of powder on the floor. Before leaving the house, N.Y. made sure he ripped the phone out and tied Bianca's hands behind her back.

"Please, I'm gonna bleed to death," she pleaded.

"Maybe you make it, maybe you don't. But it sure beats a bullet in the head, don't it?"

N.Y. hurried out to the car, threw the bag in the back seat, and headed a couple of blocks to the next apartment. If he got lucky, everything would go the same at Biggy's.

———

Blaze got a call from B that totally shocked him. *It just doesn't make sense*, he thought to himself. His favorite young bull Tyran was dead, and Biggy was in critical condition. The crazy part was, they didn't have a clue who did it.

B was on the block when the police rushed Tyran's house, so he saw everything. Plus Tyran's young jawn told B the details when he got to the hospital. After talking to her for a few minutes, B was on his way out the hospital when Biggy arrived and his sister was admitted for the same gunshot wound to the leg. Biggy's sister Sarah told B that a little guy knocked on the door claiming to be Tyran. When she let him in, he went haywire, shooting her and her mom. Then he tried to get Biggy. Biggy fired a couple of shots back, but somebody else rushed in and helped the other guy out. That's when Biggy realized he wasn't going to get a win. So he tried jumping out the window. The two guys rushed the window and shot him up.

"Then, they asked me and my mom where the money was at. After we told them, they found it and spread drugs everywhere and left," Sarah said. The whole incident, according to Sarah took less than three minutes.

When Blaze hung up with B, he put his vest on and grabbed his twin .40 caliber pistols and headed back to Chester. Blaze had been relaxing out Scranton and he wanted to get back to make sure that they didn't have his address too.

When Blaze pulled up on Twenty-fourth Street, cops were everywhere. He parked his car in St. James, found a young bull riding a bike, and paid him twenty dollars to let him hold it. The young bull was with it, but only if he rode on the handlebars to make sure he got his bike back. Sounded good to Blaze. He rode the bike around Charnetta's house to find out what was going on.

When he pulled up in front of the house he found out from Shakeya and Nikki that somebody also shot Tyran's cousin Tommy's car up. Blaze became enraged.

"Where B at?" Blazed demanded to know.

"I don't know," Nikki replied, "he ain't been on the block since the shooting."

"Yeah," Shakeya chimed in, "I heard Biggy and Tyran got shot too."

"I heard," Blaze said, "who's inside Charnetta's house?"

"Nobody," Nikki said. "She on some bullshit 'cause she think niggas told on Duck."

Blaze thought nothing of it. He didn't really like the bitch anyway. He called Tommy's cell phone and found out that B, G.L., and a few other young bulls were over Tommy's house. "All right, I'm on my way," Blaze told B before he hung up.

Blaze dug in his pocket for his keys, asking Nikki,

"Yo, you know where Tommy live?"

"Yeah, he live around Wallingford, right?"

"Right. Look, grab my car from around St. James and bring it around there. You got that for me?"

"Yeah, of course," Nikki happily replied.

It wasn't long before Blaze was at Tommy's crib finding out what the fuck was going on. Their main suspects at the moment were the Garden niggas. Who else would come at them so crazy? So logically they believed it had to be the H.G.s.

―――――――――――

Var and N.Y. were having the best day of their lives. So far, in just two jobs, they had grabbed over twenty grand and four bricks. And they hadn't even hooked the biggest fish of all yet, Blaze. They went through Twenty-fourth Street looking for him, but couldn't find him instead they ran into Tommy, so they shot at him.

Afterwards they went back to their house, grabbed some cash, and drove up to Philadelphia to get a legit car to do their dirt.

When they got done doing that they left the stolen car up Philadelphia and headed to Chi-Chester to wait on Blaze. They were hoping it was the right address, but if it wasn't they'd find out soon enough.

―――――――――――

Saturday, Tamia and Charnetta drove out to the county jail together to see Duck and Wally. They had a great conversation in the car about things they didn't know about their men. Tamia was shocked to find out that most of the females on the block hated Wally. She couldn't believe he acted so arrogantly; she always knew him as the sweetest person in the world. Tamia was definitely glad to hear that rather than hearing he was fucking everything, so she supposed it was good news. She told Charnetta about how the guys on the block had a meeting to get Wally locked up, and of course Charnetta was positive that they did the same thing to Duck. Then Charnetta laid some heavy information on Tamia that she wasn't ready for.

"It's all good though," Charnetta said, "them snitch-ass niggas getting just what they deserve."

"Why you say that?" Tamia inquired.

"You ain't hear? Somebody killed Tyran yesterday and shot Biggy up, plus shot Biggy's sister and Tyran's girl. When you do dirt, you get dirt. Nawmean?"

Tamia didn't know what to say. For the first time in her life she was stuck. Her mind was racing with the realization that she had made the phone call that brought about the murders. *What would she do if she got caught in the middle of everything? Why did she do something so dumb?*

"Feel me, Tamia? Tamia? Tamia?"

"Yo?" She finally responded from her daze.

"You all right?" Charnetta asked.

"Yeah, I'm cool, I'm all right. Just thinking about Wally, you know?"

"Yeah, I know, girl, 'cause it's been crazy not having Duck in bed with me at night."

Charnetta's words started sounding like a record playing too fast as Tamia got caught up in her thoughts again. She just couldn't wait to get to the visit.

After a quick strip search, Wally and Duck strolled into the visiting room to find their seats. They had been talking all morning about Tyran, Biggy and the shit happening at home.

Naturally, Wally hadn't told Duck he knew who was behind it because he didn't trust Duck for shit. When they got to their seats, an aisle apart, they both embraced their girls and kissed them passionately.

"Hey, baby, how you doing?" Wally asked Tamia.

"Hey, boo," she said? "Did you hear what happened to Biggy and Tyran?"

"Yeah, so?"

"You don't think if ya boys get caught they going to tell on us, do you?"

"Tell on us about what?" Wally asked back, like she had said something stupid.

Timidly, Tamia said, "You know, about telling them to do it?"

"Yo, if I tell ya to go kill the president right now, is you going to do it?"

"Naw!"

"Why?"

"'Cause I ain't crazy, that's why," Tamia replied.

"Exactly. You ain't *make* nobody do shit. You feel me now?"

Tamia looked at him and smiled. "I get ya point."

After that the talk was limited. They mainly did a whole lot of holding hands and kissing. Wally explained how he expected things to go and told Tamia not to worry. Then the hour was up and Tamia had to leave. The tears in her eyes killed Wally.

"Look, I'mma call you tonight, baby," he promised. "I love you."

"I love you too," Tamia said as she and Charnetta both made their way from the visiting room.

# CHAPTER 10

Ace was having dinner at TGI Friday's when he got the distress call from Blaze.

"What's the problem?" Ace asked.

"Somebody came at me real crazy," Blaze explained. "They slumped my young bull Tyran and took four bricks from him. Then they ran up in Biggy's crib, shot him and his sister up, and took four bricks from him too, not to mention whatever money they had." Blaze exaggerated.

"Who was it?" Ace snapped.

"I don't know," Blaze confessed. "My young bull Tommy said he think it's them same niggas and somebody shot his car up."

"Why the fuck is niggas tryna kill y'all and y'all don't know who it is?" Ace angrily questioned.

"I don't know, gangsta, but them eight birds they took hurt me."

"All right, look," Ace said, "we'll talk about making up for the loss later, that ain't nothing. Where you at right now?"

"I'm over the east side, but I'mma about to shoot to my crib right quick to drop some money off."

"All right, listen, call the bull Hollywood and tell him who you think it is and he'll take care of it."

"All right, good looking, Cannon," Blaze said with relief and appreciation.

"Yo, don't get yourself slumped, man," Ace joked.

"Dog, they gonna need the National Guard to merc me, 'cause I'm gonna ride."

Ace laughed. "I hear you. It sound good in the studio, but talk that same shit when the lead flying at you."

They laughed a bit before hanging up, and afterwards Blaze grabbed the money he picked up from Tommy and a couple of other young bulls, then he headed home.

N.Y. and Var got restless waiting down Chi-Chester for Blaze and pulled off a couple of minutes too early. They felt as though they had put in enough work for one day and decided it was time to go celebrate. They drove to Var's house and grabbed five stacks a piece out of the free money they took earlier in the day. From there they drove down to the neighborhood bar. When they pulled up at Reflections, they caught Mean Sheen coming out the bar, about to hop in his car.

"What's the deal, Mean Sheen?"

"What's going on?" he greeted as he approached their car. "I'm about to go over the Bonnets; that thing jumping. It's a party over there or some shit."

"Yo," N.Y. exclaimed, "There's too many cops over there, dawg!"

"Yeah, I feel you, but it's dead in there," Mean Sheen said with a jerk of his head in the direction of Reflections. "The party in the Bonnets is where everybody at."

"I'm there," said Var.

"All right, follow me over," Mean Sheen instructed.

They pulled up in the Bonnets' parking lot a few minutes later and had a hard time finding a parking space. They parked way in the back, hopped out their cars and headed for the door.

"Yo," N.Y. said, "we left our guns in the car. They probably checking at the door, ain't they?"

"Yeah," Mean Sheen said. "I already found that out from Ike. So I got a twenty-five in my boot."

"Ike in there?" Var asked.

"Yeah, him, Shyne, E. Marvels and all them niggas," Mean Sheen informed them.

"Aw, we ready to show our ass, Mean Sheen," Var rallied.

They got in the bar after a quick pat down and scanned the bar looking for their team. They noticed Smiley and them from Feltonville when they first came in, then they walked past a couple project and Bennett niggas before they finally saw their team. They walked up on the squad, shaking everybody's hands enthusiastically.

"What's good, N.Y.?" asked Shyne.

"Ain't shit."

"You know ya nut-ass homies Skate and them in here."

"Yeah, all right," N.Y. said indifferently, like he couldn't care less.

"Yo, I'm just letting you know so them niggas don't catch you in the bathroom and beat the shit out you. You know you can't fight, and it ain't no guns in here, so you know you got to be easy," Shyne teased in a joking manner.

"Man, I'll fuck them niggas up," N.Y. boasted. "Plus Mean Sheen got a gun in his boot."

"Yeah, well, you better get that now, before you get too many drinks in you. Fuck around and have to pee or something and get caught in that bathroom."

By now N.Y. had noticed all the Garden niggas posted by the bathroom and around the wall. Him being the type dude he was, he got mad at Shyne for all the playing and put his stunt mode into overdrive. He walked over to the DJ booth and gave the DJ a hundred dollars for the mic.

"Yo, this that nigga, N.Y., from the McCaffe. I'm buying

all the bitches in the bar free drinks! Except them bitches up the Gardens, them niggas gotta buy they own drinks!"

Var popped up on N.Y.'s heels and tapped him to get the mic. By now the DJ was trying to get it back, but Var had snatched it outside the booth.

"McCaffe!" Var yelled into the mic. "Yeah, all pussies drink for free except Garden pussies! McCaffe!"

The DJ immediately turned the mic off while Var was still ranting.

Across the bar the Garden niggas were furious. They were the ones throwing the party for their man Rat, who just came home. The pack of young bulls snapped out. Skate and Maine tried to talk them into waiting till they got outside, but they weren't trying to hear it. T-Bone and the Cut-off niggas followed the young bulls' lead. They all walked toward the other side of the bar to confront N.Y. and Var. As they made their way around the bar, Mean Sheen went in his boot to grab his gun.

Moments later, Eddie stole N.Y. and, like a domino effect, punches started flying from all angles. The brawl lasted about three minutes before the first shots went off. Mean Sheen let off three shots at York hitting him twice, that's when everything paused for a second. Then a stampede broke out as people started running for the door.

As the crowd broke up, Skate came out of the mix with Kenny, who fell from an overhand right and uppercut that Skate threw. Then Skate searched the crowd looking for the nigga who let off the shots. He caught a glimpse of the person he was looking for. Skate broke through the crowd like a raging bull. When he got in a good range, he pulled out his .380 and let off five shots. After he was sure he had hit the nigga, he tucked his gun in his pants and kept running for the door.

As Skate made his way out, he stepped on Mean Sheen's back. Mean Sheen was laid out on the floor, critically injured with three bullets in the back. Beside him, another bull was down with a bullet in the hip.

Skate hurried through the parking lot to his car. Once there, he wanted to pull off but had to wait for Maine and Rat. He could hear the sirens in the background rapidly approaching and began to get nervous. He started the car, ready to pull off, when Dre knocked on the window, startling him.

"Yo, give me ya gun," Dre demanded. "Hurry up! They shot Rat!

Skate didn't think about it, he just rolled the window down and passed Dre the .380. Dre ran back, feeling like *Rambo* as he cut through the crowd. Skate sat thinking for about three seconds, until he heard shots going off in rapid succession.

"Fuck!" Skate yelled before he hopped out the car with a .45 he had under the seat and ran back toward the bar.

Shyne's car was parked right in front of the door, so as soon as he made it out of the Bonnets he popped the trunk and grabbed two guns. The first nigga out that he saw was Rat. So without hesitation he put four slugs in his face. N.Y. came out next chasing three young bulls.

N.Y. had picked up the gun from Mean Sheen when he checked on him to see if he was cool. He didn't expect Mean Sheen to make it, so that made him snap. He grabbed Mean Sheen's gun and started chasing the first niggas he saw.

When N.Y. got to the parking lot, the shots from Shyne startled him. But once he saw who it was, he ran straight to his car.

"Yo, give me one of them guns," N.Y. demanded. "Maine still in there?"

"Man, I'm about to pull off, fuck that! The police coming!" Shyne expressed sternly.

"All right, we out," N.Y. said.

As he went to get in Shyne's car, the young bull Dre popped up and let off six at them, two of which hit N.Y. Shyne quickly returned fire, hitting Dre in the stomach. Then he ran to see if N.Y. was cool and found out he was only hit in the arm and shoulder.

Shyne helped N.Y. in the car and sped off, but not before Skate shot the back window out, hit the taillight, and struck Shyne in the neck.

Skate caught Maine coming out and told him to hurry to the car. He went to grab Dre, but Dre was bleeding pretty badly. Skate held up one of the females running past and told her to make sure Dre got in an ambulance.

Then Skate saw the police coming and knew he was in trouble. He took off running toward the street, hoping to get a nice distance on them. Hopefully Maine would pick him up in the car. But everything was happening too quickly, and Skate wasn't fast enough. The cops tackled him in the middle of the street and caught him with a .45 caliber Desert Eagle. For Skate it all ended in the blink of an eye.

It was possibly the worst night of Skate's life, and when he woke up for breakfast he was extremely mad. Skate walked from his cell to get his breakfast tray thinking about all the shit he could have done to avoid jail. Things weren't as bad as they could be, but they were bad enough. Not only did the police catch him with a loaded .45, but they also charged him with the attempted homicide on his young bull Dre. Dre was in a coma, in critical condition. From what the police were saying, he wasn't expected to make it. Skate figured he'd rather be charged with Dre's attempted murder than Mean Sheen's murder. Good thing he didn't grab his gun back from Dre.

After he grabbed his tray, Skate spun around to go back to his cell. That's when he noticed Wally and M.B. in line waiting to grab their trays. Skate was instantly enraged. Since he expected to come out later on in the day, he didn't feel there was a reason to draw. But he had pretty much made his mind up that he was going to fuck them niggas up.

The doors kicked at ten o'clock in the morning for block-out, and Wally went straight for the phone and dialed Tamia's number.

"Hello?" Tamia answered after a few rings.

"Hey, baby, how you doing?"

"I'm cool, baby. You know N.Y.'s been calling all day. He said he need to holla at you."

"All right. Pick up ya cell phone, call him, and see what he want," Wally instructed.

Tamia walked through the house, grabbed her cell and dialed N.Y.'s number. Once she got him on the line she put both phones on speakerphone so Wally and N.Y. could talk to one another.

"What's the deal, N.Y.?" asked Wally.

"Yo, that nigga Skate out there with you?" N.Y. asked angrily.

"Yeah, in arm's reach."

Skate had walked out and picked up the wall phone next to Wally, so he was standing right next to him.

"Yo, you know that nigga slumped Mean Sheen and Shyne last night."

"What?" Wally snapped.

"Yeah," N.Y. continued, "we ran into them niggas at the Bonnets last night and shot it out."

"So you want me to reach out and touch this nigga?" Wally asked.

"Basically," N.Y. replied.

"It's done."

"All right," N.Y. said, satisfied. "Listen, I got hit last night, twice, so give me a week or two to go at Blaze."

"Don't worry about it, get yaself together my nigg, he ain't going nowhere." Wally assured.

"All right, look, I'mma holla at you, pimp. Be easy," N.Y. said before hanging up.

No soon as he hung up, Tamia went into her rationale speech. She got about two sentences out before Wally cut her off.

"Look, boo, I gotta do what I gotta do."

Skate, of course, overheard enough of Wally's conversation to figure out what it was hitting for. So since he couldn't get through, he smacked Wally with the phone and commenced to punching him in the face. Wally didn't quite recover from the phone, and the punches that landed had him knocked out on his feet. The phone was dangling and Wally couldn't hear Tamia screaming his name over and over again.

Wally was a hook away from falling when M.B. saved his ass. He caught Skate from the blind side and buckled him into the wall, but Skate was too big. Even though M.B. had hit him hard, he recovered quickly and got into a scuffle with M.B.

Seconds later the guards grabbed Wally, Skate, and M.B. and took them to the hole, but not before Wally screamed, "Duck, you bitch-ass nigga! How the fuck you gonna let this nigga get out on me?"

"I just came out the cell," Duck lied.

"Man, get the phone and tell my girl I'm going to the hole, you fucking faggot!" Wally scolded.

Duck was mad that Wally disrespected him but he would definitely enjoy telling everybody how he got fucked up, since Wally wanted to talk shit. Duck grabbed the phone and explained detail by detail to Tamia how Wally got his ass kicked.

⸻

"Three... two... one... Happy New Year!" yelled the commentator on TV! Juanita blew into her party favor and feverishly waved her noisemaker in the air. Doc couldn't help but laugh at her.

"You really enjoying this? Ain't you?" He asked Juanita.

"Why shouldn't I be? Last year I met the greatest man in the whole world, and this year I'm going to marry him and have his baby," she happily expressed.

"Oh, you gonna marry him, huh?"

"Yup."

"What makes you think he gonna marry you?"

"Because he loves me," Juanita said matter of factly. "And if he knows what's good for him, he'd hurry up and put a ring on my finger before some young stud comes along and sweeps me off my feet. Plus I ain't that big, so I might be able to convince Jeremy that this baby is his."

"Oh, the young stud named Jeremy, huh?" Doc said, feeding into her game. "I guess I'mma see if I can get somebody to throw Jeremy's stud ass off a bridge."

"You wouldn't!" Juanita dared in mock astonishment.

"I got to. The sperm he busting on my son's head might change his hair color or put his eye out or something."

She laughed at Doc's response and then pulled him close and kissed him softly.

"Well, I guess to avoid all that we must be getting married," Juanita said, acting all melodramatic.

"You know, you'd make a great extortionist. How about

we kidnap Jeremy first, take him for the millions and billions of dollars he got?"

Juanita replied, "who said he got millions and billions of dollars?"

"He gotta be worth something to take you from me."

"Well, he's not. He's a goat herder."

Doc laughed, suggesting, "Guess he going to be from Zamunda next, huh?"

"How'd you know?" Juanita said, playing like she was surprised.

"Cause they said you'd say that."

"What else they say I'd say?"

"They said you'd say that you wanna be nasty," Doc said before kissing her.

"They must know me pretty well, don't they?" Juanita joked, pulling Doc's shirt over his head. "Let's do something special to bring in the New Year, baby."

Twenty minutes later they were in the woods on a blanket making love under the stars, and Juanita couldn't have had a better new year if she tried to.

---

Three and a half weeks after Duck was initially locked up, he finally had a preliminary hearing date. His lawyer, Omar Dickens, said that Duck would be on the street in a week. The hearing for the drug case was three days away and Mr. Dickens had already gotten the detainers lifted for Duck's bulletproof vest and DUI cases. The failure to appear cases were technicalities the detectives were using as a deception to get Duck to break on something really important. The CID had showed up twice to see Duck to primarily ask questions about Wally, and secondly about Tyran and Biggy. They threatened

Duck by saying they'd make sure he got the max on his case if he didn't cooperate. But Duck didn't know anything to cooperate. So for that reason, and that reason alone, he didn't have anything to say.

After his attorney's visit, Duck called Charnetta. She had been serving people that came to the house for the last two weeks, and she had his bail money on ice. She gave Doc back two quarter bricks, claiming that's all the coke Duck had. She sold everything else. She broke a lot of the weight down and sold nicks and dimes. With Tyran and Biggy getting killed and Tommy laying low after his car got shot up, Charnetta had almost seventy thousand dollars and maybe three and a half ounces worth of dimes left in her house. It wasn't that she was really trying to get money; it was just coming. Her best friend, Simone helped her hold the crib down while she made runs to her own house to stash money. Charnetta's friends, Nikki and Shakeya, were terribly jealous, but they smiled in her face while they plotted on fixing Miss High-Sidity with the new attitude.

Then finally came the day. On the day Duck got released from prison, Charnetta had big things planned. She picked Duck up after the preliminary hearing and drove straight to the airport. She didn't pack a lot of bags and she deposited ten thousand dollars into her bank account so they could have spending money. If they blew the ten thousand dollars, she brought cash.

She didn't tell Duck where they were going until they got to the airport. As she walked to pick up their tickets, Duck asked her where they were going. And since she knew he would be happy, she told him, "Where else would we be going? We going to Vegas."

*Vegas!* Duck thought. *Damn, she really know how to make a man smile!*

So they caught their plane to Las Vegas. The entire flight Duck thought about how much money he would win. This was the best trip in the world for a compulsive gambler.

———————

N.Y. and Var were laying low after the Boots & Bonnets incident. They both wanted to go to Mean Sheen and Shyne's funerals, but somebody told them the police were parked outside, so they didn't risk it. For two weeks they stayed away from the city, only coming back to pick up money for the coke they were dropping off. Since they both knew a bunch of college girls from being out Oxford with Wally, they laid low out there. They stayed out Lincoln with some chicks they met named India and Linda. Between staying at the college and paying crack houses to push their coke, time was flying.

That's what made them go back to work.

The next day they were in front of Blaze's Chi-Chester address all day. Var even knocked on the door and rang the bell to check the house for a visible alarm system. He wasn't positively sure but he thought he noticed a keypad by the door when he looked inside the window.

Var hurried back to car to inform N.Y. they were changing the plan from breaking in, to breaking shit out.

"Yo," Var said, "I definitely think that nigga got an alarm."

"Damn. What you wanna come back tomorrow?"

"Naw, we gonna bring dude to us. We gonna park about a block down the street and watch everything with binoculars."

"Okay, then what?" N.Y. questioned.

"I'mma break the fucking windows out," Var explained. "The cops gonna come first, but the security system people gonna call him and let him know somebody broke his shit."

N.Y. smiled at the simplicity of Var's plan.

Executing their plan, they parked far enough away not to be noticed by the police. Var had broken out the big bay window so Blaze couldn't patch it up easily. The two of them were laid behind the tints watching the whole scene play out.

The police responded quickly, too quickly, as far as Var and N.Y. were concerned. Then a half an hour later the golden boy popped up. Blaze talked with the cops, let them inside the house to look around, and when they were sure nobody was there they left.

Blaze was mad that he had to let the police in his house, period. But he didn't want them to get funny feelings and hang around. As soon as they left he began to gather all of his money together to load into his truck. He had about $2 million in the house, so it wasn't an easy task. He was also trying to get in touch with somebody to come board his window up.

Blaze was moving so fast that he didn't notice the two guys swiftly walking down the street. He was on his second trip back inside the house to grab the last four bags of cash from his stash when Var and N.Y. made their move.

"Yo, you grab the money. He put two bags in the trunk," Var said, laying out their strategy.

"I'mma slump the pussy and meet you at the car. Pull up out front and wait for me."

N.Y. just shook his head and rushed to grab the money. He pulled the heavy bags from the truck and turned to run them back to the car.

Var quickly walked through the open front door, scanning the downstairs for Blaze. He was clutching his gun in both hands so that he'd have an accurate shot as soon as Blaze appeared.

Var swiftly strolled through the living room, dining room,

and kitchen. On his way out the kitchen Blaze came running down the steps. Blaze was talking on the phone, so for a split second Var thought maybe Blaze wasn't alone in the house. Var hid behind the dining room wall waiting for the perfect moment. Then, as Blaze got to the bottom of the steps, Var saw the cell phone.

Var made his move. He took aim and caught Blaze with four of the six shots he fired. Blaze screamed out in pain, and surprise before buckling to the floor, face first. Var immediately rushed Blaze. Blaze was laid flat out, not moving, so Var kicked him twice.

Since Var assumed he finished the job, he grabbed the two bags Blaze had dropped and ran to the door and sat them down for N.Y.

Var figured that Blaze might've had more bags upstairs, so he ran to check. After a brief search he found two bags of cash sitting on Blaze's bed. On his way back down, Var planned to put a few more slugs in Blaze's head to make sure Blaze was dead.

Blaze had been on the phone with his girlfriend, Janisha. As soon as she heard the shots and heard Blaze scream, she hung up to call the cops.

For a brief moment Blaze had the wind knocked out of him. As he tried to roll over he realized that something might be broke, but Blaze's will to live kicked in, and thanks to his vest he wasn't fatally wounded.

As Var ran up the steps, Blaze crawled for cover. He made it behind the couch as Var was coming back downstairs.

When Var got back to the living room he was momentarily shocked to find that Blaze wasn't in the same spot he left him. In the split second that Var lunched, Blaze took aim. As Var headed for the door thinking Blaze was trying to run to his truck, Blaze let off four shots from his four-pound Desert Eagle.

Var wasn't as lucky as Blaze. Three of the four shots hit him in the back and forced him to stumble out onto the steps. He fell face-first down the steps with a bag of cash in each hand.

Blaze was in the process of trying to get to his feet when N.Y. charged through the door. They saw each other at the same time and exchanged a hail of gunfire.

Blaze dove behind the couch, ripping shots at N.Y. N.Y. ducked behind the door as Blaze shot through the couch trying to hit him.

Then N.Y. heard a siren in the distant back ground, so he ran down the steps. He rolled Var over and realized his homey was dead. Before N.Y. could retrieve the two bags of cash from Var's hands bullets came whizzing by him causing him to retreat.

As he put the car in drive to pull off, Blaze stumbled to the door reloading his gun. N.Y. peeled off, screeching up the street as Blaze emptied a fresh clip in his direction.

N.Y. felt bad for leaving Var, but he couldn't risk going to jail. All he thought about on the way home was how Blaze managed to kill Var when Var had the drop on him. Then it dawned on him Blaze must've had a vest on.

The next day, N.Y. bought a newspaper and found out that the police found Var dead with three shots in the back and two in the head. They also found $1 million dollars cash in two duffel bags on the front steps. The owner of the house, Carlos Corbin, was found laid out behind the couch with the smoking gun in his hand. Since the gun was registered to the house, Blaze was more than likely to escape prosecution for the homicide, but he was being held under federal investigation for possession of the cash.

Corbin was also admitted to the emergency room with fractured ribs and bruised lungs in critical condition. He also received a gunshot wound to the arm from a different caliber weapon than the one police took off the intruder. Police were looking for anyone with information about the incident.

"Damn, how the fuck I leave $1 million dollars?" N.Y. cussed at himself after reading the article.

He wasn't upset though, because with what he did grab, he still committed the biggest robbery of his life.

# CHAPTER 11

Doc got up early Saturday morning, took a shower, and got dressed. By then his cell phone was ringing. When he picked it up, it was just who he expected it to be. It was Tamia asking if he was ready yet.

"Yeah," Doc answered, "I'm about to hop in my car now. Where you wanna meet me at?"

"I don't know. Is the bowling alley down Chi-Chester cool?"

"Will it take you long to get there?" Doc asked her.

"About thirty to forty-five minutes," Tamia estimated.

"All right, I'll see you then."

Doc hung up, then kissed Juanita and told her he'd be back later on in the evening. He grabbed his Rolex and car keys before rolling out.

It took him forty minutes to get to the bowling alley. Once there, he hopped from his car to Tamia's.

"Hey, beautiful," Doc greeted her, "How you holding up?"

"I've had better days," Tamia replied, "but I've been working a lot of overtime to keep my mind off it. Wally said you got in touch with two of the witnesses."

"Yeah, it was some young girls from down Third. I gave them five stacks a piece and told them I got five more when the case gets thrown out."

For the rest of the ride they conversed casually. It took them twenty minutes to get to the county lock-up, and another twenty before they got in. Wally came out shortly after they were situated in their seats. Correctional Officers escorted him to the visiting room in handcuffs. When Doc saw his face he knew Wally had gotten himself in the middle of some dumb shit. The guards un-cuffed him and let him walk over to their table, where Wally hugged and kissed his girl. Then Doc let loose with the questions.

"Goddamn, gangsta, what happened to you?"

"Me and ya bull Skate was tearing it up. That nigga stole me while I was on the phone with Tamia," Wally explained.

"She told me about that part. But what was it about?"

"N.Y. told me Skate slumped Mean Sheen."

"Yeah, well, you know Blaze slumped da bull Var last night," Doc informed.

"Man, get the fuck outta here!" It was news to Wally.

"Yeah, Var and somebody else ran up in his crib, robbed him and shot him up. If the nigga ain't have a vest on he'd probably be dead right now."

Wally had a somber expression on his face while Tamia looked shocked. Doc knew something was up, but he didn't know what.

"What's up, you all right?" Doc inquired.

"Naw, I need to tell you something."

"What's good?"

Wally said, "You know Duck told me that ya boy Blaze had a meeting and told them dudes to get me locked up."

"Man, I can't believe that!"

"I'm serious, old head. The police was sweating them niggas, and Detective Nutsack told them if they turned me in he'd cool down the heat."

"Yeah?" Doc replied. The news had him fucked up, but he tried to keep his composure as he asked, "So, what, you put Var on them niggas?"

"Naw," Wally lied.

But it didn't matter; Doc knew the truth. They talked for forty-five minutes about things the lawyer had told them and about what Doc was doing as far as trying to find the last witness. Doc told Wally about his plans to leave the game at the end of the year and how he was going to marry Juanita on her birthday and buy her a Benz. They also discussed a few business endeavors Doc wanted to put together. Then Doc hugged his young bull and left him to talk with Tamia for the last 15 minutes of the hour visit.

Once the visit was over, Tamia took Doc back to his car and dropped him off. He told her if she needed anything to call. He gave her a hug, then hopped in his car and sped off to investigate the accusations he'd just been made aware of.

Biggy and B had a set of keys to Duck's house the entire time he was gone. Charnetta had left her keys with Simone, explaining that she didn't want anybody in the house except B, Biggy, Kiana and Kelly. For the first couple of days Simone managed to keep Nikki and Shakeya out, but at the end of the week they weren't going for the Charnetta-don't-want-nobody-in-the-house story anymore. Especially since Simone was letting everybody else in. So Simone just came out and told them, "Look, Charnetta said she don't want y'all in her house." That news hit Nikki and Shakeya hard at first, but after a day or so they weren't mad anymore; they wanted to get even.

The two of them started putting together a plan, so when Charnetta and Duck got back from their little vacation they would have something special waiting for the two of them.

Biggy didn't sense the hostility because the two of them still spoke to him and B. Plus, occasionally, Biggy would give them weed and liquor to keep them happy.

Saturday afternoon everything was going the same as usual. Biggy and B were staying indoors as much as possible, trying to get money on the low. They had plenty of weed and liquor, and being that they heard what happened to Blaze, they were both wearing vests.

Doc pulled up in front of the house at a little after four. He didn't waste time speaking to Nikki and Shakeya, who were out on the steps. He knocked on the door, tried the doorknob, and walked in.

When he got to the living room he found Biggy and B playing video games and smoking weed. The place was a mess. Old pizza boxes were laying around and empty beer bottles were all over the coffee table. Doc tried to overlook the condition of the house as he called the two of them to the kitchen to interrogate them away from the three females they were keeping company with.

"Yo, what's going on with y'all?" Doc asked.

"We just laying low," said B. "I know you heard about what happened to Blaze."

"Yeah, I heard. That's why I'm here, I wanna go put an end to this. But I need y'all to tell me something."

They both stared attentively, waiting.

"Blaze told y'all to tell on Wally?"

Biggy and B looked at each other, then back at Doc. Biggy took the initiative.

"I don't know what you talking about, Doc."

Doc was instantly mad. What, did they take him for a sucker?

"Well, you know what?" he said. "The niggas who coming for y'all already know where ya live. What, y'all think this shit coincidence? They shot you once Biggy and they meant to kill you. They just ain't catch up with you yet, but believe me they trying to. Somebody told Wally y'all niggas told on him and he got them niggas on y'all head. So either y'all talk

**128**

to me and work this out, or y'all can keep snitching and end up in jail or dead. Matter a fact, clean my girl shit up and get the fuck outta her house."

Doc was snapping. He was already sick that they had done what they did and were now trying to play him. Doc spun to leave in disgust when B grabbed his shoulder and said, "Hold up, Doc, it wasn't like that. Tyran told everybody to meet up down his house. It was originally his plan, but I ain't gonna act like we didn't agree to it, because we did. By the time Blaze got there, everybody was down, even Duck. So Tyran told Blaze the deal, and he asked us how we felt. After everybody spoke their peace, Blaze said when Wally got knocked we never had this conversation, so it died right there. So it wasn't Blaze's idea, but he just didn't object to it."

Doc looked at the two of them after B finished talking and became sick to his stomach. He didn't feel like arguing about the shit, so he decided to leave.

"You gonna squash this shit for us Doc?" Biggy asked in a pleading manner. Fearing that the next time he was shot, he might not be as lucky.

Doc turned around, looked at the two of them wearing Gucci faces, and smiled.

"Yeah, I'mma do what I can. But if I was y'all, I'd probably go holla at Wally."

He stared at them blankly for a minute before leaving. His whole outlook on life had changed in one day. For all Doc knew, Blaze might have been talking to the feds about him. He just didn't trust Blaze anymore. Doc really couldn't understand how Blaze got arrested, made the front page of every newspaper, and was home the next day. Early in the morning Blaze had called and told Doc he was under a federal investigation, that he just paid bail and was about to lay low.

Doc knew what Blaze meant, so he didn't talk over the

phone. Now he was driving out to the lay low spot wondering what Blaze had to say about the whole situation. Doc decided that no matter which way the talk went, after their conversation, this would be the last time they'd see each other. He would make sure Juanita signed the house over to Charnetta, then he'd rent out his couple of apartments and move down south. Maybe Atlanta, Virginia, or somewhere fun, but country enough for him to stay out the way.

At Blaze's Lancaster apartment an hour later, Doc parked in the back alleyway and knocked on the back door. After a few minutes Blaze opened the door. He had a lot of papers in his hands, so he didn't stand around to formally greet Doc; he just walked back into the living room. Doc closed the door behind himself and followed Blaze into the living room.

Blaze had receipts scattered everywhere, a calculator, and pay stubs from his fictitious job. Blaze was hard at work making a fake trail for his money. The feds had called his business associates, and while they were still loyal to Blaze, he intended to use that to his advantage.

"So, what's the deal?" Doc asked.

"Man, I'm tryna get this money situation straight. The feds took $1 million bucks from me, and they tryna get me for tax evasion and maybe RICO for dealing and racketeering. But the personal trainer thing is getting my ass out the sling. Then I got receipts from all my apartments I'm renting out. Plus I got a couple more plans to protect my ass. You feel me?"

Doc didn't answer, he just looked at him. He couldn't believe a nigga he'd known so long would do such slimy, underhanded shit.

Blaze said, "Yo, you know the bull that tried to rob me was from up the McCaffe, right? The bull Var?"

"Yeah, I heard," Doc replied to that old bit of news. Then, bluntly said, "I also heard that you gave Tyran and them the green light to get Wally knocked."

"What? Who told you some dumb shit like that?"

"The people that was at ya little meeting down Tyran's house."

"Man, don't come at me like that. If you talked to them niggas I know they told you I told them I wasn't with that shit. They already had they minds made up, it wasn't shit I could do," Blaze explained. "And you know what? It struck me as kind of odd when I pulled Var's mask off. But I guess if you heard about this shit, Wally must've heard too. So what he say when you told him?"

First of all, it went more like, what did *I* say when *he* told me. And honestly, at first, I couldn't believe it, but I went and questioned Biggy and B when I left Wally. And they told me the same story Wally told me. It's still kinda unbelievable, you know?"

"Yo, Doc, them niggas had they minds made up, even Duck. I don't know what he said to Wally in there, but all of them niggas crossed him. I know you love that young bull, but if he beat that case, I'mma kill him."

"I knew when I took Var's mask off he had something to do with it. Plus I knew somebody had to give them niggas my address, not to mention Biggy and Tyran's addresses. But it's cool. Wally caught us sleeping. But when I catch ya young bull, I'mma blow his fucking brains out."

Doc didn't respond. He would merely inform Wally ahead of time and hope Wally caught Blaze before Blaze caught him.

"So now there's one of them little pussies running around the McCaffe with $1 million dollars of my money. I know you don't know who did it, but if you find out who did, I'll split whatever's left with you when I kill that mothafucka and get my money back."

Blaze watched Doc closely to see if he could read his thoughts.

"I'll see what I can find out and I'll let you know," Doc replied, keeping a stone expression on his face so Blaze couldn't tell he was lying through his teeth.

"It's cool, he'll fuck up and spend too much money. When he do, it's about his ass!" Blaze vowed.

Doc was tired of hearing the bullshit Blaze was talking, so he grabbed his keys and cell phone off the table. Just as he got up to leave, Blaze asked him, "So, what side you choosing? You riding with ya young bull?"

The questions came as a shock to Doc. They paralyzed him momentarily as he looked at Blaze. Blaze had his arm in a sling and a brace around his leg, yet his demeanor still screamed for war. Doc took a minute to choose his words wisely before speaking.

"Yo, I'm not choosing sides. I'm thinking about giving all this shit up and moving out west to Vegas or Cali."

Blaze just stared at Doc already knowing that Ducky was out Vegas. That's when the realization came to him that Duck was the person who told Wally everything, and then to avoid retribution his scared ass ran out to Vegas. That's why he left Biggy and B the house. Now Doc was running scared too.

"I always knew you wasn't built, Doc. I can't believe you lasted this long. That's what you and ya soldiers wanna do, huh? Move out to Vegas. You know Vegas the gambling capital of the world" Blaze paused to add emphasis to his words, "so make sure you're a good gambler, because at any given time you could lose it all!" Blaze chuckled afterwards and smiled, but he meant every word of it.

"Yo, have a nice life, pimp," Doc stated.

As he walked toward the door Blaze stopped him to shake his hand. Doc was hurt by their conversation, but he still gave a fake hug and handshake and wished Blaze luck.

Doc was feeling like he lost a brother as he started his car. Everything went sour when Flame died, Doc believed. And now it was time for him to choose sides, just like Blaze had insinuated, so he picked up his cell and called Tamia as he pulled off.

"Yo, Mia, tell Wally I'm coming for a visit Monday night. I got some serious rap for him."

"All right, Doc, I'll tell him when he calls tomorrow."

Charnetta and Duck stayed in Vegas eight days and seven nights. On their first day on the Hollywood Strip Charnetta was mesmerized by the Mirage Hotel. It was the big pool with the dolphins that attracted her the most. She spent most of her day shopping for gifts and watching the dolphin show, and that night they stayed cuddled up in the room having wild sex.

The next day Duck got on his serious gamble. He won forty-five thousand dollars the previous day but lost twenty-five thousand dollars on his second. After that he decided to check out some of the other casinos. He went to Bally's, the Tropicana, and Planet Hollywood on his third day before checking into the Stratosphere that night.

The Stratosphere was on the end of the strip, on Sahara Avenue. For Duck that was perfect. The hotel's rooms were nice and, more importantly, cheap as hell compared to the ridiculously extravagant rates of the Mirage. Duck had found out about the Stratosphere and Circus Circus from a guy he had met named Gilbert. Gilbert was from Phoenix, but he had moved to Vegas to become a professional gambler. So naturally Gilbert knew where all the cheap spots were because he'd been down and out on numerous occasions.

The next day Gilbert came to holler at Duck early in the morning. He took Duck and Charnetta to Arizona Charlie's and treated them to a steak and egg breakfast. That afternoon Gilbert and Duck gambled at the Stardust, Circus Circus, the Hilton, and the MGM Grand. When they got to the MGM Mirage, Charnetta bought a ticket to go see the Siegfried and Roy show. By then Gilbert had picked up a girlfriend for Charnetta to hang with so he and Duck could devote all of their time to gambling.

Gilbert had a nice strategy. He always quit gambling when he won fifteen to twenty thousand dollars. If he was losing, he'd quit once he lost five grand and try somewhere else. He normally won more than he lost though, because for him the name of the game was knowing when to quit. For Duck, knowing when to quit was something he couldn't fathom. Duck was good at not going completely broke, so he didn't need a strategy.

On his sixth day, Duck came real close to losing it all. He was down to a thousand dollars but Charnetta was doing great at the Stratosphere. She didn't like gambling, but since they had a cute little refund policy she tried her luck.

By then Duck and Gilbert picked her and Gilbert's girl-friend, Cynthia up and took them to Mr. Lucky's. There, they had a steak and shrimp dinner and a lot of conversation. When Charnetta found out Duck was losing so badly she gave him the whole five thousand dollars she had won. All she wanted was for Duck to come in some time during the night and have sex with her.

Duck didn't make it in that night. By the next morning, when he did show up, he was fifty thousand dollars richer. Somehow he had managed to hit big and quit. He wanted to keep playing, but Gilbert persuaded him to call it a night.

The next day Duck spent the entire day pampering his girl. He took Charnetta to a suite at the MGM Grand and four or five different shows. When they left they had about forty thousand dollars and the ten thousand dollars that Charnetta had in the bank. As far as she was concerned they had a great time. They met some new friends and picked up plenty of souvenirs.

When they got back to Philadelphia the first thing Duck did was catch a cab to a car dealership. He would've liked to have won enough to grab a Bentley or a Maybach, but Charnetta was just as content with the XJ Jaguar Duck bought her. It was a candy apple-red with peanut butter guts. She could just imagine how the bitches would be hating when she pulled up.

---

After thirty days in the hole, Wally and Skate both went back to D-block. Now that the Correctional Officers were aware that the two of them didn't get along, they were kept separated. Skate was housed on the top tier and Wally on the bottom. Since the top and bottom never came out at the same time, the guards assumed their problem was over. Wally didn't plan on talking to Skate, but two days after they were back on the block something changed his mind.

Skate made a small power move and had a Correctional Officer, drop a carton of cigarettes and a half ounce of weed off. In a smoke-free environment, cigarettes were like crack. So a day after Skate got his package damn near everybody knew.

M.B. and Wally tried to indirectly buy some weed and a pack. They sent one of their homies to Skate who wasn't from their project. Ash hollered at Skate that afternoon and showed Skate the fifty-dollar bill Wally had given him, but Skate wasn't doing anything. He knew where the fifty was coming from,

Wally had just tried to spend it with a Correctional Officer a couple days earlier.

That night Wally and M.B. locked in, mad that Skate wouldn't serve Ash. Then it hit Wally like a bolt of lightning. He would try to kill two birds with one stone.

The next day when he came out for his two hours, Wally immediately walked up to Skate's cell. He knocked on the door, and Skate looked up, totally surprised.

"What's up?" Skate asked cautiously. "What you knock on my door for?"

"Yo, I'm tryna cop some of that weed and a pack of cigarettes," Wally sternly replied.

"You knocked on my door for that?" Skate was more scared that Wally would draw on him more than anything, but when Wally bobbed his head in the affirmative it made him furious. "Man, what, you fucking crazy? I don't fuck with you like that. I wouldn't sell you water in hell, nigga!"

"Damn, well, that's too bad," Wally said casually. "I thought you might wanna know who killed ya six young bulls down Third a while back."

It was a comment Skate wasn't expecting. So when Wally started to step off, Skate called him back.

"Yo, how I know you ain't bullshitting?"

"Man, look," Wally said, "I don't need that shit that bad. I was just tryna squash the bullshit between me and you, for real. But you playing me like I'm some nut-ass, dick-eating dude. You know I get money, and I know you get money. So you can come off that corny shit and hear some real rap, or we can keep on gang warring and go through it until one of us die. It don't matter to me, either way."

Wally was taking a risk putting the info out there because everybody knew Doc and Blaze were cool. But he figured if he spun it the right way he could have Skate put his team on Blaze immediately.

They rapped on the door for a while. Wally explained how after the shit went down with him and Flame got slumped, Blaze promised to get them back. Wally told Skate how Blaze had hired professional hit men to kill all of them.

Skate believed every word of it. By the time Wally was done, he had Skate convinced that Blaze was behind everything, even both of them being locked up.

In gratitude, Skate slid Wally a nice bag of weed and half a pack of smokes for free. They planned on talking the next day, and Wally spun off to get a shower and use the phone.

# CHAPTER 12

Hollywood was beginning to really enjoy his new hustle spot. His bull Blaze picked him up about a week ago and rented him an apartment at Wallingford, dropped a quarter brick on him and told Hollywood to do his thing.

A week later Hollywood was dug in. He kept a vest and a Desert Eagle on him and stayed in all black. He was prepared for anything that came his way, even police.

The best part about his new neighborhood was the females. In a week he had intercourse with Tyran's girl Bianca, Nikki, Shakeya, Carla, and Sheila. Almost a different girl every night. It was good being the new guy in the neighborhood; Hollywood felt like a celebrity.

When Blaze pulled up in front of Larry's Pizza Shop, Hollywood was in the process of setting up a date with a smut named Micah. He was really feeling Micah until Blaze told him she had six kids. That changed his demeanor dramatically.

"Listen, shorty, call me up later on tonight. I'm about to take a ride with my man," Hollywood said, as he wrote down his cell number and handed it to her while Blaze ran in Duck's house and dropped off some coke.

While Blaze was inside, hollering at Biggy and B, a car pulled up and three guys got out and walked into Larry's. In the store, Maine told his young bulls that he assumed Blaze was somewhere in the vicinity. He pointed to the money green Benz S-500 and told Eddie and D to wait out front for dude.

Eddie posted up out front of the store, keeping their eyes on the S-500 across the street. Hollywood sat a few feet away from them on some steps beside the store. Since everybody was a potential threat to Hollywood he kept a watchful eye on the duo.

Just when Maine was paying for his food, Blaze walked out the house. Eddie tapped on the window, signaling Maine that their mark had appeared. Maine, of course, quickly finished paying for his food and headed for the door.

Eddie and D were already in the process of approaching Blaze. Blaze thought nothing of it as he made his way to get into the car, until Hollywood hollered.

When Blaze came out the door, Hollywood peeped the one guy knocking on the window and the other pulling out a gun. When they started walking toward Blaze, he went into action.

Hollywood pulled out his four-pound and hollered to warn Blaze. When he yelled, D instinctively spun around. The gunshots rang out like a school bell. Eddie started shooting at Blaze, forcing him to run back toward Duck's house to get a gun, while Hollywood and D got into a wild western shoot-out with just a few feet separating them.

Hollywood's Desert Eagle ripped holes through D, who wasn't wearing a vest. Maine, on the other hand, had one on. So when he came out to help D, Hollywood's .45 slugs only knocked the wind out of him. He in turn caught Hollywood with three shots. The shooting ceased momentarily as Hollywood took cover behind a car.

Maine immediately limped to his car. The blood-covered T-shirt D now wore let Maine know nothing could be done for him. Eddie hopped in the passenger's side a second after Maine.

"Maine, what about D?" Eddie hollered.

"We can't help him," Maine said unhesitatingly.

As he started the car up, Blaze ran out the house with a

Mac-11, sending round after round tearing into the car as Maine stomped on the gas. Blaze wasn't satisfied, so he ran to the corner and ripped shots in the car's direction as the car slipped farther away. When he realized his shooting was in vain, Blaze ran to see if Hollywood was okay.

Hollywood was laying up against a car trying desperately to breathe better. The three bullets he took to the chest did more than just knock the wind out of him, they felt as if they broke some bones, but he quickly got his shit together and ran to Blaze's car. They peeled off, leaving one dead body and plenty of witnesses. The only good thing about the situation was Blaze had Biggy, B, Tommy, Kiana, Kelly, and Simone – the whole team – outside to make sure nobody said anything.

Officer Minor was the first cop to arrive on the scene at Twenty-fourth and Madison. When he pulled over, a small crowd had already congregated on the corner. Most of the neighbors were unaware of what happened, so they were spreading hearsay they picked up from people who witnessed the crime. Simone, Kiana and Kelly supplanted that story. The only people who had a different version were the ones in the pizza shop. Their story didn't come to light until an hour after Detective Nutsack pulled up.

Detective Nutsack stumbled across their story accidentally when he went to the store to purchase a pack of cigarettes and a soda. The owner of the store, Larry, assumed Detective Nutsack knew what had actually happened. He was completely ignorant to the truth of the matter as he began to run his mouth a little bit too much.

"How you doing today, Detective?" Larry idly said as he rang up Nutsack's purchases.

"I hope you lock those guys up and throw away the key. I knew something was up when those guys walked inside my store."

"The suspects were in here?" Nutsack replied, confused as

he popped the top on his Pepsi.

"Yeah, it was three of them. They came in, talked briefly, and two of them went outside. The one guy stayed and stood right where you're standing now and ordered a turkey club, and right before they started shooting, one of them other guys tapped on the window."

"Are you sure, Larry? Cause we got about two dozen witnesses claiming that it was a drive-by."

"Yeah, I'm sure!" Larry argued. "The guys were shooting at one of the guys who hangs out across the street. I don't know the guy's name, but he was just on the front page of the newspaper last week. If I'm not mistaken, somebody tried to kill him and the feds found $1 million dollars in his house. I'm sure it was him," Larry said emphatically. "When they started shooting at him, he ran in that house over there across the street. Then he came back out the house as the guys were pulling off and chased the car, shooting at it."

Nutsack said, "Do you think that you could come down to the station and maybe pick the shooter out of a mug book and give us a statement?"

"I'd need about ten minutes to close the shop down. But, sure, why not?" he said, removing his apron.

Nutsack thanked him and walked outside to wait for Larry to lock up. He called Detectives Jones, Banks, and Edmunds over to inform them of this latest development. They went over everything Larry shared with the detective until Larry came out and left with Nutsack. Banks, Edmonds, and Jones stayed behind to investigate the house the suspect allegedly ran into.

When Simone answered the door she was almost floored to find three detectives on the stoop.

"Is this your house, ma'am?" Banks asked.

"Naw," Simone said. "I'm just house-sitting for a friend

that's out of town."

"Okay. Well, we need to talk to you and whoever else is in the house, Ma'am."

Simone looked like she just lost fifty IQ points. But since she knew Biggy and B had already taken the coke out of the house, she told the police to give her a minute. When she ducked inside to tell Biggy and B the situation, they were mad as hell. But to avoid the police getting a warrant they all complied.

───────────

The first time the Jaguar XJ came through Chester followed by Duck's Denali heads were turning. People who knew Duck and Charnetta were waving and beeping their horns as they made their way through traffic. When they pulled up on Twenty-fourth Street, the looks on everybody's faces made them feel like superstars.

They got out their cars in front of their house and spoke to the usual group sitting out front. Charnetta took a seat on the steps with Nikki, Shakeya, Kiana, and Kelly to catch up on the gossip, while Duck took their bags inside.

"That's your car, Charnetta?" Kelly inquired.

"You know it," she boasted.

"Oh my God...you go girl!" Kelly and Kiana both said as Charnetta took a seat next to them.

"So, what's been going on?" she asked.

"Girl, you know somebody tried to kill Blaze yesterday," Kelly said, eager to be first to share that tidbit.

"Yeah," Kiana chimed in, "the cops was questioning us and everything. Plus, on the day you left, somebody ran up in Blaze's house and shot him up and almost killed him!" Kiana refused to be outdone.

Charnetta was shocked by the news. *Why were people trying to kill all the neighborhood guys?*

"Yeah, girl," said Kelly, back in the limelight, "Blaze was in the paper and everything. The guy shot him six times, but Blaze had a vest on and he killed the guy."

"But they still locked him up because the feds found $1 million dollars in his house," Kiana said.

"Get outta here!" Charnetta sounded.

Kelly said, "I heard it was more than that. But one of the guys who tried to kill Blaze got away with $1 million during the shoot-out."

"Damn, shit been crazy around here, huh?"

"That ain't the half of it," Kelly and Kiana voiced in two-part harmony.

Charnetta looked over at Shakeya and Nikki and began to wonder why they weren't adding their two cents.

"What's up, y'all?" she directed at them. "What's going on?"

"What's up?" Shakeya returned sarcastically, rolling her eyes.

Her manner took Charnetta by surprise so she didn't comment right away until Nikki opened her mouth, saying, "Don't nobody fuck with ya fake ass!"

"What?" Charnetta said, perplexed.

"You heard me, don't nobody fuck with ya fake ass! What, everybody suppose to hail the queen 'cause you the fuck back with ya brand new car? Bitch, please!"

Charnetta was over her shock now, asking, "Well, what the fuck is you sitting on my steps for, bitch?"

"Cause I want to," Nikki declared. "What, you gonna fucking move me? Imagine that!"

"Imagine that?" Charnetta retorted. "You right, bitch. We gonna see if you move when I punch you in ya fucking mouth."

Charnetta got up and began to approach Nikki.

Kelly and Kiana quickly stood up and stepped between the two women. Shakeya and Nikki were both now standing, and Shakeya was pulling her hair into a ponytail in preparation for a fight. Their actions made Charnetta go on tilt.

"Oh, y'all bitches think y'all gonna get out on me? Get off me, Kelly!" Charnetta shouted, but Kiana and Kelly were already pushing her into the house.

In the house, Biggy and B were telling Duck about everything that happened while he was on vacation. More importantly, they were telling him that Blaze knew about him telling Wally about their meeting. Duck wasn't taking it too seriously at first, until B informed him about the two attempts on Blaze's life. Then they told Duck about how the police had questioned everyone in the house, and just as Duck was about to give his side of the story, Charnetta rushed in the house.

She ran straight to the closet and grabbed a baseball bat. Kelly and Kiana stood in front of the door, pleading with her, which made Duck quickly jump up to find out what was going on.

"What's the matter, baby?" he asked as he took the bat and put it back in the closet.

"Ain't shit wrong with me!"

She broke from his grip and ran upstairs and changed into a sweatsuit. Simone immediately awoke from all the commotion, asking, "What happened? What's the matter?"

But Charnetta didn't have time for explanations. She broke back downstairs, wiping Vaseline on her face. Duck tried talking to her as she pushed her way past him to run back outside to confront Nikki and Shakeya. Kiana and Kelly had explained what happened to Duck and tried to tell Charnetta that Shakeya and Nikki were just mad they weren't allowed in the house while they were away. But it was no use. Charnetta was furious. She rushed back outside expecting Shakeya and Nikki to be gone, but they weren't, and that just added fuel to the fire.

*These bitches must think this shit a joke*, Charnetta fumed. She ran down the steps and started swinging on Nikki as soon as she got in arm's length.

The first punch caught Nikki in the head, but she was expecting it. Nikki rolled with the punch and pulled Charnetta toward her. As quick as rain falls from the sky on a cloudy day, Nikki whipped a box cutter from behind her back and sliced deeply into Charnetta's face. Her scream was that of a wounded animal as Charnetta lunged forward and grabbed the cutter.

Everything happened so fast it took everyone a few seconds to react.

But Shakeya jumped in then, since she was the closest. She pulled out her can of mace and sprayed it directly into Charnetta's eyes. Then she tried turning around to spray whoever decided to assist Charnetta, but it was too late, Duck came running down the steps as soon as his girl got sliced and landed a solid right hook on Shakeya's jaw with a cracking sound. Her limp body fell headfirst into the pavement.

Simone came to help Charnetta when Duck hit Shakeya. She caught Nikki from the blind side with a strong, solid blow. Nikki never saw it coming because the mace had blown into her eyes too. She immediately lost her grip on the box cutter and stumbled up against Charnetta's car.

Simone grabbed her by her neck and slammed her head into the windshield of Charnetta's car over and over again. By the third time the window on the Jaguar gave way to the torment and shattered, sending shards of glass deep into Nikki's face.

Once the window broke, Simone let her go. But Charnetta

wasn't letting Nikki off that easy. Even with her eyes burning and blood rushing down her face, Charnetta managed to find the box cutter on the ground. She grabbed a hold of Nikki's ponytail and quickly wrapped it around her wrist. Just as she was going for Nikki's throat, Duck hollered, "Baby, no!"

Then he grabbed her arm and tried pulling her away from Nikki.

Charnetta looked up at Duck and saw the fear in his eyes. It was enough to bring her back to herself. She shook her head, letting him know she understood. But as soon as Duck released her, she cut a chunk of Nikki's hair out with the words, "Hating bitch!"

"Come on," Duck told her, "we gotta go before the cops come."

Kelly came running down the steps with a dishtowel to stop the blood from pouring down Charnetta's face, and B handed Duck the bag he asked him to get. Duck and Charnetta rushed to his truck, Charnetta tossing her car keys to Simone.

"Get outta here before the cops come," instructed Charnetta.

"Hold my car down until I call you."

Having said all she needed to say, they pulled off. Duck drove to Riddle Memorial rather than to Crozer because they had no intention of going to jail. They would stay at a hotel for a day or two, and when shit died down maybe they'd go back home.

---

Life was beautiful for the young kid from the projects that never had anything. After finding out about Var's death, N.Y. took fifty thousand dollars to Var's mom for the funeral. That same day he decided it was in his best interests to leave. N.Y.

called his family down south and planned a visit. Then he sent his two sisters to rent two cars. When they came back he loaded one of the rentals with his gun and all his money. They packed up a few of their belongings and loaded them into the same car. When they got done they kissed their mother, told her they would call when they got there, and left. N.Y. got straight on the highway behind his sisters and tailgated them all the way to Virginia.

When they got to their aunt's house, N.Y.'s sisters, Karen and Fiána, went sightseeing with the family. N.Y., on the other hand, made it his business to find a house. A week later he bought a five-bedroom beauty in Blacksburg, Virginia for one hundred and fifty thousand dollars. It was ten miles off the campus of Virginia Tech, so that was a plus. N.Y. needed action and excitement and figured living near a college would provide that. But N.Y. was a city nigga. So after a month in Virginia, he was on his way back to Chester, Pennsylvania.

For the eight-hour ride back home N.Y. thought about all the things he did with his money. He dropped another two hundred and fifty thousand dollars decorating his house, then he gave his aunt eighty thousand dollars to get him a car, a fully loaded Benz. He bought his sisters an Escalade for fifty thousand dollars and spent about another fifty thousand dollars on clothes, food, and partying. When he decided to leave, he packed up sixty thousand dollars and left his sisters eleven grand to hold them down while he was gone. He stuffed the rest of the money inside a wall safe that he had built in the bedroom of his new home. Should ever something happen to him, he told his sisters to unlock his room and look inside the dresser drawer for a will, and in the envelope contained the combination to the safe.

When N.Y. finally reached Booth Street he got the response he'd been looking for, ever since he took the money, people went crazy!

What's the point of taking money if you can't enjoy it, he thought as he climbed from the Benz, shaking his friends' hands?

When N.Y. first took the money he was a little nervous, but now, a month later, he was feeling like he couldn't be touched. He was feeling like a boss, and with the type money he had now, it wouldn't be shit to get a squad to rob Blaze again.

The first person he informed of this idea was Ike, a true gangster. When N.Y. ran down the plan, Ike liked it right off, since he knew that the feds found $1 million dollars in Blaze's house. Ike didn't waste time asking the new million-dollar question.

"So, how much money you get the nigga for?"

N.Y. just smiled. Some things you just don't tell because you don't want niggas to think you're stunting. He simply said, "Something nice."

"That ain't answer my question, nigga," Ike asked impatiently. "What you sitting on?"

"About as much as the feds got."

"You ain't shit!" Ike attested, smiling. "You got all that cash and just rolled out. I don't know why you came back. You must've fucked it up."

N.Y. couldn't help but laugh. "You really know me, don't you, Ike?"

"You know I do. Shit, if you still had that cash you'd be somewhere laid back."

Ike knew the car N.Y. was driving ran almost one hundred thousand dollars. He could only imagine what else he bought. That alone was enough to inspire him. Ike's mind wandered towards what he would do with that much money, making him even more eager than N.Y. for the *Let's Rob Blaze, Part II*.

"So," Ike said, "when we gonna do this? I say we may as

well try tonight."

# CHAPTER 13

Officer Minor stopped at the emergency room's desk to find out what room the second victim was located in. A short conversation with the receptionist pointed the police officer in the right direction.

Once he got inside the room the family rushed Officer Minor to tell him about the staples in Nikki's head and the stitches in her face. He sympathized for the woman. The family tried telling him as much as they knew, but Officer Minor wanted to talk to the victim himself.

"Is she able to talk?" he inquired.

"Yes, she can talk," Nikki's mother responded, "she's just talking very slow."

Officer Minor walked over to Nikki's bedside and believed her to be in the worst condition, compared to the other girl.

"Are you okay, miss?" he asked Nikki.

She nodded her head in the affirmative.

"So what happened?"

Being that she was in surgery on her first day admitted, this was the first time an officer was able to talk to her. Nikki slowly began to fabricate her side of the story. She conjured up the gruesome details of how Charnetta and Simone jumped her for nothing. She told Officer Minor that Shakeya tried to break it up, and even went as far as spraying her mace and how Duck broke her jaw for that. Nikki then claimed that Charnetta and Duck sold kilos of cocaine from their back door. According to her they were the biggest drug dealers on the east side and were planning to murder Blaze because he worked for Duck. Duck was mad that Blaze had been popped with his $1 million dollars. She blamed the attempt on Blaze's life and all the problems that Twenty-fourth Street had on Duck.

By the time she got done telling her story she was sure Duck was going to jail. Him and his nasty-ass bitch.

Officer Minor had Nikki sign a few statements and asked if she'd be willing to testify in court.

"I'd be more than willing to cooperate with you, Mr. Minor, because I believe people like that don't deserve to be on the street."

Officer Minor thanked her for all her help, wished her well, and said he would be in touch.

---

It was his third preliminary hearing court date, and according to his attorney, if the witnesses failed to show again, Wally would be released. That alone made him pray like hell while he was sitting in the holding cell. They finally called him to court after an hour passed. The sheriffs came to get Wally and escorted him to the courtroom.

When Wally walked inside the courtroom he was happy to see his girl and surprised to see the two people with her. N.Y. and Ike gave Wally the thumbs up, letting him know they had his back.

"I'll be out in an hour!" he proclaimed.

Wally sat down with his attorney, conversing, expecting the case to be thrown out momentarily.

After a few minutes the bailiff walked in and announced

the judge: "All rise.... The Honorable Judge Keaton presiding."

Once Judge Keaton took his seat the prosecutor asked the judge if counsel could approach. Keaton gave permission. Moments later, the two attorneys were in a heated debate. Then the judge decided, and both lawyers sat back down.

"What's the problem?" Wally asked Dickens.

"The prosecutor said that they have a missing witness in court today, some girl named Michelle Gay. I tried to argue that she was never on the witness list, but the judge doesn't care. But don't worry, I'mma chew her up."

A half an hour later, Wally was returned to his holding cell to await trial. His lawyer did grind the witness up, but she did her job, she foiled Wally's plans of going home. The only good part was that N.Y. and Ike said they would handle it. Later, they were both with Wally's girl when he called and she passed them the phone. Ike knew Michelle Gay well, so he would snatch the bitch up. N.Y. promised to give her ten stacks, but the only thing they were really worried about was Blaze.

"Yo, we got you, don't worry," N.Y. assured Wally.

"But, listen, you got another address on that nigga Blaze?"

"Naw, I don't know his other address. But I know he be out Lancaster and Scranton. When Doc come holler at me I can probably maybe get some more addresses. Just make sure that bitch don't come to court on me, man, *for real.*"

"We got you!"

A couple of hours later, the duo were parked in front of Michelle's house. Ike knocked on the door, and when she answered it was clear sailing.

The car parked in front of D&G's Chinese store went unnoticed for over an hour. Inside the car, Rashawn sat patiently waiting for the third day straight, hoping that the person he was looking for might show up. Rashawn eventually got lucky. He hollered at his old head to ask him what to do.

"Yo, Maine, I think I just seen the Philly bull run up in that crib."

"Yeah?" Maine happily replied.

"Yeah. Dude just hopped out of a squatter with a duffel bag and ran up in the crib."

"Okay, he probably making drops for Blaze then."

Rashawn agreed, "I was thinking the same thing."

"All right," Maine said. "Don't let him outta ya eyesight. I'm on my way, I'm around the corner."

Maine took about ten minutes to get around the corner. He pulled up in D&G's parking lot from nowhere and hopped in the car with Rashawn.

"He come out?" Maine breathlessly inquired.

"Naw, not yet."

"Good, cause I got a carload on the way. We gonna grab this nigga and take him somewhere and do the thing to him."

A blink of an eye later his plans were completely ruined. The police rushed the block from everywhere. It was like SWAT, the way they ran up to the door and crashed through it with a battering ram.

"Oh shit!" Maine exclaimed. "Yo, you got ya gun on you?"

Rashawn nodded. "Yeah."

"All right, hop in my car and take it around the corner for me."

Rashawn hopped out quickly and climbed into Maine's car. He pushed the Mac-11 off the front seat, started the car, and pulled off. Since the cops were preoccupied they never noticed him. They were busy chasing Hollywood.

Hollywood ran out the back door as the police rushed the crib. From living in the neighborhood he knew what cuts to take to slip away. He ran between two houses, came out in an alley on Meade Street, and ran through the alley to a pathway, which led to St. James. By the time he made it there the police were all over the walkie-talkies.

Hollywood still got away. He ran in the back of one building and out the front across the street to another one. When he got to building C, the cops were just rushing into building A. He was happy he was knocking so many chicks off because he just ran upstairs and knocked on Micah's door. Fortunately she was there. She was always there.

———————

Detective Nutsack orchestrated the perfect sting. He was staking out the Twenty-four hundred Madison Street for two days. Now he possessed enough evidence to put a lot of people away for a long time. Even though one of the guys got away, it wouldn't be long before the ones that he arrested broke. The police arrested seven suspects; Biggy, B, Simone, Kelly, Kiana, and two of B's young bulls. Three kilos of cocaine, a quarter pound of weed, four bulletproof vests, and five guns ranging from .40 Ali to Mac-11s were confiscated.

Since nobody wanted to claim the drugs, all the suspects were held without bail. The women were the first to talk, and they all had different stories. The house was everybody's' from Duck's to Blaze's to Doc's. However, the lease belonged to Juanita Davis, but her name was the only one the police hadn't heard. So after a quick huddle to get their game plan together, the detectives went back to interrogate the suspects again. They wanted to know who Juanita Davis was and what kind of role she played.

---

Not only was being sick kicking Juanita's ass, but she was starting to feel alone. She decided to take a warm bath to relax herself, but that didn't work. On top of that, Doc had been gone all day. That had her worried. She tried calling his cell, but Doc never answered.

*He always answered my fucking calls before I got pregnant!* She angrily thought. After trying again for the tenth time, she decided to give up. Juanita was almost seven months pregnant and too big and too sick, as far as she was concerned. When she got out the tub and looked at herself in the mirror, she felt she wasn't as sexy as she used to be.

*That mothafucka probably fucking some old skinny whore. I'm too fat for him now.* She dried herself off, lotioned up, and put on a black Prada sweatsuit. She didn't feel like doing her hair, so she pulled it back into a ponytail. After putting on her sneakers she was about to call her girlfriend from her Lemaze class when the phone rang. Automatically assuming it was Doc, she snapped.

"Where the hell you at?" she barked.

"Who me?" Charnetta replied, mystified.

"I'm sorry," Juanita apologized with an uncomfortable giggle. "Who this?"

"It's Charnetta, boo. How you doing?"

"What up Charnetta, I'm all right. What's up with you?"

"Girl, shit crazy. You know I had to fuck hating-ass Nikki and Shakeya up."

"Get outta here!"

"Yeah, the bitch Nikki sliced my face with a box cutter,

mad 'cause Duck brought me a brand new Jaguar. So you know me, I commenced to whooping her ass. Then Shakeya maced me, so Duck broke that bitch jaw. Finally, Simone bashed Nikki's face through my car window."

"Goddamn, girl!" Juanita voiced with awe.

"Yeah, but you know them bitches told the police on me. They ran up in ya crib yesterday and locked everybody in the house up."

"No they didn't," Juanita said, stunned.

"Yeah," Charnetta went on, "The bitch Nikki got staples in her head and stitches in her face. Simone called me and said they got her on an attempted homicide.

"Oh shit, so what you gonna do?"

"Shit, I'm going down south. Me and Ducky leaving tomorrow. I just called to say bye, and tell you we wasn't gonna be in the house no more in case you wanted to change the locks."

"How about that?" Juanita replied. "You think I should go do that?"

"Yeah," Charnetta advised. "You don't want them bitches or some niggas from out on that corner in ya house."

"Yeah, you right," Juanita agreed. "I'mma go do that right now."

"Well, look, write down my number and call me if you see my car parked out front."

"I got you. You said it's a Jaguar, right?"

"Uh-huh. A red XJ."

"All right, I'll call you when I get back."

After their conversation, Juanita hung up and called Doc again to tell him that she was going to Chester to put padlocks on her house. She grabbed the keys to Doc's BMW 745 and drove to a hardware store first. From there she went straight to Chester.

When she pulled up on the block she saw Charnetta's

Jaguar parked on the corner and called her from the cell to tell her she was there. Then Juanita got out and walked a couple houses down to her neighbor Mike's.

When Mike answered the door he was taken aback to see Juanita. They talked for a bit, before Mike agreed to help her padlock the door. They walked down to Juanita's house, and as Mike went to work Juanita went inside to check out the house's condition.

Juanita was upstairs, furious at how poorly her house had been taken care of, when Mike called out to her. She walked back downstairs to find Mike standing with two police officers.

"Hello, are you Juanita Davis?" Officer Minor inquired.

"Yeah. Why, what's up?"

"We need you to come with us for a minute," Edmunds said.

"For what?" Juanita indignantly asked.

"It's in reference to your house, Ma'am."

"All right. Well, ask me now, 'cause I got shit to do."

"Listen, miss. You can come willingly or unwillingly, but, point-blank, you're coming," Officer Minor informed her.

Right then and there Juanita knew she was in trouble, and her only request was to get her cell phone. She had to get in touch with Doc and probably a lawyer. Now she was wishing she never got that phone call from Charnetta.

━━━━━━━━━━━━━━━

The conclusion was a no-brainer, they both knew they had to leave, they just didn't know where they wanted to go. Duck wanted to go back to Vegas, but Charnetta disagreed. She knew their money wouldn't last a year in Vegas, and she wanted a more stable life. So she suggested Atlanta, or Virginia, near Virginia Beach. Neither one of them enthused Duck at all, so she came up with another one.

"What about Miami, next to South Beach somewhere?"

It was a winner, something they could both agree on.

"So we might as well roll out tomorrow then, huh?" Duck asked.

"What about my car?"

"What about it?"

Charnetta whined, "Ain't you gonna go get it for me?"

"Man, I think we should leave that jawn there. The cops all over the crib. Matter a fact, call Juanita and ask her to bring it to you."

As Charnetta grabbed her cell phone to call Juanita. Juanita picked it up on the first ring, hoping it was Doc.

"Hey, you still at the house?" Charnetta asked.

"Naw, I ain't at the fucking house. I'm locked up!" Juanita snapped.

"You kidding me?" Charnetta queried.

"For real! Why you ain't tell me B and Biggy got caught with all them drugs? You know the police think it's yours and Duck's. They only locked me up because they want me to testify against y'all when they lock y'all up."

"Damn," Charnetta exclaimed, "You agreed to sell us out like that?"

"If I was going to sell y'all mothafuckas out, the police would've already been there locking y'all up."

"All right, I'm sorry girl," Charnetta apologized. "What you need us to do?"

"I need twenty thousand dollars to get out on bail. Get in touch with Doc, or come get me the fuck out. The money ain't shit!"

Charnetta insisted, "I'll call Doc right now. And if he don't call back, we'll send somebody."

"Well, hurry up, 'cause you can't pay bail after six o'clock and I ain't tryna go to no damn county," Juanita said, furiously.

"We'll take care of it. We on our way."

Charnetta and Duck got up and got dressed right away. Duck called Doc's cell and got in touch with him on the first ring. Doc was out Oxford, hustling, and he told Duck there was no way he could get back by six since it was already three. So Duck volunteered to take care of it himself, knowing good and well that it was his fault that Juanita was jammed up in the first place.

Duck didn't waste time explaining the whole story, he just hung up and made some more calls. He knew he couldn't go and pay the bail himself, so he called the only person he felt he could trust.

"Yo, where you at?" Duck asked.

"I'm on the block," Rick replied on the other end. "Why, who this?"

"It's Duck. I need you to make a move for me."

"Duck, what's going on, pimp? Where you at?"

"I'm about to meet you somewhere if you give me a minute."

"My fault," Rick apologized. "What's up?"

"Yo, you got ya car?"

"Yeah."

"All right." Then it hit Duck—that feeling you get when you know you're in the middle of a bad decision. "Yo, who you with?"

"Nobody," Rick said.

"Well, who there?"

"The regular chicken head bitches that always out here."

"All right, look, meet me at the McDonald's out Eddystone by yaself. Can you do that now?"

Rick said, "Yeah, I can handle that. I'm on my way."

"Okay. Hurry up and I got something nice for you."

As soon as the phone call was terminated, Rick called his connect.

"Yo, Blaze, you still got ten stacks if somebody tell you where Duck at? Yeah? All right, well, he want me to meet him right now... Uh-huh, yeah, I'll take a half a brick... All right, so you want me to pick Hollywood up right now? Is he gonna have the half a brick on him? All right, say no more."

Rick hung up and headed straight to pick Hollywood up. Hollywood came out with the half a brick in a bag and two guns on his waist and asked, "So, what you going to meet this dude for?"

"I don't know yet," Rick replied. "He just said he need a favor."

Hollywood immediately starting thinking. First and foremost, he didn't want to kill Duck at the McDonald's. Secondly, he didn't want to kill him in front of Rick, because he didn't like leaving witnesses. Thirdly, Blaze said the chump had a couple of dollars, all of which Hollywood could keep after the job was done. Then he realized, "Yo, when you get over Sun Village, I want you to let me get inside ya trunk until you find out what he doing."

"That'll work," Rick said agreeably, "cause he told me to come by myself."

"But listen," Hollywood added, "don't let dude pull off without finding out where he going, all right? If he do, you gotta give the coke back."

The look on Rick's face said it all. There was no way he was going to part with the coke; that was out of the question. So he assured Hollywood that he would find out exactly where Duck was going.

When they got two blocks away from the McDonald's, Hollywood let down the seat release and climbed into the

**160**

trunk, then he pulled the seatback toward him so that it looked as if the seats didn't even fold down.

Moments later, Rick pulled into the McDonald's lot and hopped out and approached Duck's truck. Rick knew that he would possibly never see Duck again after that day, but he didn't care. Ever since Duck had started staying at Juanita's house and started getting major coke he fronted on Rick. Not to mention he had snuck Rick when he was all drunk down Jack's one night-bustin his lip; something Rick never forgot. It was all catching up with Duck.

"What up, Duck?" Rick greeted casually.

"What took you so long?" Duck asked, all irritated.

*I was signing ya death warrant, ya fat mothafucka!* Rick thought to himself, but said, "I had to go get some gas. Plus I had to wait for a sale to get gas money."

"All right, fuck it," Duck said impatiently, "listen. Doc's girl is locked up. I called a bail bondsman and he's going to meet you there. Give him this five thousand so he can pay her bail. Then, when you get done doing that, grab my Jag that's parked in front of her house and get her to drive it back here for me. You follow her out here, I'll give you five stacks and then you can take her home or wherever she going."

"Goddamn, that's a whole lot, man," Rick complained.

"You going to be here the whole time?"

"Naw, I'mma go to Cancun. Just hurry up before I change my mind and let somebody else make an easy five stacks."

"You right, just make sure you don't go nowhere with my five stacks."

"You think I'mma go somewhere when you got the keys to my car? Come on, use ya head sometimes."

Duck passed Rick the bail money and the keys to the Jag and watched him leave as fast as he came. He wished he could've called somebody else to go take care of business, but he didn't trust too many people with that much responsibility. Duck didn't actually trust Rick, he just believed Rick was too much of a bitch to cross him. Not to mention he'd have Doc to deal with if he disappeared with Juanita's bail money.

*Maybe I shoulda told him it was Doc's money,* Duck thought after Rick drove off, then realized: *What the fuck's wrong with me? He ain't the fuck crazy!*

Duck cut the engine of his truck off and walked inside the McDonald's. He decided to get a Chicken McNugget 20-piece, a large French fry, a large Coke, and a Double Quarter Pounder. That should hold him until Rick got back. But if he needed to waste some more time, when he was done with his meal, he'd just order a sundae or two.

When he got inside, Charnetta had already ordered herself a salad and soda, acting impatiently. "Is he taking care of it?"

"Yeah, he wasn't going to pass that deal up."

After sitting down for fifteen to twenty minutes casually conversing and eating, Charnetta had grown impatient.

"Honey, they taking too long. Since we leaving as soon as they come back, I wanna run to my mom's house, if you don't mind."

Duck looked at his girl with a sly smirk. "You the one that was worried about the car, wasn't you?" he said.

"I know, baby. But it'll only take me a second to run and say good-bye to my mom. And plus I wanna get my aunt's address down Miami."

Charnetta was using that whining baby voice that always seemed to melt Duck like butter.

"All right," he agreed. "Just don't get pulled over with all that money in the trunk."

"I won't," she cheerfully promised.

"I'mma go on back to the room, so you can meet me there."

Duck kissed her passionately before she left. And as she

walked out the door, he wondered why he didn't follow his first instinct and leave when they found out Juanita was locked up. Maybe if he'd been more persistent about it Charnetta would've agreed. But at least he convinced her that waiting until the following day was a bad idea.

He knew that Doc would be extremely upset when he found out why Juanita was locked up, and he'd rather avoid that confrontation all together if possible.

After Rick explained what Duck wanted him to do, Hollywood insisted that Rick park around St. James and walk around to grab the car before he picked Juanita up. How else would he get inside the trunk without anyone seeing him? Rick followed the instructions to a T, but when he was getting inside Duck's car, Shakeya and Nikki tried to stop him from pulling off.

"Hold up, Rick," Nikki called. "Where you going with this car, and how you get the keys?"

His response was brief and to the point.

"Man, mind ya mothafucking business and get the fuck out my way before I run you over."

Since he wasn't thinking past go, Rick only assumed Blaze must have told them to keep tabs on the car. The reward for Duck was common news around the neighborhood, so Rick gathered that the two hood rats were trying to cash in. Rick pulled off swiftly and hurried around to St. James to pick up Hollywood. Hollywood was standing under a tree in front of the apartment complex when Rick pulled up.

Rick met the bail bondsman in the Chester Police parking

lot shortly thereafter. He hopped out the car and gave the five stacks to the bondsman, who told him, "She'll be out in ten minutes."

Rick related this to Hollywood, now concealed in the trunk, when he climbed back in the car. The cocaine Rick was so desperately waiting to get home, was sitting on the back seat. He imagined bagging it up and hitting the block with nicks the size of Halls. He was counting the profit in his head while he waited for Juanita.

Juanita opened the door fifteen minutes later and jumped in. She was highly agitated, so she lashed out at Rick unconsciously.

"Where the fuck Charnetta at?" She abruptly asked him.

Rick snapped out of his daydream instantly, startled.

"I don't know. I guess she still at the McDonald's with Duck. They just paid me to come get you," he replied in a *why-you-mad-at-me voice.*

Juanita looked over at him, realizing he wasn't the person at fault.

"I'm sorry," she said, catching herself. "Could you take me back to my car, please?"

"Where's it at?" Rick asked, not knowing she was talking about Twenty-fourth Street.

"It's in front of my house, across the street from Larry's."

Then it hit Rick he hadn't seen Juanita in so long that he had forgotten she used to live on Twenty-fourth Street.

"Oh, yeah, my fault," he said. "You think you can drive me back to my car after we meet Duck and them, because he scared to drive through Chester?"

"Sure. No problem," Juanita replied.

She reached inside her purse and grabbed her cell phone to check her messages to find that Doc had called five different times. She didn't waste time calling to cuss him out.

"*Now* you wanna be worried," she mused aloud.

Doc picked up the phone, and heard the concern in her voice. "Baby, what happened? Are you okay?" He asked, worry in his own voice.

"Don't act worried now, mothafucka. I've been calling all day. Don't baby me!" Juanita continued.

"I'm for real. I'm in route to your house now. Where you at?"

"I'll see you when I get there, Doc," she said harshly before clicking off. Then she dialed Charnetta's number.

"Hey, baby," Charnetta answered cheerfully on the first ring, hoping it was Duck.

"I'm not ya damn baby," Juanita said with shortness.

"Girl, I thought you was Duck. Where he at?"

"I don't know, wherever the fuck you left him. Y'all sent Rick to get me, remember?"

"Where y'all at?" Charnetta asked now.

"We on our way to get my car!"

"Did Rick pick up my car?"

Juanita was becoming furious at the lack of concern she was getting from her alleged best friend.

"Yeah," Juanita said. "We in your precious car now, and we about to take it to your precious Duck. And since that's all you seem to be concerned about, I'll holla at you!"

"Naw, it ain't like that," was all Charnetta managed to get out before Juanita hung up on her.

"Oooh! That bitch lucky I'm pregnant!" Juanita exclaimed after hanging up. She couldn't believe she got locked up because of their irresponsibility. Now she was starting to see exactly what kind of friends they were.

A few minutes later she and Rick pulled up in front of her house, and Rick volunteered to drive her car so he could hop out of Charnetta's car with his bag of coke. Juanita rolled the window down to speak to Shakeya and Nikki.

"We don't fuck with you, bitch," Shakeya spit, her voice dripping venom. "Get ya snobby ass outta here. You don't belong around here."

It took everything inside of Juanita not to get out of the car. She pulled off with tears in her eyes, her mind full of humiliation for not jumping out and smashing one of them bitches in the face.

"They would have never talked to me like that if I wasn't pregnant. Never!" she fumed aloud.

Not long after, she pulled up in the McDonald's parking lot and hopped out of Charnetta's car. For the first time since the ordeal began somebody seemed genuinely concerned. Duck acted like she'd just come from a funeral, considering all the dramatics he was pulling. He kissed her ass for five minutes before he went on to tell her that he believed Shakeya and Nikki sent the police to her crib. But Juanita was ready to go. Duck swore on his mother that he wasn't keeping coke in her house and promised to reimburse Doc for lawyer fees.

Then, when Duck realized he was wasting time, he pulled out twenty-five hundred dollars for Rick and stepped off as quickly as he gave it to him and hopped in his car.

"Duck, this shit short!" Rick hollered as Duck was on his way out the parking lot.

Rick hadn't actually counted the money that fast, but he didn't believe Duck would pay him the whole five thousand dollars for the little bit of errands he ran.

"You lucky you got that much!" Duck yelled back as he peeled off up the street.

"We'll see who has the last laugh!" Rick shot back in frustration, knowing Duck couldn't hear him.

# CHAPTER 14

After Omar Dickens, Esq. filed a ***Rule 600*** to address the violation of a defendant's right to a speedy trial, a court date was set for Laneer "Wally" Jones. Mr. Dickens dug so much dirt up on the witness that if she decided to take the stand her credibility will be shot. Wally already knew the witness wasn't showing up, but he didn't trust his attorney enough to tell him.

A month later, Wally's trial date came around. As soon as he got inside of the courtroom and saw N.Y. and Ike sitting in the back row he knew everything was going to go right. The prosecutor requested a month delay to locate the witness, but Mr. Dickens immediately objected.

Mr. Dickens wanted the ***voir dire process*** to determine whether a pool of jurors can weigh the evidence fairly and objectively to begin, since the witness wouldn't be taking the stand today. The prosecutor then asked for a five-minute recess, and both the prosecutor and defense attorney went inside the judge's chambers.

The prosecutor couldn't bear losing the case, so he dropped from seven and a half to fifteen to a one to two. Dickens went to consult his client about the deal, but Wally declined.

After another brief conversation, the judge granted the state one more week to locate their witness. The prosecutor ordered a subpoena to secure her testimony and agreed that trial would begin in a week with or without their witness.

After court, the prosecutor talked to the lead detective and another officer he had scheduled to testify and stressed to them, "Without that witness we have nothing. You've got to find her!"

———————————

Duck pulled into the hotel parking lot and was glad he hadn't turned his room key in. He unlocked the door, entered his room, then closed the door back but forgot to re-lock it. He flopped down on the bed and opened up a bottle of Hypnotic he bought earlier from the liquor store. Then he flicked the remote and turned the TV on. He surfed through the channels a bit before he sat the remote down and headed into the bathroom to take a shit.

Hollywood waited for three to four minutes before he slid from out the trunk. He checked his surroundings to make sure nobody noticed him, then he pushed call on his cell phone.

"Hello," Blaze answered.

"Yo, it's me. This chump out the Red Roof Inn."

"You know the room number?"

Hollywood walked up to the door the car was parked in front of. He tried the doorknob. When it opened he smiled.

"It's one twenty-five," Hollywood informed Blaze.

"I'm in route. I'll be there in five minutes. Keep that pussy on ice for me. I wanna see his face before he die."

"Got you."

Hollywood hung the phone up and slowly crept inside the room. He closed the door behind himself, careful not to make a sound. Then he pulled his .45 automatic from his waist. He swiftly scanned the room and noticed the television on. The room wasn't that big, so Hollywood gathered Duck was in the bathroom. Hollywood cautiously approached the half-open bathroom door with his gun tightly gripped in his hand. When he got to the door he could tell by the smell what Duck was doing just before he kicked the door open. Duck was straining like a woman on a delivery table, until he saw Hollywood. The infrared beam of Hollywood's gun was aimed straight at Duck's face, which was filled with sheer terror. His bowels released instantly.

"Surprise!" Hollywood said with a sinister grin.

Tears started rolling down Duck's face. He almost started to plead with Hollywood but knew it was useless.

"So," Hollywood said, "you was planning on leaving, fat boy?"

"Naw, who told you that?" Duck lied, his voice cracking as he trembled with fear.

Hollywood's voice was filled with doom. "Don't worry about who told me. Worry about who sent me."

"Well, who sent you?"

"In due time! You got a gun in here?"

"Naw."

"All right, kick those pants off and slide them to the door."

Duck kicked his pants off and slid them toward Hollywood. He was hoping and praying that maybe it was just a robbery.

"Yo, hand me that Hypnotic too," Hollywood demanded as he checked Duck's pants pockets and found his cell phone, money, and car keys. After he was sure Duck didn't have a gun or anything else of value, he threw Duck his pants back.

"I'm gonna leave now," Hollywood said. "But I want you to stay in this bathroom for fifteen minutes. Now, if you do what I say, maybe I'll be gone. But if you run out of here after I close this door and I'm still here, I'mma kill you. It's ya choice, shitty. Now, you gonna sit ya ass on this toilet like you suppose to, right?"

"Yes," Duck replied, thinking maybe this was his way out.

He was almost getting happy.

"Anymore money in here?" Hollywood questioned.

"Naw, my girl left with it, man, I swear to you."

"All right. Fifteen minutes. I hope you can follow instructions."

Hollywood stepped back and shut the door. He sat on the bed drinking Duck's Hypnotic, laughing to himself, thinking, *this fat mothafucka really thinks I'mma let him live.*

For the next few minutes Hollywood waited patiently for Blaze to show up. Before long, Blaze arrived. Hollywood smiled and put his finger up to his lips, letting Blaze know to be quiet. Then Hollywood re-opened the room's door and slammed it, making sure that Duck heard it.

Duck fell for the bait. He rushed out the bathroom, only to be stopped in his tracks as if he'd seen a ghost. He was hoping Hollywood hopped in his car and drove off so he could call the cops. Instead he felt as lucky as a klutz when he saw Blaze and Hollywood standing together.

"Hey, Hollywood," Blaze said, "I know that ain't the nigga responsible for me losing $2 million dollars and almost getting killed, is it?"

"Yeah, that's that rat-ass nigga right there."

"What is you talking about, Blaze?" Duck pleaded. "Me and you always been cool. How'd I make you lose $2 million dollars? You got the wrong dude."

Blaze said, "You think I got the wrong dude, Hollywood?"

"Naw, I doubt it; he the right dude."

"I swear. Blaze, it wasn't me. Whatever y'all talking about, I couldn't have done it. I was in Vegas."

"Yeah," Blaze said, "they said you'd say that, Duck. But I distinctly remember you, B, Tyran and Biggy calling me to the coke house to tell me y'all was going to get Wally knocked. And I clearly remember telling y'all I ain't approve of that shit, but do what y'all gonna do. Remember that?"

"But, Blaze, I—"

"Shut the fuck up, Duck. I also remember saying that the conversation died right there because something like that could get niggas killed. But all y'all niggas were worried about at the time was getting money. Now that one little conversation done got Tyran killed, and me shot up." Blaze's eyes became an evil squint. "So what the fuck is I'm suppose to do, Duck, huh? What is I'm suppose to do?"

"It wasn't me, Blaze, it was Doc. Wally asked me about it 'cause Doc told him. I swear!" Duck continued lying.

"Only problem with that, Duck, is...Doc didn't know."

Blaze drew his gun from his waist to kill Duck, but then Hollywood stopped him.

"Naw, Blaze," Hollywood protested, "Don't kill this pussy. Maybe it wasn't him. Right, Duck?"

"It wasn't! I swear to y'all on my mother. Please, don't kill me!" Duck was crying crocodile tears by now, and he pissed himself a long time ago. He was praying a million times a minute and was hoping God was listening.

Blaze looked at Hollywood crazy, because for a split second he actually thought Hollywood was buying the bullshit, until Hollywood smiled.

Then Blaze realized Hollywood was just fucking with Duck and decided to play along.

"All right," Blaze agreed, "maybe you right. I'mma go ask Doc and see what he say."

"All right, come on, we out," Hollywood said.

He and Blaze walked toward the door, and as soon as they got to the door Hollywood spun back around, saying, "I almost forgot—I told you if you came out that bathroom before fifteen minutes was up, I was going to kill you, didn't I?"

It was all over for Duck and he knew it. As Hollywood reached for his gun Duck tried to rush him. Duck screamed like a raging madman as he ran toward Hollywood, hoping to scare and overpower him in that brief second. He didn't have a chance. The shots went off in unison as Blaze pulled his gun at the same time as Hollywood and started firing. Hollywood was a lot closer than Blaze, so the blood from Duck's face splattered all on his clothes.

As Duck's body fell limp to the ground, Blaze walked up on him and put four shots in his face to make sure it was a closed-casket funeral.

Then Blaze turned to look at Hollywood as he headed for the door, saying, "For a minute I ain't know what the fuck you was doing."

"Yeah, I know. I was just bidding off the chump," Hollywood said with a smile.

Blaze said, "Boy, you lucky I was there to get him off ya ass."

"Imagine that! I ruined my Rocawear hoody with that pussy brains," Hollywood complained.

The two of them joked with each other all the way to Blaze's rental car. As they jumped in and pulled off, Blaze's cell rang. He leisurely conversed with his girl as he pulled onto Industrial Highway and headed for Chester.

As they drove away from the hotel, Charnetta headed toward it. She passed them in traffic and never noticed them. She pulled up and parked next to her car two to three minutes after they left.

"Yes!" she proclaimed to herself, happy to see her car parked out front.

When she hopped out the truck she was expecting to run in the room and have wild sex with Duck before they left. When she opened the door, the sight horrified her.

"Oh my God!" Charnetta screamed.

Charnetta froze up, she didn't know what to do. She thought about calling the cops but knew they would more than likely lock her up.

*And what if they take my money?* She thought.

She was stuck in a daze until a guy walked up and asked her if she was all right, and then simultaneously noticed what she was staring at.

"Oh my God!" he yelled.

Charnetta instantly snapped out of it. She turned and looked at the middle-aged white man. They stared at each other briefly before Charnetta's survival instinct kicked in. She brushed past the man and ran to her truck at top speed. She jumped in it and peeled off so fast that the tires screeched and left smoke. She headed straight to I-95. All she could think about as she sped down the highway was how she had left Duck and more importantly, her Jaguar.

---

Doc was feeling terrible. He sped down the highway hoping to get home before his girl did. He couldn't believe the police locked Juanita up. He faulted himself more than anything, because if he hadn't avoided her phone calls, he would've known what was going on.

Doc had stayed out for the past three days. The first day he wasn't actually lying when he said he was at Wally's trial all day, because he really was. The next two days were an altogether different story. He spent most of that time with his side jawn, Yazmeen.

Yazmeen was a Muslim chick he met while he was in a halfway house. She was beautiful. Light-brown skin, pretty hazel eyes, and jet-black shoulder-length hair. She could pass for a video girl all day. Yazmeen was Doc's heart, and he'd been messing with her on and off for the last two years. It wasn't that Juanita didn't please him, because she pleased him in every sense of the word. It was the constant nagging that he had to deal with every time he came home. That shit really worked his nerves. He knew it was because of the pregnancy, but some days it pushed him straight into Yazmeen's arms.

Besides, Juanita hated going out now. She was always tired. And whenever Doc stayed home, she acted like he was Benson or Mr. Belvedere. That wasn't the worst part though, the worst part was the days she didn't want to be touched. When their relationship started they'd have sex two or three times a day. On a good day, maybe five. Now Doc was lucky to get some every other day. He couldn't help but cheat; he'd never met a nigga in his whole life who never cheated. Not out of the niggas he knew. For the first time in months he was actually worried sick over her. Juanita's close call brought Doc back to his senses. Juanita was his heart. He couldn't fathom life without her, and as he rushed home he planned on making it up to her.

As soon as Doc got in the house he put the dozen roses he brought her in the vase on the coffee table. Then he pulled out those vanilla candles she liked so much and placed them around the house in candleholders before lighting them. When he was done doing that he turned the CD player on and played a little Keith Sweat; she wasn't nothing like some crying-ass Keith. He walked into the kitchen and opened up the bag of steamed shrimp he bought. Juanita loved steamed shrimp, and while she was pregnant she usually wanted a bowl of Fruit Loops and some cookies-n-cream ice cream on the side. Doc was finished trying to figure out what made her want all the crazy shit she wanted. He just bought it and fixed it.

After the shrimp was heated up, he put them in a bowl, melted a stick of butter, and mixed in a little bit of bleu cheese salad dressing. After the sauce was the way she liked it, he poured a little hot sauce in it and sat it next to the shrimp. He made sure to sit the fresh box of Fruit Loops on the table next to the shrimp and then sat the ice cream out with a spoon on top of it.

When he was finished preparing her food he walked into the bathroom and changed into some pajamas. Doc knew to take a shower at his other apartment. He wouldn't dare make a mistake and come home smelling like perfume or some shit; Juanita would kill him - literally.

Shortly after he sat down and started playing some NBA Live on his PlayStation 2, Juanita walked in. She was still somewhat upset, but when she saw the flowers and smelled the candles she was just glad to be home. She momentarily smiled when she noticed Doc staring at her with the hurt puppy look. *This mothafucka think he slick*, she thought.

Doc immediately started ass kissing. He didn't waste time making stupid excuses. He was wrong, so he told her exactly what she wanted to hear the truth. Not the whole truth—he wasn't crazy. Just a tiny bit of the truth. Enough for him to be able to swear on his moms if he had to.

Baby, I'm sorry," he began. "I know you mad at me, and you have every right to be, because this is all my fault. I feel like a fool, the whole time you was calling, I thought you ain't wanna do nothing but argue or complain about ya back hurting or send me to the market. Baby, I can't lie to you, that's why I wouldn't answer my phone. And you know how I hate when you be nagging me. So I turned my phone off. I'm sorry, boo. Can you please forgive me?"

Juanita was caught off guard because she expected Doc to make excuses about having so many responsibilities, or need-ing money to pay all of their bills. She thought maybe he'd try the Wally story, about being in trial all day and going straight out Oxford and going to sleep. The fact that he accepted responsibility for his actions shocked the shit out of her.

Doc, seeing he had her on the ropes, got up and grabbed her hand and led her into the kitchen. The sight of all her favorite foods was just too much, and she chuckled as she said, "You think you getting off the hook that easy, you crazy."

"I'm not tryna get off the hook, baby. I'm dead wrong. I was trying not to get killed."

Juanita laughed, but as he reached to hug her, tears welled up in her eyes.

"Baby, I was scared!" she confessed. "They tried to make me tell on you, Blaze, Wally...everybody! They asked me all types of crazy questions. I just kept telling them I ain't know. They called me a liar and screamed at me... Boo, I don't wanna never go through that again."

"You did right," Doc said compassionately. "Don't ever worry about what they say to you, they just say that stuff to scare you. They probably told you our baby gonna be born in jail and everything, didn't they?"

Juanita looked at Doc with surprise.

"I know," he said, voice full of experience. "That's the tricks they use to scare you. You shoulda known I was gonna pay ya bail. You think I'mma leave my snuggy bear in jail?"

Juanita couldn't help but smile and blush.

"Baby," he went on, "I don't care if ya bail $1 million dollars, I'm coming to get you. Always remember that."

After their brief moment, Juanita told Doc about Rick picking her up, her conversation with Charnetta, how Shakeya and Nikki tried to stunt on her. She almost left out the most crucial detail but brought it to his attention as she sat down to eat.

"Oh, you know I had to give the bail bondsman our address."

"You gave him *this* address?" Doc asked hoping otherwise.

"Yeah, what address was I supposed to give him?"

"The address around Twenty-fourth Street," Doc said, stating the obvious.

"I told the police I didn't live there no more."

Sadly, Doc said, "So you gave them our address too."

Juanita immediately got mad.

"I had to get out of jail."

"Nooo," he groaned, "you don't tell them nothing, baby!"

"How was I suppose to know?" she said with tears filling her eyes again. She couldn't help but defend her actions by using his words against him. "It's your fault," Juanita accused. "If you would've called my nagging ass back I would've never gone to Chester. Ever since I got pregnant you've been acting funny. You think I like dealing with ya bullshit? I'm carrying ya baby and I got to put up with ya ass running the streets and ya lame-ass excuses all the time. But do I get tired of it! Nooo! I just deal with it."

Her tears were streaming down her face now. Doc wasn't the stupidest nigga in the world, so to cut the argument short he pulled her close and kissed the tears from her face. He went from her face to passionately kissing her lips, and as he kissed her, Juanita's body melted in his arms. He refused to waste time and kill the mood, so he tenderly lifted his girl's dress up and sucked on her neck and breasts. Moments later he had Juanita sitting on the kitchen counter top while he ate her pussy. After she had an orgasm Doc didn't waste a single second before he laid down on the kitchen floor. Juanita, of course, climbed on top of him and started riding him until he ejaculated deep inside of her. When they were done, Doc sat at the table and fed his wifey her shrimps, ice cream, and cereal.

After eating they cuddled up on the couch in the living room and watched a movie.

A week seemed like a month for Wally while he waited on his next court date. The trial began October 24th and lasted three days. The prosecutor's case was so weak that the judge didn't even understand why it was being tried; the witnesses were a bunch of cops who kept trying to interject hearsay testimony into evidence. Omar Dickens continuously objected. By the time the District Attorney was done presenting the state's case, Mr. Dickens had half of the testimony struck from the record.

When the defense finally got a chance to present its case, the prosecutor was already trying to cut deals as low as time served. The prosecution's whole case centered on Laneer Jones driving an X-5 with Ben Franklins painted on it. The fact that the truck didn't even belong to him was never brought up until Mr. Dickens called Tamia Adams to the stand.

Her story was the most crucial to the case, because she was the owner of the truck. Tamia told the same story she told when the truck was impounded. She insisted that her boyfriend, Ali Thomas, was driving the truck and was killed the night in question in retaliation.

After Tamia's testimony, Mr. Dickens called Ali's baby mother, Shana Joyner. She testified that she was aware of Ali and Tamia's relationship. She then told about how she had caught Ali driving the truck once. She even claimed she broke the windows out of the truck. That was the most vital part of her testimony because, according to the District Attorney, Wally purchased the truck the day of the shooting. But since the dealer was paid off, no paperwork could be produced to support the allegations. Mr. Dickens, on the other hand, produced a receipt for the damages and introduced it into evidence.

**178**

Then, for his last witnesses, Wally's lawyer called three girls who were at the scene of the crime: Stephanie, Jennile, and Meeka.

On Wally's last court date they were scheduled to show up but couldn't be located. Doc had found them, however, and gave them a grand apiece. Now their testimony was solid: It wasn't Wally; it was Ali

After closing arguments, both sides rested their cases and the jury was sent out to deliberate. Two hours later, they came back with a unanimous decision not guilty.

Laneer "Wally" Johnson was acquitted of all charges. After court, N.Y. showed up at the county jail to pick Wally up. When he got in the car, N.Y. handed him a bottle of Dom Perignon and a blunt of Hydro. For the whole forty-five minute ride they plotted on some serious shit. Doc had already informed Wally that Blaze planned on killing him, so Wally was on his toes.

After N.Y. dropped Wally off at his house he went straight to snatch Ike up. Wally had provided N.Y. with Blaze's Lancaster and Scranton addresses. The plan was for N.Y. and Ike to check the houses out while Wally got in touch with Doc to find out exactly where Blaze was.

It was a long day for Juanita Davis after being arrested on a drug charge. That night the police rushed her house with an arrest warrant for murder and conspiracy to commit murder. The news almost made her have a miscarriage. The police raided her house at eleven that night with guns drawn. They were also hoping to find a ton of drugs.

It wasn't until after she was in custody that the Essington

Police got a call from the Chester Police Department about a murder.

When the Essington Police had shown up at the Red Roof Inn, they found Sammy "Duck" Green DOA. The one witness at the scene identified a woman as his killer. The witness claimed he walked up and startled her after the crime. He didn't get the license number on the truck because he was startled himself when the woman ran out the room with a smoking gun.

Officer Minor and Detective Nutsack went to view the videotape and stumbled across the red Jaguar that was parked out in front of Juanita Davis' house. Then it came to them. Officer Minor sent the Essington Police to take fingerprints off the car. It was funny to him how Duck, the guy who was hustling out of Juanita's house, got killed the same day they locked Juanita up. Somebody was trying to protect her, and Duck knew something, so he thought.

An hour later the police had prints lifted from the car and Nutsack took them straight to headquarters to get a match. The match came back 100% positive – they belonged to Juanita Davis. The only problem after reviewing the videotape that they could see was a platinum Denali. Officer Minor decided to go work a couple of his snitches. And after a little talk with Nikki and Shakeya he had the missing pieces of the puzzle.

A guy named Rick picked Juanita up by himself, they found out from a bail bondsman. Then the two of them drove to Twenty-fourth Street to pick up her car. After that they drove off, following each other. Minor and Nutsack watched the tape again after talking to Nikki and Shakeya and Louie, the bail bondsman, to find Juanita's car. But no BMW 745 ever entered the parking lot. The Jaguar pulled into the parking lot by itself. There were two cars with tints that pulled into the parking lot. Since they didn't have a camera right over Duck's door, the surveillance tapes they were watching were from the front of the hotel.

By ten o'clock, Nutsack and Minor had talked the Essington cops into believing that Juanita had Duck killed. By the time they got done telling their story, she was a cold-blooded killer and drug lord that just got a whole block locked up for a drug ring she operated from her house. Essington went for it hook, line, and sinker. And why wouldn't they? It wasn't Minor or Nutsack's investigation; they didn't care if Juanita committed the crime or not. The two of them were playing a friendly game of shake the tree and see what falls. A snitch was born every day with that trick.

When they banged on the door, Doc answered it with a baseball bat. By the time they came in and slapped the cuffs on his girl, they had him on terrorist threats and assault on a police officer.

The old man of the house took a swing at Officer Nutsack. Split his mouth pretty good too. Of course the police beat him up and gave him a fifty thousand dollars cash bail, which he paid the next morning. But his girl wasn't that lucky. She was held without bail until a preliminary hearing could be held.

Doc snapped again and almost got himself locked up two minutes after Omar Dickens paid his bail. Omar Dickens sent Doc out to his car while he went to talk to Juanita. He promised she'd be out in a week or two. He asked her a few questions and took a message to give to Doc.

"Tell him I said, "Get his snuggy bear out of jail ... *now.*""

And once again, tears came streaming down her face.

# CHAPTER 15

Rick took the twenty-five hundred dollars Duck gave him and bought a pound and a half of Hydro. Then he bagged up four and a half ounces of coke and hit the block with dimes the size of Peanut M&Ms. He sat on the block with Shakeya and Nikki and smoked two blunts. Afterwards, they didn't have any problem holding his coke for him while he hustled. It only took an hour for smokers to find out he was giving away coke. The rumor was Rick had dimes the size of birthday presents. In no time at all he was sold out.

Rick made thirty-six hundred dollars off the four and a half ounces and put three thousand dollars in the house. Everything was going just like he planned. Rick bagged up eight hundred dollars off every ounce. He could have bagged up fifteen to sixteen hundred dollars, easy, but his mission was to establish major clientele. By the time he drove down Jack's bar at one o'clock in the morning, his beeper was on fire. Junkies were walking all the way down to Jack's to cop. Rick had no intentions on going home to get more coke. By now his only plan was to take his two new best friends — Shakeya and Nikki — to the hotel for a threesome. The girls were definitely with it, being super high, and Rick had weed for days. The three of them lost count after their eighth blunt but smoked five more after that.

At two that morning all three of them left the bar together. They were famished. Rick took Industrial Highway straight to Denny's, where they all ordered more food than they could eat. Piles of food were on the table after Rick paid the eighty-dollar bill.

They checked into the Radisson for the night after eating. As soon as they got inside the room the three of them took a shower together. They thought it would be a good idea to bring their highs down. The shower scene was like a porno as both women took turns giving Rick head. It was like they were competing against each other.

When they got done he banged Nikki first, and imagined he was having sex with Nia Long. While he played with Shakeya's pussy he envisioned Nivea. Twenty minutes later he rotated the women and banged Shakeya while he kissed Nikki and fingered her to keep her aroused.

An hour and a half had passed by the time they got out the shower. Their highs were completely gone, so they rolled a couple of blunts that they passed among each other while Rick gave both of them oral sex. When those were gone, Rick rolled the last three blunts in the box. Good and high again, they got in the bed together and went to sleep.

For Rick, this was the best night of his life. He knew it would only get better, and he couldn't wait until tomorrow.

———————————

After slumping Duck, Blaze and Hollywood picked up Janisha and China. Blaze had been messing with Janisha for five years. She was his equivalent of a "girlfriend." She was originally from the Philippines and somewhat resembled the chick in the movie *Tomb Raider*. China was her best friend, who Blaze had hooked Hollywood up with. Hollywood didn't take long to lock her in. And ever since the first night he met her he took her personal. China looked like she was Chinese and black—that's where she got her nickname from, and to say she was gorgeous was an understatement.

Just to be on the safe side, the four of them took a ride over Atlantic City. Blaze and Hollywood rented rooms at the Taj Mahal and spent most of the night gambling. The sixty thousand dollars Blaze had brought with him was halfway gone when he counted his money later that night.

Hollywood, on the other hand, turned his twenty grand into forty-five, minus the five stacks he gave China as soon as he got there. He was usually tight with his money, but since Blaze gave five stacks to Janisha from the drive, he followed suit.

Both China and Janisha did good with their money. They hit the slot machines and the Black Jack table and won a few thousand.

Janisha turned her five thousand dollars into twelve thousand dollars, and China was sitting on almost eight thousand dollars. She gave Hollywood four thousand dollars back on the strength that he claimed he lost big, which he gladly accepted. Hollywood only said he lost because he knew Blaze had lost a little over twenty thousand dollars. Hollywood didn't want Blaze to be all in his pockets if he kept gambling and lost all his money, so it was best if Blaze didn't know how much money Hollywood was holding. That was just the type of dude Hollywood was.

After ordering champagne and room service, which Janisha and China paid for, the small group split up for the night. Hollywood started tearing his clothes off as soon as he got through the door. He couldn't wait to beat China's back out. They hadn't spent much time together in their three months together, because Hollywood was too caught up in the streets. His motto was: M.O.B.—Money Over Bitches. So even though China was wifey material and prettier than a full moon and stars twinkling on a clear night, she wasn't prettier than the duffel bag of money he had under the bed. Halle Berry or Stacy Dash wasn't as pretty as the old-ass presidents on the forty-five stacks, and Hollywood had a crush on both of them.

Hollywood didn't waste any time laying China down and giving her the pipe. He had her climbing the walls like a squirrel up a tree. China made more noise than a hungry infant that was being ignored. It was a wonder somebody didn't walk past her door and think he was abusing her.

After an hour of good fucking, Hollywood laid next to China smoking a cigarette. She was talking to him about getting a house together, but he was barely listening. He was thinking about how much money he could make if he video-taped him and China having sex. Or better yet, how many girls would want to have sex with him after seeing him in action. It would be a great hustle, he imagined. He'd name it some old fly shit like *Rumble in the Jungle* or *Ice Yaself Down* and charge nineteen dollars and ninety-five cents a tape.

He finally snapped back to his senses when China pinched him.

"Are you listening to me?" she asked him.

"Yeah, I'm listening, baby..."

"No, you ain't," China accused. "What I say?"

Hollywood didn't feel like the games, so he knew exactly what to do to shut her up.

"You said you want me to do something nasty."

Hollywood kissed her passionately to stop her from talking, and worked his way down her body. Moments later he was up inside of her, making her scream like a mother at a murder scene. When he was done China went to sleep while he sat up and schemed on how to get more money to go home with.

The next day Blaze woke up early and traded his rental in at the nearest Enterprise, then he did a little shopping. He went to the Gucci shop and bought himself a bucket hat, a nice shirt, and some jeans to match his sneaks. He grabbed Janisha a nice-ass dress and some sandals, spending and easy five thousand dollars.

The four of them spent the day sightseeing and shopping. The least of their worries was the trouble that was brewing at home.

Doc was on a mission. For the entire ride to his house he explained to his lawyer all the things he went through in the last year. He started with the case Wally caught and how that got his brother killed. Then he talked about his life and how the game changed him. He needed somebody to talk to; he was stressing. Doc was ready to give everything up and get married, but now the only person he loved and needed was locked up.

Omar Dickens listened to Doc attentively. He was visualizing Doc's life as a good movie, or maybe a book.

When they got to Doc's house, Doc ran straight upstairs, leaving Omar Dickens in the living room on the couch. The police had pretty much ransacked the place. Doc wasn't concerned with the condition of the house. He pulled the electric fireplace out of the chimney inside his room just far enough to squeeze inside. Then he stood up and reached for the shelf where he had two duffel bags. He pulled a bag out of the chimney and counted out twenty stacks of five thousand dollars. He put the one hundred thousand dollars in another bag and then slid the remainder back where it belonged and slid the fireplace back. Since the top of the chimney was sealed, that was the safest place in the house for his money. He ran downstairs with the bag in his hand a little dirtier than he left.

"What, you was working on a car?" Omar Dickens asked at the sight of Doc.

Doc said, "I got to be one step ahead of the game to make sure my money safe."

"If I had to go through all that, I would just put my money in the bank."

Doc didn't waste time explaining why he didn't fuck with banks. He just rushed Omar Dickens back to his car, which was parked at Chester Police Station.

After a handshake, Doc was out. He drove straight around Twenty-fourth Street. When he pulled up on the corner of Madison, he spotted exactly who he was looking for. Rick was walking out the alley where he had just served a fiend a fifty-dollar piece. Something inside of Doc snapped.

He jumped straight out the car and choked Rick up, saying, "Pussy, you tried to set my girl up!"

"What is you talking about?" Rick barely managed to speak windpipe being squeezed.

"Pussy, you slumped Duck and got my girl locked up for that shit!"

Rick's eyes got as big as oranges. The news shocked the shit out of him.

"Doc, it wasn't me!" Was all he could squeak out before Nikki and Shakeya came to his rescue.

Nikki jumped on Doc's back, screaming, "Let Rick go, pussy!" Shakeya was pulling up the rear, about to bust Doc with a bottle, when he spun around to confront them. The move flung Nikki off of him, and she fell against the wall. Before Shakeya could hit him with the bottle, he punched the shit out of her. She fell to the ground and dropped the bottle.

By now Rick had gotten himself together and started to

run, but was scared that Doc might pull out a gun and shoot him. He also wanted to make sure his name wasn't caught up in the middle of the murder.

"Doc, let me explain. Please," he pleaded.

Doc had rage in his eyes and was two seconds from shooting somebody, but he briefly stopped to listen.

Seeing he had this one chance, Rick jumped right on it.

"Duck called me and told me ya girl was knocked, and that he needed me to pay her bail. Rick explained. So I met him out McDonald's and got the money for the bail and that's when he gave me the keys to his car. When I came to get it, Blaze had his man watching the car, so he made me take him with me in the trunk. I picked Juanita up, dropped the car off, and that's all I know." After waiting a brief moment to see how Doc reacted, Rick asked the most important question of all. "My name ain't caught up in that shit, is it?"

Doc stared at him with a granite expression as Shakeya and Nikki began regrouping. Nikki was getting up off the ground and Shakeya was waiting on Nikki to set it off. Doc collared Rick up and practically dragged him to the car.

"We calling the police!" Nikki yelled as the two of them got in Doc's car.

"Yo," Doc warned Rick, "tell ya little buddies to fall back or they might not never see you again, because I'll turn you in myself"

That was the answer Rick was looking for. He was petrified. He looked at Doc, then back at Shakeya and Nikki.

"Yo, let me holla at them right quick, Doc. That way they'll know it's cool."

Doc released his grip on Rick's jacket and told him to hurry up. Rick rushed over to his new best friends and did some real fast-talking. It took a moment to convince them, but when he was done they realized they had too much to lose if they called the cops and Rick got locked up. They were both planning on playing him out of all his money. They didn't really like Rick, especially after how he fronted when he picked up Duck's car, but they let that slide due to the fact that he smoked about a quarter pound of weed with them.

Now they despised him even more for telling on Blaze. But they knew if things went right they would be able to get all his cash, set him up for telling on Blaze, and get some money and good dick from Blaze and Hollywood. They had it all figured out.

"All right, go head, Rick," Nikki said. "But if he don't bring you back or you don't call us in a couple of hours, we calling the cops."

Rick nodded his approval before walking to Doc's car and hopping in. Doc had just hung up with Omar Dickens and assured him that he was on his way. As Doc pulled off he began telling the lie about how Rick's fingerprints were found all over the car, and how there was a McDonald's surveillance tape of Juanita and Rick pulling off. The police were charging Rick with conspiracy to commit murder. After hearing it like that, Rick ran the story down to Dickens, piece by piece. When he was done giving his taped statement, Omar Dickens assured Doc that Juanita would be out soon, but he also told Doc that the police might try and lock Rick up on a conspiracy charge.

Rick was waiting out in the lobby, wondering what was taking Doc so long as they had their private conversation.

"So, what should I do?" Doc asked his attorney.

"Tell your buddy to lay low for a while. Then, after I get your lady out of this mess, if they try to lock him up, I'll pick his case up for half price."

After Doc and Dickens were done talking, Doc and Rick left. Rick had ninety-nine questions but Doc didn't have the answers for any of them. By the time he got to Twenty-fourth

Street, he knew exactly what to say because Rick had exposed his worst fears.

"Look," Doc said, "I don't know if they going to charge you or not. But I do know that if Blaze think you talking to the cops, you're dead. So your best bet is to lay low."

"Yeah," Rick agreed, "I should just lay low."

He shook Doc's hand before getting out the car, and no soon as Doc pulled off, Rick had Shakeya and Nikki in his car going off in the opposite direction. He didn't plan on letting anybody catch him.

───────────

After going through intake and being processed into the jail, Juanita was sent straight to the infirmary. She was having major labor pains and was scared something might be wrong. She spent twenty-four hours up medical before being sent to D-block. There, she immediately became fearful of the muscular women with bald heads and missing teeth. She thought she was on the men's block for a second.

As Juanita wobbled to her cell, following the Correctional Officer, she noticed several women smiling at her.

When Correctional Officer Lamyra Morris opened the cell door the odor almost made Juanita sick to her stomach. An old lady named Pearl, who was a typical dopefiend and alcoholic, instantly got up off of her bunk and started yelling and complaining about not taking cellies.

───────────

Simone was on another block playing cards. Correctional Officer Nasheema Northern called her out into the hallway to get a mop and bucket. Since Simone was the hallway runner that was naturally part of her job. Most of the Correctional Officers liked Simone alot, so she was always doing something she wasn't suppose to be doing. Simone was presently gambling, and the thought of quitting a game to go and get a mop and bucket made her mad.

"Who need a clean up, Northern?" Simone asked, her tone expressing her irritation. She rolled her brown eyes, popping her contraband chewing gum, looking up at Nothern.

"Uh, Pearl need one to clean her filthy-ass cell."

"Pearl? That dopefiend bitch wasn't cleaning her house on the street. Now she wanna complain about living conditions."

Northern waited until Simone was done throwing her little tantrum, then she explained why Pearl needed a bucket, explaiing, "Pearl's dirty ass don't really wanna clean up. She just got a new cellie and she *got* to clean up."

"Oh God, who they putting in there?"

"I didn't hear her name," said Northern, "But I seen her coming in yesterday. She had on some fly shit. She pregnant though, and I think she from out Chester."

That was all Simone needed to hear. She heard that Juanita had gotten locked up, but Charnetta told her Juanita made bail. Still, the description sure did fit Juanita. So Simone walked straight from A-block to D-block to investigate. As soon as she arrived, she excitedly said, "Juanita...girl! What the hell is you doing in here?"

Juanita turned around toward the voice. Her grim expression slowly changed into a smile as Simone rushed toward her and hugged her tightly.

"What's up, girl?" Simone went on. "I heard you got caught. What happened?"

Juanita couldn't hold the tears back any longer. She started breaking down right there on the tier.

"I don't know what's going on," Juanita complained. "First they locked me up for the drugs they caught y'all with in my house. Then I bailed out and they came back and gave me a murder charge. The police talking about if I don't help them book Doc I'mma do life in jail. Then they talking about taking my baby. I don't know what to do!" she wailed.

"Calm down, not right here, boo," Simone cautioned. "Go down to my cell—I'm in two-twelve."

Simone helped Juanita pick up her stuff and pointed her toward her cell. As soon as Juanita walked down the tier, Simone pulled Northern to the side.

"Yo, that's my girl from my block. Put her in my cell and move Wanda into the open runner cell."

Northern looked at Simone with the wish-I-could face. "If I could, you know I would," Northern said with sincere regret. "But this is Morris' block."

Simone turned to face Lamyra Morris, knowing good and well she was going to have to go through a song and dance. Looking Morris up and down, stopping to take notice of the soft leather Reeboks Morris was wearing. *A Reebok broad* she thought to herself, popping her chewing gum defiantly.

Simone was petite with well-proportioned assets. Her grey Baby-Phat sweatsuit that she wasn't supposed to have in jail, fit her perfectly. It also magnified her nice hips and plump ass. It was rumored that she got it from a male lieutenant that she was close to. Most of the regular guards were already warned by their superiors to overlook it. That way, when Rookie guards like Morris worked the block, they would know automatically that Simone is to be treated special.

"Is you gonna do that for me, Morris?"

Morris replied, "You know I can't do that, Simone. She ain't no block worker."

Simone became mad, but she refused to take no for an answer. The only thing she could think of saying was the shit chicks like Morris respected.

"You gotta call somebody," Simone told her. "That's my best friend. I got locked up in her house with a bunch of niggas that hustle for her boyfriend. Her boyfriend's the richest nigga on our block. You can't put her in Pearl's cell, pregnant, he fuck around and get somebody killed for that shit. Ten to twenty stacks ain't shit to him; that's her sneaker money. We ain't no bag of weed bitches fucking to get hair-dos. We push Lambos with our hair blowing in the wind and shit."

Nasheema Northern just smiled at Simone because she already knew Simone was a fronting bitch. She gave Simone all the help she could, and after that it was all up to Morris.

"I'm saying, I'll call a lieutenant, if Morris worried about getting in trouble—and explain the situation."

Morris went right for the bait, stepping dead in the shit.

"I ain't worried about getting in no trouble," Morris said. "I don't need this job; I got money, girl."

"Well, what's the problem?" Simone asked. "You see she pregnant. Putting her in the cell with Pearl will make her lose her baby."

Morris and Northern couldn't help but laugh, and just like that it was done. Morris walked down to Simone's cell and told her cellie, Wanda, to move into 210. Wanda was a bit upset, but she tried to hide it as she packed all her belongings into laundry bags. A couple of minutes later she was out and Juanita was in.

Simone moved all her stuff from the bottom bunk to the top; there was no way Juanita was going to be able to climb up there. So Simone re-arranged her stuff to make her girl comfortable. While they were getting situated Juanita explained the last twenty-four hours to Simone. By the time she was done telling the story her face was full of tears, and Simone felt like she didn't have any problems at all.

**Whatever Starts on the Streets... Stays on the Streets**

# CHAPTER 16

Mr. Dickens started his investigation at McDonalds. His first move was securing the surveillance tape from the restaurant. Once he got that, he knew the statement Rick gave would be the most crucial part of the case. The tape didn't come easy though. The manager tried telling Mr. Dickens that it was against policy to give tapes away unless they were needed because a crime occurred. For a minute the manager even stuck to his guns, until Mr. Dickens offered him five hundred dollars. That made the tape more readily accessible. Dickens reviewed the tape to make sure it was the one he needed and smiled graciously at the manager when they made their exchange.

After that tape was secured, Mr. Dickens went to obtain surveillance video from the Red Roof Inn. Unfortunately that one had already been confiscated by the Essington Police and they refused to give Dickens a copy of it. So he had to call the judge for an order to get the tape. It took a day, but once the judge granted the order the tape came up missing. At that time Dickens had no idea what Minor and Nutsack were trying to put together. The only problem with that was, they didn't expect the Essington Police to tell Mr. Dickens.

When Dickens couldn't get the tape with a court order, he went back to the judge. His Honor, in turn, sent the District Attorney to go get it. The next day, after talking with the Chief of Police, District Attorney Kovan found out Minor and Nutsack had the tape. He went to the Chester Police station shortly thereafter and had a talk with the two officers.

Their story was compelling, but the District Attorney was already aware of the McDonald's surveillance tape and the recorded confession of Charles "Rick" Wilson. So Kovan knew they didn't have a case against Juanita, but a good case against Rick for conspiracy if Juanita testified on him. That, in turn, would get Rick to roll over. The District Attorney had it all figured out.

It wouldn't go the way the Chester cops wanted it to exactly, but with their help and the tricks up District Attorney Kovan's sleeves, it was an open and shut case. All the officers had to do was issue a warrant for Rick.

After getting the McDonald's tape back, District Attorney Kovan took a copy of it to Dickens and told Dickens that he was willing to withdraw prosecution against Ms. Davis if she agreed to testify that Rick came to pick her up and was aware that Hollywood was in the trunk and would kill Duck.

Dickens, realizing how crucial it was for Juanita to get out, questioned Kovan's motives, asking, "You know and I know that you don't have a case. So why should I get my client to agree to something like that?"

"Because," Kovan explained, "it would get her out of jail today, and she's been in there, pregnant, for three days so far. Besides, it's nothing that the bail bondsman and numerous witnesses on Twenty-fourth Street aren't already going to testify to."

"I understand where you're coming from, but I'm not sure my client will agree to that."

"Well, maybe you should go talk with her and find out then," Kovan suggested.

"Maybe. Or maybe I should just wait until the preliminary and just call her and tell her in four days she'll be out."

"Well, we're going to get Charles Wilson with or without her help. You do know that?"

"Yes, I know," Dickens replied cynically.

As Omar Dickens left, he wondered what Doc would think of the D.A.'s offer. He started to call Doc when he got in the car, but he didn't want to stress Doc out more than he was already—it was an open and shut case at the preliminary. So he just worked on making his case rock solid.

---

As soon as Rick got in Doc's car, Nikki called Blaze. She loved Blaze too much to see him go to jail, and she made sure to tell him so the moment he answered the phone. Then, as soon as she had him wondering what the fuck she was talking about, it would be time to play out the little scenario she worked out with Shakeya. Nikki knew Blaze was a snake, so she was hoping that she thought everything through thoroughly.

"Baby, I don't want nothing bad to happen to you," Nikki said sympathetically.

"Well, what the fuck's going on?" Blaze asked impatiently.

Then, just before she had a chance to give him the news, Shakeya snatched the phone and said, "Yo, you gonna give us some money, ain't you?"

"It ain't about no money!" Nikki hollered in the background.

Blaze said, "Yeah, I got some money for y'all."

Since they had planned for it to go like this, Shakeya immediately recapped how Doc jumped out and choked Rick up, and how Rick started telling. Then she told Blaze that Doc had let Rick go, and he walked back and told them that the police were looking for him. So he had to clear his name.

Since he promised to come back and get them and leave the city, the girls were sure that they could take him someplace and have Blaze and Hollywood meet them.

"Sounds good to me," Blaze informed Shakeya. "Don't worry, I got something nice for y'all."

"Yeah, well, I'm telling my family that you picking us up. So don't get no crazy ideas."

"Yeah, I hope he don't!" Nikki said loudly off line.

"Girl, what would make you think some shit like that?" Blaze said, somewhat mad that they had him figured out.

"Well, what you got special for us?" Shakeya asked. "I hope it's some good dick to go with that money you gonna give us."

"Oh, most definitely. Just give me a ring when you get to where y'all going. Try to take the chump down Baltimore, Maryland, or Jersey."

"We got you," Shakeya assured Blaze. Then she hung up and gave Nikki a high five. "Girl, he with it," Shakeya gleefully informed her girlfriend.

"Shit, they fuck around and eat our pussies," Nikki said hopefully.

"Who you telling? I'mma go get a strawberry douche."

The two of them laughed as they thought of how their night was destined to become better and better. They couldn't have made a better move if they tried. They were about to rob Rick, get him killed, get some money for doing it, and fuck the most desirable niggas on Twenty-fourth Street. Of course they knew it was some grimy shit to do, but their philosophy was simple: Shit happens.

———————

Wally must've beeped Doc twenty times that night he got home, but for some reason Doc never called back. Wally found out the next day that Doc and Juanita were locked up when Doc finally called back. Then Wally heard why, and decided it was time for Blaze to get dealt with.

"Yo, old head, dude just running around killing everybody. Don't you think that eventually he gonna try and kill you?" Wally asked.

Doc's reply was, "So what do you think I should do?"

That was all Wally was waiting for; he already had it mapped out. All he had to do was run the plan across Doc. After he ran it down, Doc was convinced. It sounded like it would work...if it didn't backfire. Doc tried to convince Wally that they should re-think it a little, but Wally had it all worked out and that's the way he wanted it to go. So it was agreed. Within the next couple days Doc would put the plan in motion, but for now he had business to take care of, so he told Wally he'd holler at him later.

Doc hung up and called his lawyer. Juanita had been in jail for three days. If everything went right, Doc was expecting to see her in three or four days.

─────────────

As soon as Blaze and Hollywood dropped Janisha and China off, they headed straight to Maryland. They got another call from their two friends that Rick was heading for Virginia. Since they were high and had a long day, they persuaded Rick to stay at the Hilton in Baltimore. Blaze and Hollywood told Shakeya and Nikki they would call when they arrived. Once they got inside the room, Blaze intended on making the girls commit the murder so they wouldn't run their mouths.

By three o'clock in the morning Blaze and Hollywood

were outside the hotel. Since they knew which room the girls were in, they requested a room on the same floor. After they purchased the room they called Nikki and Shakeya. Nikki, of course, was waiting for the call. So when her cell phone rang, waking her up, she quickly answered it and headed for the bathroom, hoping she didn't wake Rick and Shakeya up.

"Yo, it's me," Blaze said when Nikki groggily answered. "If dude is sleep, walk down here. If he not, tell him ya mom on the phone and she said the police just rushed ya house."

Nikki opened the door to see both Shakeya and Rick looking at her. She knew that everyone was paranoid for their own separate reasons, so she went right into acting mode.

"Shakeya, it's my mom. She said the police just kicked my door down. She asked me if I'm in Virginia, and I told her no." She continued on the phone, "Yeah, Mom, I know. I'm not... I love you too." Then Nikki hung up.

"I'm ready to leave," Shakeya fretfully declared.

"Man, we leaving in the morning," Rick said. "Ain't like we nowhere near Chester."

"Boy, this room in our name," Nikki pointed out. "What if they put out an APB or some shit?"

"All right, it's cool, but I'm going down to the cigarette machine and get a soda and some candy. Y'all want something?" Nikki asked, sliding into her T-shirt and sweatpants, but leaving her bra and panties on the floor.

"Yeah, get me something," Shakeya asked. "Matter a fact, want me to come with you?"

"Naw, I'll be right back."

With that said, Nikki grabbed the room key and a twenty dollar bill and suggested someone roll a blunt as she left the room. She quickly walked out, locking the door behind her, and headed to Blaze's room. There she found him and Hollywood smoking a blunt.

"Hey, baby!" Nikki exclaimed, giving Blaze a hug and

**200**

making sure her perky breasts rubbed up against him through her T-shirt.

"So what's up?" Blaze asked.

"He thinks I'm going to get some cigarettes and sodas. I kinda got him scared, so we gonna be leaving early in the morning."

"Good. Hollywood, go grab them sodas and cigarettes for her right quick."

Since Hollywood knew what Blaze was up to he grabbed the money and rolled. As soon as he walked out the door Blaze pulled Nikki close and kissed her as he rubbed on her ass. Then he pulled away and hesitantly said, "Boo, I need you to do something for me."

"Anything, baby," Nikki said excitedly. At the same time she reached down his pants and rubbed his dick.

"Oh, we going to have plenty of time for that. But first I want you to slip Rick this roofie." Blaze handed Nikki two date-rape pills. "Make sure you get these in his soda. And as soon as they kick in, while he fucked up, walk him down to the car."

"Anything else, baby?" Nikki asked, massaging his fully erect penis.

"Yeah, if you do this right, I got ten thousand for you and Shakeya."

Nikki's eyes lit up; she couldn't believe her ears.

"Plus take a shower and wash up real good," Blaze said suggestively. Then, with a cocked eyebrow, he asked, "You ain't fuck that nigga, did you?"

"Naw, baby, hell naw. You know he ain't on my level. I been saving this pussy all for you."

Blaze knew she was lying, but to seal the deal he pulled his dick out and gently pushed Nikki down to his crotch. She immediately went to work, giving Blaze some of the best head he had in a while. Hollywood walked in just as she was finishing up; swallowing all of his cum down her throat. She turned and looked at Hollywood, thinking of how good he would taste too if she had enough time. The eye contact she made with him said enough as she finished up Blaze with a long lick and a loud, "Uhmm!"

Hollywood couldn't help but smile. And Blaze couldn't help but smile back. He fixed his clothes as Nikki got up off the floor, wiping her mouth.

"Yo, what you got under them sweats?" Blaze asked.

Nikki graciously pulled her sweats down, letting Blaze see her pussy and Hollywood see her ass.

"Blaze, that thing look good from back here!" said Hollywood. He had never made it past the door, he just stood there, watching the show.

"Yeah, I can't wait until she handle her business." Blaze played with her pussy for a minute while Hollywood walked up, rubbing her ass and feeling her breasts.

"Can you handle both of us?" Hollywood asked.

"If Blaze want me too," she returned.

Blaze said, "I want you to be as freaky as possible, baby. But first go handle ya business."

Blaze kissed her on her forehead and stepped away from her, while Hollywood took his erect penis from off her back and zipped it back in his pants.

"Boy, I hope she hurry up," Hollywood said, anxiously.

"Me too. Don't forget to take a shower for me, baby we might wanna get freaky."

With that said, Nikki fixed her clothes, quickly grabbed the sodas and cigarettes, and hauled ass back to her room. When she got there, Rick and Shakeya were fucking hard as shit. Since Shakeya was riding Rick, Nikki jumped right in. Her pants dropped to the floor and she climbed on top of Rick's face, placing her pussy in his mouth. He gladly ate her while Nikki kissed Shakeya.

Shakeya was stunned. It was the first time Nikki had ever did that so she knew Nikki had some good news.

Before Rick could ejaculate, Nikki got up to get the bag with the sodas in it. While Shakeya was still fucking Rick, she opened a soda and handed it to Shakeya. Then, while Shakeya was drinking her soda, Nikki secretly opened Rick's and slipped the pills in just as he was asking Shakeya for some of hers.

"Naw, don't give him none, boo!" Nikki exclaimed, then calmly said, "I don't want him to change position, anyway, so he can eat ya pussy while I get some of that dick."

Shakeya was with it. She didn't care. She was high as shit, and when she was high she liked to fuck; get her pussy sucked, get banged in her ass, she didn't care, as long as she was cumming.

While Shakeya dismounted from Rick, Nikki awaited to climb on top of him, but not before handing him his soda. It took about twenty minutes for Nikki to cum. Then she got up and headed for the shower. By that time she got done showering and douching, the pills had kicked in and Rick was very disoriented. Nikki came out the bathroom whispering something to Shakeya, and while Shakeya went to shower up Nikki made the call.

"It's done," she said into the phone.

"All right, walk him to the car," Blaze instructed.

Ten minutes later, Shakeya and Nikki walked a stumbling and drowsy Rick to his car. When they got him in the passenger seat, Nikki hopped in the car and pulled off. Next stop, down by the harbor.

After a twenty-minute ride, Nikki pulled to a secluded spot by the harbor. By now Rick was completely knocked out. Nikki cut the car off and waited for Blaze and Hollywood to pull up. When they finally arrived she got out the car quickly to tell Blaze, Rick was passed out. She was very nervous, her stomach was fluttering, and she was sweating profusely.

"He's passed out! Hurry up and throw him in!" Nikki frantically demanded.

Blaze could see that she was scared, so he and Hollywood couldn't help but laugh. Her facial expressions went from scared to confused as she wondered what was so funny.

"Baby, you did the hard part, so calm down," Blaze said soothingly. "Nobody knows nothing but us. You ain't gonna tell on yaself, is you?"

Blaze's subtle voice made her feel more comfortable, but she couldn't believe that she was actually helping him commit murder. For him it seemed so easy, but for her it was like having sex for the first time.

"Naw, I ain't gonna tell on myself," Nikki said with confidence. "I ain't going to tell on shit. I just wanna get this lame-ass nigga out the car so you can drown his dumb ass."

Blaze smiled. He and Hollywood got out the car and grabbed the cinder blocks they had picked up.

Blaze said, "Look, after we tie these shits to his feet, cover the nigga with this syrup."

Blaze handed Nikki the syrup and headed for the car. A few minutes later they were done and Rick was sinking to the bottom of the harbor.

"Hold up, boo," Blaze called to Nikki. "Don't throw that bottle in there, it got ya fingerprints on it."

Blaze explained to Nikki and Shakeya how to clean the car out. Then they drove to a different hotel about thirty miles away from the Hilton they had stayed in. When they got there, Blaze and Hollywood went and got the room while Nikki and Shakeya cleaned Rick's car with disinfectant. They made sure to put all his money, drugs, and valuable possessions in their bag, and they put the rest of the stuff in a trash bag. When they were satisfied with the job they'd done, they hurried up to the room and had the best orgy of their lives.

———————————————

Juanita was exonerated of all charges after she spent a whole week in jail. She wanted to leave straight from the preliminary when she saw Doc in the courtroom with her lawyer. But she had to go back to the jail, and it seemed like forever before she was finally discharged.

Juanita was sitting in her cell, reading a newspaper. She had packed her belongings as soon as she got back. Then she told Simone that she would retain Omar Dickens for her case. That made Simone very excited. She was talking to Juanita about all the plans she had for the future when Correctional Officer Cross called out, "Juanita Davis!"

Simone got up and hurried to the door. She was hoping Juanita was being discharged, but she honestly had mixed emotions. She wanted Juanita to go home so she could handle her pregnancy properly and take care of her lawyer situation. But she felt like when Juanita left she would be all alone. Simone opened the cell door and looked out.

"Ya cellie going home, Monie," Cross said.

"All right, she getting ready now," was Simone's response.

A few minutes later, Simone was following Juanita down the steps, carrying all her belongings. Simone carried them as far up the hallway as she could, gave her friend a hug, and waved to Juanita as she waddled her way down to intake to be discharged.

Fifteen minutes later, Juanita was escorted out the front doors of the jail. She sat waiting momentarily while Doc pulled up from the parking lot to the front gate to pick her up. When she slid into the car her emotions could be concealed no longer. She reached out to hug Doc and the two of them cried together.

"It's going to be okay, baby. It'll never happen again," Doc promised.

It sounded good, and Juanita really wanted to believe it but she knew nothing was promised to go right. Not in the life they lived.

Doc said, "Don't worry, baby. I got a surprise for you."

Doc could tell by her face that there was an intense fear in her eyes. He knew she would never feel safe in her old life. So he was buying her a new house far enough away for her to start a new life.

# CHAPTER 17

*Thirty Days Later...*

The cell phone rang for the sixth time, and just as the caller was about to hang up, Wally finally picked up.

"Yo, what's up?" he queried, half asleep.

"Yo, what's up with you, you bitch-ass nigga?"

"Who the fuck is this?"

"You know who it is, it's ya worst enemy, mothafucka."

"Skate?" Wally asked, astonished to hear his voice.

"Yeah, it's me mothafucka! When we gonna handle our business? Don't tell me you done got scared now, you bitch-ass nigga."

"Imagine that!" Wally retorted. "I'm ready whenever you are. I been waiting for ya bitch ass to come home since the day I got out."

"I hear you," replied Skate. "I hope ya loaded ya gun with cop killers, 'cause I loaded mine with Talons."

"Look, this just between me and you, nobody else included."

"Yeah, sure," Skate said indifferently. "Just give me the location and I'll meet ya bitch ass there."

"All right. I'll call you back with it before the day over."

With that said, Wally hung up and made a quick call.

Blaze picked up his cell phone, wondering who was calling him from out of state.

"What's the deal, pimp?"

"Doc?" Blaze was surprised to hear the familiar voice. "What the fuck, you hiding out?"

"Hiding out for what? Imagine that!"

"I don't know, dog," Blaze said, "You ain't been around since ya girl got out of jail. So what's the deal now?"

"Damn, Blaze, you acting like me and you going through something or something."

"Oh, naw, it ain't nothing like that. I'm just saying, a lot of shit been going on and you ain't been around for nothing. Last I heard, you took Rick to the police station so ya girl can come home."

"Yeah, right," Doc said. "Imagine that I took the nigga to my lawyer so my lawyer could figure out a way to beat the case. All Rick did was tell him where he drove at to meet Duck, and my lawyer got the videotapes and my girl spanked all the charges. Why I'm explaining myself? I don't even know!"

But, Doc continued to do so. "Anyway, my girl was stressed out from everything that happened, so her doctor said it would be a good idea for her to go on vacation if she wanted to have a successful pregnancy. So I brought her to Virginia Beach."

By now Doc was tired of justifying himself, so he got straight to the point.

"Anyway, while I been down here, I met a couple dudes. But I ain't gonna do no whole lot of talking over the phone, we better than that."

"Yeah, I guess you right," Blaze said, but thought, *he's about a spineless-ass nigga. He ain't crazy enough to set me up!* So Blaze asked, "So what's up with you?"

"Yo, shit hectic... I'm on my way back. I got fifty large

and I need to meet you somewhere," Doc practically pleaded.

"What, you fucked up?" Blaze said, not believing that Doc only had fifty thousand dollars to spend.

It killed Doc's pride, but he had to suck it up and say, "Yeah, I'm fucked! Them lawyers killed me. Wally's, Juanita's, my bail, my bills, plus the police took a couple hundred thousand when they ran up in my crib. They pocketed that. Then I've been down Virginia Beach for a month with my girl. Shit been fucked up, dog!"

After Blaze thought about it thoroughly he guessed Doc was telling the truth. He calculated his living expenses, lawyer fees, and how much money he figured Doc as having. Thinking about all the bills he was paying and how Doc seemed to be scoring less and less ever since Flame died. Then after it all added up, Blaze smiled to himself as he thought, *damn, this nigga broke.*

"Yeah, I feel you, dog," Blaze empathized. "You know you can always count on me. So when you coming back?"

"Well, my mans went to get me a plane ticket, so I'll be there tonight. Where you want me to meet you at?"

"Just call me when you get to the city," Blaze said, thinking, *damn, he ain't even got his own plane fare, broke-ass nigga.*

Doc said, "All right, that's what's up."

Then, before Doc could disconnect, Blaze asked the question he'd been most concerned about since he got on the phone with Doc.

"Yo, what's up with Wally? He down there too?"

"Naw, I ain't seen him."

"So you ain't talked to him neither, huh?" Blaze asked, not believing Doc completely cut Wally off.

"Not since I left. Last I heard from him, he was out Oxford, hiding out with his girl."

The news was enough to stroke Blaze's ego. He was happy with what little info he got, so he left it alone. He'd merely bribe Doc with a couple of extra bricks to set Wally up. Then he'd eventually kill Doc a month or two later.

"Yeah, okay," Blaze said. "Well, I'll see you tonight. Call me when you get to the city."

Blaze hung up and made a quick call to Hollywood. He didn't say much, just enough to let Hollywood know the deal.

"Yo, I need three platters," Blaze told him.

"The fish or the mixed?"

"Fish."

"All right," said Hollywood, "I'm on my way."

Blaze hung up, thinking that if he gave Doc the fish scale instead of the re-rocked, Doc would depend on him to get back. Blaze usually saved the fish scale or what is known as the best coke you could buy for his main customers and workers. People didn't usually like the mixed coke because it was cut and re-compressed to rock form so that you couldn't tell it was cut at all–hence, re-rock. But since Blaze still half-ass liked Doc, he would treat him real good for a short time. A very short time.

---

♪♪ *We can bang out! / We can clap out! / We can on sight ... shoot it out!/ Bitch, we an bang it out.... Bang out! / Bitch, we can clap it out.... Clap out!/ Bitch we can shoot it out/ On sight, shoot it out!/ You wanna bang me, bitch?/ I ain't hard to find. Hanging on 24th, I'm on the front-line, you ain't./ Shoot at my head, I don't plan on dying/I got the vest and the Tec, mothafucka, I'm riding/ I got the fifth on my lap, quick to start firing/ Catch you riding by, and spit while I'm driving.*

*Innocent victim snitching to the sirens/ I coulda been killed!*
*Bitch, stop crying. Nosey-ass bitch, wanna run to a problem/*
*Bullets start flying, the bitch can't dodge them/ Now motha-*
*fuckas wanna see me bid, because I shot shit up like Billy the*
*Kid/ I live for this shit;! I want you to slump me!/ I love*
*shootouts; I'm the adrenealine rush junky/ I get my dick hard*
*when I'm ducking from bullets and breathing all fast. Nigga,*
*go ahead and blast!/ 'Cause when I catch you  pussy, it's*
*about ya ass. I'mma dump on you like you collect trash/ Hope*
*ya duck game right, when I shatter ya glass. Hit you with the*
*fifth and splatter ya mask. Bang out/Bitch, we can bang it out!*
*Clap out. Bitch, we can clap it out! On sight. Shot it out!* ♪♫

The Escalade came to a stop in front of Jack Denny's. The
music blaring out the speakers turned every head in the vicinity. Skate took another deep pull on the blunt and let the smoke
seep into his soul. Intertwined with the feeling of intensity he
got from listening to his music pound from the system. He was
ready. He exhaled the weed, passed the half of blunt to Maine,
and downed the Heineken he was holding in his hand. Then he
pulled out his .45 and cocked it.

"Yo, you sure about this shit, dog?" Maine asked Skate,
not really comfortable with the situation.

"I'mma soldier!" Skate proclaimed. "I ain't got to be sure
about this shit. If it's gonna go down, it's gonna go down. Just
play ya position."

Then Skate shook Maine's hand before tucking his four-
pound and hopping out the truck. Maine pulled straight off. He
kept straight through the light about fifty yards, then he made
a right into the fast food restaurant parking lot and parked.
Something wasn't right, Maine was sure of it.

Skate pulled out his cell phone and speed-dialed Wally's
number. Wally picked up as if he was waiting for the call, and
Skate was surprised.

"How you expect to kill somebody pulling up like that?" Wally admonished.

"So, you watching me, huh?"

"Of course. Ain't I supposed to be? Now listen, you done already drawed, so just walk across the street."

Skate crossed the street and headed toward Crozer Hospital parking lot. He was nearly to the middle of the lot before Wally spoke again.

"Yo, turn around."

Skate spun around almost in slow motion and noticed the door to a black Mustang GT with jet-black tints fly open. Behind the door was young Wally, full of smiles.

"Hop in, you bitch-ass nigga."

Skate cracked a smile, jumped in the passenger's seat, and said, "So what's the deal?"

"Dude should be here any minute," Wally replied. "My old head just called dude and told them he was in the bar. Now this is what I need you to do, my truck over there on the side of the bar. He should come out the bar and run up on it, when he pulls up. Either way, I need you laying in the cut to make sure this dude don't catch me slipping."

"So, what, you going to get in the truck?" Skate asked.

"Yeah, why not?"

"Why not?" Skate repeated incredulously. "It's stupid! Why not park this car a few cars behind your truck, and when he run up on ya truck, you can jump out with the drop? That way you ain't putting ya life all in my hands, because I might let y'all kill each other. You know I don't really like ya bitch-ass anyway," Skate said, half-jokingly.

"All right, that's what's up," Wally agreed.

Wally was never one to argue with a good point. He pulled out the hospital parking lot and drove the long way around the whole block before he pulled over about thirty feet behind his truck.

"This good?" he asked his companion.

Skate shook his head in the affirmative before taking his four-pound out and sitting it on his lap. Then he went inside his pocket and pulled out a bag of weed and a blunt.

"Yo, open the door when you crack that," Wally requested.

"Man, how we suppose to be creeping on a nigga opening doors?"

"Shit, how we suppose to be creeping on a nigga smoking?" Wally returned rhetorically.

"Easy. This shit keeps you on point. This shit makes you notice a tree branch move a block away."

Wally couldn't help but laugh. He knew Skate was shot out. *He* particularly didn't smoke weed when he was trying to kill somebody. But this wasn't something he ran around practicing either. So fuck it. If Skate wanted to smoke, then they were smoking. Wally reached in his waistline and pulled out his nine and sat it on his lap. Skate, in turn, smiled as he opened the door slightly, emptied the blunt, and closed the door back quickly. He filled the empty blunt with weed, rolled it shut, and licked it to keep it rolled. Then he lit it.

"This thing pearled good too," Skate said with satisfaction as he puffed on the blunt.

Doc was in the bar for about fifteen minutes. He was sipping a drink and a Heineken while learning from Darnell what's been going on in the neighborhood. Doc figured that Blaze should be pulling up at any time because he had called an hour ahead of time to tell Blaze where he would be. Doc knew Blaze wouldn't be expecting Wally to be with him, so this would be a hell of a surprise for him. But Doc failed to take the most critical thing into consideration; Blaze was far from average.

As Doc finished his drink and prepared to order another one, a ring of his cell phone interrupted his conversation.

"Yo," Wally said after Doc quickly answered, "me and my worst enemy getting restless. When dude gonna show his miserable face so we can blow it off?"

Doc instantly thought his young bull was crazy because of the mindset he had.

"Yo, you shot out! But listen, he suppose to be on his way. So keep ya eyes peeled."

With that said, Wally hung up and kept his focus on the truck and the front and side doors of the bar, the side being more visible. Then, as he and Skate started to argue with each other about the last of the weed, Blaze's money-green

S-500 rode by and stopped on the side of Wally's truck. The passenger door opened, and Hollywood jumped out and looked in the car. But when he noticed it was empty he hopped back in the car with Blaze.

Skate saw Hollywood hopping back in the car with what appeared to be a gun and snapped out of his daze.

"Yo, somebody just checked ya truck," he said to Wally. "I think he got a gun. Look, look." he said, pointing. "They pulling off, they pulling off."

Wally gazed up from the seat he was slouched in and saw the figure hop back in the car, then watched it pull over at the side entrance, where Blaze got out—Calico in hand—and walked into the bar. Hollywood took the front door. This instantly made Wally nervous.

"Oh, shit!" Wally exclaimed. "They ready to kill my old head!"

"Naw, they probably looking for you, Wally. Be easy," Skate reasoned.

"Man, fuck that," Wally snapped. "I can't take that chance."

Wally jumped out the truck with his 9mm and approached the side door. Skate caught up with him just before he got to the door and pulled him into the little alley behind the bar.

"Yo, at least call him and see what the deal is before you rush up in the bar like this."

"Good idea," Wally said, quickly pulling out his cell phone. When Doc answered, he asked, "You cool?"

"Yeah, baby, I just got here. I'm with Blaze right now. I'll call you later."

Relieved, Wally disconnected the line and told Skate, "He ain't in trouble, but it's a crucial situation."

"Crucial situations call for crucial measures," expounded Skate. He chirped to Maine, "We need a diversion down here."

Maine said, "I thought you'd never ask."

Blaze was watching Doc closely as he sipped on the drink he ordered. He didn't trust Doc since noticing Wally's truck parked outside. He felt like Doc was up to something. His story didn't make sense, and he seemed nervous. So even though Blaze had the coke in his car, he'd make a phone call. He'd say he had to have somebody bring it so one of his young bulls could get in a good position to follow Doc to take Wally his truck back.

Doc claimed he wasn't taking Wally the truck back because he already had it, but Blaze wasn't going for it. He was too suspicious.

For Doc, the plan seemed to be going perfect. He knew Blaze didn't believe him. All Blaze had to do was give him the coke and follow him to the highway, out the city, and deep down into a dark, wooded area. And that would be the end of Blaze. But Doc didn't realize Wally changed the plans.

Maine pulled up by Blaze's money-green S-500, and his young bull Eddie hopped out and put slugs up in the car, shattering the windows and flattening the tires. After putting ten shots up in the car, he hopped back in with Maine, who peeled off as the crowd piled up sneaking glances out the door.

"Somebody's car got shot up," came a voice from the

crowd.

Blaze and Hollywood immediately got up. As they approached the door somebody called out, "It's a green Benz."

Blaze instantly spun around and looked at Doc. "What's the deal, dog?"

Innocently, Doc said, "I don't know, dog. You know as much as me."

"Yeah, I hope so. Come on, let's roll then."

It was weak, too weak. So Blaze sent Hollywood out the back, and Blaze cleared through the crowd, with Doc following him closely. Blaze knew for sure now that Doc had brought Wally with him. And he knew this was a set up. But he had a plan of his own.

When Blaze and Doc got out on the sidewalk, the man of the hour stepped from the shadows into the light, right in front of Blaze's car.

"Looking for me?"

Blaze was already on guard for anything, so in one swift motion he spun around and grabbed Doc as a shield, pressing a gun to his temple extremely hard and said, "Tell ya young bull to throw his gun down if you wanna live and see that whore-ass girlfriend of yours have that ugly-ass baby!"

Doc had no choice. His hands were tied. He yelled out to Wally, wondering why the fuck Wally didn't follow the original plan.

"Wally, he got the drop on me. He want you to put ya gun down."

Wally, being fully confident in his new plan, called Doc's cell phone. He yelled across the thirty-some feet and told Blaze to pick up the phone. Blaze in turn reached in Doc's pocket and grabbed the phone. When he turned it on and put it to his ear, he couldn't help but smile.

"Doc ain't got shit to do with this," Wally attested. "Let him go, and I'll shoot it out fair and square with you and ya

**216**

homey that's hiding on the side of the bar. Now you know the cops on they way, so we ain't got much time."

Blaze was amused, but he had the upper hand. Or so he thought.

"Listen, pussy, fuck the police," Blaze spat. "By the time they get here, ya old head's brains will be all over this pavement, and you'll be wearing ya chest and face mixed with ya clothes."

"Sure. Now listen here, pussy. Let my old head go and my man won't blow ya brains out. Did I forget to mention somebody's behind you?"

Blaze turned around quickly, hoping that Wally was just joking, but he wasn't. A big guy with a mask gripped Hollywood up, and a young bull had the drop on him.

"Now let Doc go, and me and you can shoot it out until you die. Or don't let Doc go, and die without the chance of being able to kill me."

Blaze was instantly enraged. Still, he said, "I let Doc go, they back up and it's me and you, huh?"

"Yeah, why not?"

Blaze pushed Doc to the ground and aimed his gun at Wally. As Doc got up and ran for cover, Eddie and Skate backed up toward the alley with Hollywood.

Then, as if somebody heard Blaze's silent prayers, a car pulled around the corner. Before it even stopped, shots went off at Eddie and Skate.

Blaze's young bull, Tommy, who was supposed to be bringing the coke, started cutting at the dudes who had Hollywood pinned up. The driver of the car, Ock, slammed on the brakes and was about to jump out shooting when Skate started shooting back.

That started a frenzy of gunfire. Eddie was hit twice. Skate hit Hollywood in the head, pushed him to the ground, and ran for the car, shooting at the blue Maxima that pulled up to Blaze's rescue. Wally started shooting at Blaze immediately. Blaze returned fire as he half ran, half ducked behind a car to shield himself from the fire. Skate made it to the Mustang GT unscathed, but as he tried to hop in, Tommy hit him with three shots in the back. Skate fell to the ground from the impact, but his vest stopped the shots from being fatal.

As Tommy and Ock bent the corner to close in on Skate, a car came peeling down the street at top speed. And for the brief second that Tommy stopped to look and see who it was, that's all it took for Maine to run him over. Ock spun around and aimed at Maine's car as it sped around the corner. The screeching tires let Skate know that Maine wasn't going too far. Even though he was hurting, Skate knew he had to make it to the car because he could hear the police sirens in the distant background.

Wally had emptied his clip and didn't know what to do when Maine screeched around the corner and crashed into the car Blaze was hiding behind. Blaze jumped for cover, cartwheeling toward a trashcan. He aimed at Maine and took a couple of shots because he thought Maine was trying to kill him.

The total shock of Blaze's life took place. A person came running out the alleyway, and as Blaze tried to spin around and shoot, Doc kicked the gun out of his hand. Then he kicked Blaze in the face.

Wally saw everything happening and knew he had to act fast. Blaze was dizzy from the kick, but he recuperated fast. He grabbed Doc's leg before he could kick him again and pushed him back. As Doc tumbled to the ground, Blaze scurried toward his gun. He was an arm's length from grabbing it when Wally dove over top of him and grabbed the gun. He crawled to his feet staring Blaze in his eyes.

"I guess we know how this is going to end." He could

hear the sirens getting closer and closer and it seemed at that moment that everything seem like slow motion even though the whole incident happened in about two or three minutes.

"Wally, look out!" It sounded like a tape dragging. When Wally turned around he knew he was in trouble. He spun right into the shots, two of them. One hit Wally in the throat; the other one hit him in the head. Skate came to Wally's rescue, but it was a split second too late. Skate emptied his new clip in Ock's head and back. As Ock fell, Skate noticed Blaze aiming the gun he took from Wally dead at his face ... three shots went off. One hit Skate in the mouth. The second one hit Skate in his left eye and came out the right side of his face. The third shot hit Skate in his stomach but wasn't fatal because of the vest he was wearing, a necessary accessory in an ugly situation.

Blaze tried to get up and hop to his car, but the rage inside of Maine wouldn't allow Blaze to get away. Maine had been knocked unconscious briefly, but when Skate screamed for Wally to turn around, the shots woke Maine up. And as he woke up the first thing he saw was his brother getting killed. Even though he was broken up from the car accident, Maine managed to hop out, take the gun out of Hollywood's dead hand, and catch Blaze before he could pull off.

"Blaze!" Maine screamed as if he was a drill sergeant. Blaze spun around to shoot the voice that called to him, but Maine's bullets were already in the air. The shots hit Blaze in the chest and he slid down the car, but his return fire finished Maine off. Blaze tried to climb into his car to escape the sirens, which were screaming in the background. But as he got to his feet a white X-5 with Ben Franklins pulled up on him and rolled down its tinted window.

Blaze raised his gun and told the driver, "Too bad you ain't gonna be around to see your whore-ass girl have no ugly-ass kids for you, you slimy punk mothafucka."

Doc squeezed five shots into his face. The adrenaline in him made Blaze continue to raise the gun after the first two shots, but when he squeezed, the gun was empty. So Doc's four-pound just continued to rip chunks out his face before he screeched off.

———————————

It was a gruesome scene for the police. The only thing that saved some of the victims was the fact that it all happened across the street from a hospital.

Officer Minor searched for witnesses, but everybody's story was the same. When the shooting first started, everybody rushed out. But when they got outside, it turned into the O.K. Corral, and everybody rushed back inside in fear for their lives. Most victims were DOA, though three people made it to ICU after immediate surgery.

Detective Nutsack felt as though it was good news to see all the people he wanted to arrest dead. He had murder charges on Blaze and Hollywood, thanks to all the investigative work of Juanita Davis's lawyer and the taped confession of Rick. That helped them figure out how everything occurred.

After watching Juanita beat her preliminary, Minor and Nutsack went to shake down Shakeya and Nikki for information. Their demeanors had changed drastically, which let the officers know that they were onto something. Now all the work they had to do was done. Not to mention Maine Wilson was dead. Dennis "Skate" Wilson was in critical condition along with Laneer "Wally" Jones, and there were three John Does that the two officers weren't familiar with.

As Dennis and Laneer were transported to the hospital, Officer Nutsack said a little prayer—he prayed that they both died! He felt as though the streets would be ten times safer with scum like Skate and Wally in a grave.

---

*Three days later...*

Doc and Tamia showed up at the hospital to visit Wally early Wednesday morning. When they got to the nurses' station, one of the nurses told Doc that Wally's room was being monitored. The news made Tamia worry instantly, because she knew before Doc told her that the police would try to lock Wally up as soon as he got healthy. When they got inside the room, both of them were surprised to find Skate housed in the same room.

"Isn't that the guy y'all were shooting at?" Tamia whispered.

Smiling, Doc told her, "Naw, he cool; he on our side."

They sat down and talked quietly for a little over an hour. Then finally Wally's doctor showed up. He explained Wally's condition and told Tamia that it was too early to tell if he would make a full recovery. The doctor left them, and shortly after the nurse came in to check Wally's fluid bag. Nurse Beverly gave the two of them a little hope, only to tear it back down when she said, "I think Mr. Johnson opened his eyes last night, before his vitals started slipping."

"His vitals started slipping?" Tamia repeated, more like asking, astonished by the revelation.

"Oh, I'm sorry, the doctor didn't tell you?" the nurse said, suddenly sorry she ever opened her mouth.

"Naw, he didn't say anything about it."

Nurse Beverly sensed the fear and grief in Tamia's voice and decided to sit down and explain the situation. She informed Tamia and Doc of how the medication Dr. Solosky prescribed made Wally have a seizure. She went further on to relate how Wally had to have his heart hit with electric shocks so it could start beating again. Nurse Beverly said since changing his medication he'd improved dramatically and they didn't expect to have any more problems out of him.

The news had Tamia engulfed in sorrow and pain. She leaned on Doc's shoulder for support and covered his shirt with tears. The two of them stayed in Wally's room until visits were over.

Doc told Tamia before they left that he was going back to Virginia within the next three days. He recommended that as soon as Wally got healthy that she should take him out of the hospital and shoot him straight out of state.

Tamia agreed that it was a good idea and promised to call Doc as soon as Wally got a little healthy so that he could help her. From what Nurse Beverly said, the nurses had instructions to call the police as soon as either of the two patients made a recovery, so that they could charge them with murder and post a Correctional Officer out in front of their door. But someone in room 312 wouldn't have to worry about being charged. At one o'clock in the morning his vital signs went flat-line.

The nursing staff and doctors rushed to his room and tried desperately to revive him, but neither CPR nor electric shock could bring back the patient that slipped into another life. It was all over for him. His time in this world was done, and he had moved on into the serenity of a bright, bright light!

# CHAPTER 18

*FIVE YEARS LATER...*

Juanita packed the last of her clothes into her suitcase. She was trying her best to get everything done as quickly as possible during each commercial break. She was being distracted by all the excitement in her favorite soap opera, *General Hospital*. And *Oprah* was coming on next. At this rate she would never be ready.

She sat down just as the commercials ceased and was about to glue herself to the TV set when her son ran into the room.

"Mommy, Mommy, when my godpop and my godbrother gonna get here?" Duron Ali tugged at her shirt, shaking her back and forth.

"They'll be here shortly, baby. Go finish packing ya stuff up."

"Mommy, I need you, come help me. Come on!"

"Okay, here I come right now, baby."

Juanita wouldn't dare move, at least not until the next commercial. But for now her son thought she was telling the truth and hopped down from her bed and ran back to his room. About ten minutes passed before Juanita got another break. When the commercials came on she ran to see what her son was doing. When she opened his door she found him in the center of the floor playing with a few of his toys, with clothes flung all over the floor and scattered across the room.

*I knew he was too quiet!* she thought.

As she rushed through the door his innocent baby face

made her smile, but she would still get him.

"So, you wanna mess up ya room, right?"

Duron, sensing he was in trouble, jumped up and tried to run.

"No, Mommy, no!"

Juanita grabbed him before he could get far and lightly slammed him on the bed.

"I got you now!"

"No, Mommy! I'm sorry!"

Juanita, of course, ignored his pleas and tickled her son vigorously. He laughed hysterically for over a minute and then she began to pinch his legs.

"Aww, Mommy, no! I'mma clean it! I'mma clean it!"

"No, I don't want you to clean it now, bad ass."

As Juanita stopped pinching Duron and started tickling him again, somebody snuck up behind her and started tickling her. Startled, Juanita immediately jumped.

"Boy, stop," she managed to say between laughs.

"Y'all suppose to be ready to go. Why y'all in here playing?" Doc asked half mad, half joking.

"You see what ya son did with his bad behind self." Juanita stated, getting up to face her man. She kissed him quickly before brushing past him to see if her stories went off.

"Where my girl at?" She asked on her way out the room.

"She downstairs with Duron's godbrother."

"My godbrother downstairs?" Little Duron asked happily.

"Yeah, so clean this stuff up so you can leave for the weekend."

Doc spun around and headed to his room, only to find Juanita sitting down having a talk with Tamia.

"Girlfriend, we got dinner reservations in an hour and a half."

Doc ran downstairs to Wally and his godson, with little Duron fast on his heels.

Wally was sitting on the couch playing the PlayStation 2. Doc sat down and grabbed the second joystick as Wally set up the NBA Ballers game. Duron ran over and hugged his little godbrother and they right away began to complain about playing the game. But the fathers wouldn't hear it. They hadn't played a good game in a month.

"What we playing for?" Wally asked as he started the game.

"What you wanna play for?"

"If I win, next week you got the kids, I get the Bentley GT, and you run the barbershop for me while I take Tamia to South Beach. Okay?"

"Yeah, sure. But if I win, you get the kids for a month and you watch my car lot so I can go to Cancun. Deal?"

The two of them shook hands and the game began. They both wanted to win badly, so it would be a very intense game.

---

B came speeding down Twenty-fourth Street from St. James. He bent a left on Madison, and pulled over in front of Larry's Pizza Shop.

The system in his H3 Hummer was crazy, so people heard him coming a mile away. B quickly shut the engine off, hopped out, and walked across the street to holler at his team. It was the beginning of spring, the weather was breaking, and he knew it was the perfect time to cop something new. It was a hustling ritual.

Biggy and Tyrese were both sitting on Simone's steps, along with Kiana, Kelly and their new protégé, Tanya. They were all laughing at the jokes Biggy and Tyrese were telling about Shakeya and Nikki. It was no longer a secret – everybody in the neighborhood knew that they both had AIDS. The jokes usually began whenever they walked through the block. The two of them appeared to be disintegrating, and after all the slimy stuff they did, not one person felt sorry for them.

When B pulled up, the conversations momentarily ceased as everybody stared at his new truck in awe and disbelief. Everybody knew B was sitting on some major cash, but nobody expected him to hurt the block like this not even his girlfriend, Kiana. In just one year B had managed to take control of Twenty-fourth Street, establishing himself as the new boss.

Out of everyone who got locked up five years ago, B got the most time. Due to his prior record, he was sentenced to four to eight years. His girl got eighteen to thirty-six months running concurrent with a one to two years for assaulting Shakeya and Nikki while her sister Kelly got probation. And Biggy got a two to four year sentence. When they were all released, for one reason or another, they all ended up right back on Twenty-fourth Street.

Simone, thanks to Juanita, now owned the house that was the cause of their jail sentences. Juanita also left Simone all the furniture, clothes, and personal belongings she had at her house up Philadelphia before she sold that. So Simone was doing very well, thanks to her best friend.

The only thing Juanita asked was that since Simone was little Duron's godmom, she never let anyone stash drugs in her house and find a job. She wanted Simone's house to always be safe for her son whenever he chose to go there. And even though Simone was loyal to her block and team that was a promise she never broke.

Kiana and Kelly, on the other hand, both rented apartments on St. James. One, which Kelly lived with her boyfriend, Tyrese and one in which Tyrese and B stashed whatever drugs or guns, they needed to. Kiana and Kelly were as loyal to the block as someone who grew up and lived there their whole entire life. Kiana was B's backbone while he was knocked. She worked two jobs and sold a little weed to make sure his commissary stayed right. Plus, B had something nice to come home to. Now, after weathering the four-year storm with her better half, she knew it was all worth it.

Biggy lived across town. He didn't usually come around until Friday, Saturday, and Sunday because during the week he worked as a bouncer at a club in Delaware. He still sold plenty weight to the young bulls in the neighborhood, but hustling was not a full-time job anymore. He was starting to grow up.

A lot of things around Twenty-fourth Street were the same as before they all got knocked. There was plenty of money to be made, plenty of cops trying to lock people up for anything and everything they could, and plenty petty shit for petty niggas to go to war over.

But for the small group of friends that got time in on the block like L.L. had in the rap game, the few friends were as loyal to each other as the army was to our country. For all of them that sat on the steps sharing their thoughts and lives with each other, the only thing that mattered that day besides – B's new truck – was being the most important people in their neighborhood and filling the positions that they deserved in the streets.

Up the McCaffe a similar scene took place. N.Y. pulled up in the projects in a brand new Range Rover with Ike. For the last five years the two of them had become inseparable. After locating all of Blaze's stash houses and robbing them once he was dead, they made off with close to $4 million dollars. The two of them undoubtedly became the biggest drug dealers in Chester. Due to the quantity of drugs they handled, it was unusual to catch them hanging out on the corner. But today was different.

It was the beginning of summer and they were throwing the biggest block party Chester would ever see. Due to the success of most of their team, everybody was either copping bikes or cars for the upcoming Greek festival. And what better way to stunt than to throw a block party for the whole city. They had tons of food, tons of liquor, and tons of weed. The only thing they overlooked was the tons of problems that come along with being the center of attention in the life they chose. That would abruptly bring their lives to an end sooner than they expected.

But, hey, that's the life...whatever starts on the streets, stays on the streets...

*The End*

**Blue Gambino**

# Coming Soon!
## Fall 2007

# SUCKA 4 LOVE

## BY

## GENE I

Geovanni Cotto is a 20-year-old Puerto Rican boy who is living a normal everyday life in the mean streets of Elm City, New Haven, Connecticut; but when he falls in love with his next-door neighbor, a beautiful Black woman named Crystal Betha, his normal life turns into a raging nightmare.

Geovanni, known to his hood as White Boy, gets caught up in a life-or-death battle with a ruthless drug dealer named Lex. He knows he can't win; but for the sake of love and defending the honor of Crystal, he's willing to risk it all; for all Geovanni wants is Crystal's undying love… but will he find it, or become a sucka for love? This is an urban tale about love, race, drugs and murder; a ghetto story about the traps some fall into when they fall in love in the hood…

# Coming Soon!
## Spring 2008

# Money And Murder

by

## Frederick Brown

Money is a young kingpin controlling the drug trade in New York City. He's rich, ruthless and a self-made millionaire. Murder is the best high school basketball player in the country destined for the NBA. However, he refused to stop balling in the deadly streets of Wilmington, DE. *Money and Murder* meet at a family reunion in NYC, before walking away from the streets for good; they form an allegiance and take the game to another level, one...last...time.

# ORDER FORM

## A NU Direction Publishing

A Divison of MeJah Books Inc.
333 Naamans Road
Tri-State Mall, Suite #12-13
Claymont, DE 19703
(302)793-3424
(302) 793-1632 Fax

**Purchaser Information**

Name: _____

BI#: _____(if applicable)

Address: _____ Apt#_____

City: _____ State:_____ Zip Code_____

| Book Title | Quantity | Price | Total Price |
|---|---|---|---|
| Whatever Starts On The Street...Stay On The Street | | $15.00 | |
| That Was Dirty | | $15.00 | |
| The Lies Hustlers Never Tell | | $14.95 | |
| A Sucka For Love | *Coming Soon* | $15.00 | |
| Money and Murder | *Coming Soon* | $15.00 | |

Shipping & Handling (via U.S. Media Mail)... $3.00
*Add $1.50 postage for each additional purchase*
*Shipping & Handling to prisons/institution... FREE*

Please make cashier checks, institutional checks, or money orders payable to:
A NU Direction Publishing

Credit Card Payment Form
Cardholder's Full Name_____
Address_____
City_____ State_____ Zip Code_____
Card Number_____
Signature_____ Exp. Date_____
Phone_____Email_____
☐ Visa      ☐Mastercard      ☐Discover      ☐American Express

# DELAWAREBLACK.COM

## THE PULSE OF URBAN DELAWARE

## Mission

DELAWAREBLACK.COM's mission is to provide the Africa-America
community an online resource which will help promote the growth of
Black-owned businesses and community organizations and encourage
support for African-American events.

## About Us

DELAWAREBLACK.COM, launched on September 1, 2006, is the #1
online resource for African-American in the state of Delaware. Owned
operated by Delawareblack.com LLC. DELAWAREBLACK.COM is a
online pacesetter providing valuable information to our ever growing p
ulation of web-savvy internet users.

## Website Features

-Black Business & Community Directory
-Event Calendar
-E-mail Newsletter
-Local/National Headlines
-Banner and Delawareblack Page

## Stay Connected Through
## DELAWAREBLACK.COM

**Delawareblack.com LLC**
2207 Concord Pike #375, Wilmington, DE 19803 (302) 378-6576
**Website**: www.delawareblack.com      **E-mail**: info@delawareblack.com

# OCJ GRAPHIX

## Book Cover Designs

The Lies Hustlers Never Tell
Stiletto 101
Bruised
Born In The Game
The Takeover
That Was Dirty
Whatever Starts On The Streets Stays On The Streets

*Services:* *Automobile Wrap Design-Ad Layouts-Bookmarks-Stationary-Web Design-Logos-Posters-Business Cards-Anything Graphics*

Contact:
Kevin Carr
Telephone: (302) 898-4543
Toll Free: 1-800-963-6309
Website: www.ocjgraphix.com
E-mail: info@ocjgraphix.com

**ghettoheat.**

## ORDER FORM

Name_____

Registration#_____(If incarcerated)

Address_____

City_____State_____

Zip Code_____

Phone_____

E-mail_____

Friends/Family E-mail_____

Books are $15.00 each. Send me the following number of copies of:

___CONVICT'S CANDY      ___GHETTOHEAT®
___AND GOD CREATED WOMAN    ___HARDER
___SONZ OF DARKNESS      ___LONDON REIGN
___GHOST TOWN HUSTLERS    ___BOY-TOY
___GAMES WOMEN PLAY      ___SKATE ON!
___SOME SEXY, ORGASM 1    ___HARDER 2
___AND GOD CREATED WOMAN 2 ___TANTRUM

Please send $4.00 to cover shipping and handling. Add a dollar for each additional book ordered. Free shipping for convicts.

Total Enclosed = _____

Please make check or money order payable to GHETTO-HEAT®. Send all payments to: P.O. BOX 2746, NEW YORK, NY 10027

**GHETTOHEAT®: THE HOTTNESS IN THE STREETS!!! ™**